THE COULTER LEGACY

A novel by
MICHAEL LINDLEY
Sage River Press

THE COULTER LEGACY

Book #10 in the Amazon #1 bestselling "Hanna Walsh and Alex Frank" Low Country mystery series.

Hanna and Alex land themselves in the crosshairs of a dangerous drug cartel when the deadly fentanyl crisis finds its way to the Low Country of South Carolina.

Acting sheriff, Alex Frank, leads a taskforce of law enforcement agencies to confront a growing scourge of fentanyl overdoses and drug cartel violence. Attorney, Hanna Walsh, offers to help the wife and family of one the cartel drug runners at her peril, and neighbor, Quinn Burke, returns with more drama and chaos surrounding a new boyfriend.

In a dual narrative, the story of Hanna's ancestor, Mathew Coulter, whose family controlled the liquor trade in the South during Prohibition, continues in the 1930's and long-hidden family secrets and scandals are discovered in a lost manuscript.

The *"Hanna and Alex"* saga continues as our crime-fighting couple faces new danger and suspense in the idyllic setting of Pawleys Island and the South Carolina Low Country.

Other novels by Michael Lindley

The *"Troubled Waters"* Series

THE EMMALEE AFFAIRS

THE SUMMER TOWN

BEND TO THE TEMPEST

THE *"Hanna and Alex"* Low Country Mystery Series

LIES WE NEVER SEE

A FOLLOWING SEA

DEATH ON THE NEW MOON

THE SISTER TAKEN

THE HARBOR STORMS

THE FIRE TOWER

THE MARQUESAS DRIFT

LISTEN TO THE MARSH

THE FIRM OFFER

THE COULTER LEGACY

DEDICATION

My sincere thanks to the many readers of the *"Hanna and Alex"* novels. Your kind notes and words of encouragement inspire me every day.

"In the tapestry of time, each generation adds its own vibrant color."

- Unknown author

Foreword

My third novel, *BEND TO THE TEMPEST*, was first published in 2011 and chronicled the saga of the Coulter family, who controlled the liquor trade in the South leading up to and during the Prohibition years of the 1920s. The story features the Coulters' youngest son, Mathew, who, in 1918, lies in a Paris hospital recovering from a devastating wound received in a battle in the French countryside. His nurse, Celeste, will not only tend his wounds but also capture his heart—but her ties to her local French village and a soldier still lost in the conflict of the Great War will be the first of Mathew's most difficult life choices.

Returning to his home in America during the tumultuous years of Prohibition, Mathew ultimately finds new love, but a bitter betrayal and his ruthless family's ties to the liquor trade in 1920s Atlanta force him to leave and seek refuge in a friend's secluded cottage in a remote Florida beach town. He meets a young blind girl, Melanee Dalton, who will lead him on a journey that may be the final salvation for her wayward mother and Mathew's own haunted soul.

Through the last few years of writing my *"Hanna and Alex"* Low Country mystery and suspense series, I established the connection of Hanna Moss Walsh's present-day family, particularly her father, Allen Moss, with the Coulter clan in the 1920s—and then back to the Paltierre family in the mid-1800s, who first owned the Pawleys Island beach house that Hanna and Alex reside in today. The ghost of Amanda Paltierre still makes occasional visits with Hanna to warn her of impending danger and to help guide her path.

It occurred to me after the release of the last *"Hanna and Alex"* novel, *THE FIRM OFFER*, that featured her attorney father, Allen Moss, and again the familial connections to the past with the Coulters and the Paltierres, that it was time to revisit the story of Mathew Coulter in this sequel to *BEND TO THE TEMPEST*.

While this new book can certainly be read as a standalone novel, I would encourage readers to go back and start with *BEND TO THE TEMPEST* to really experience all of the backstory of Mathew and his family.

I hope you enjoy the story!

Michael

Chapter One

Barcelona, Spain. March 1939.

The dark sky cracked with thunder and another flash of lightning lit the looming buildings along the walk up from the waterfront pier. The night air smelled of Spanish food cooking in the cafes and bars on the Carrer de Sant Pau. Despite the heavy rain, windows and doors were open, and the sounds of hearty revelry echoed among the rumble in the sky above.

I held my wife Sara's hand tightly in my own and an umbrella in the other as we rushed forward to find refuge and a bite to eat. We were ending our trip to Europe to promote the release of my latest *Mathew Coulter* novel with a cruise along the Mediterranean coast of France and Spain. The White Star Line's grand ship, the *Brittanic*, had been forced ashore in Barcelona earlier in the day from high winds and heavy seas from a storm front that blew in off the continent.

The crew of the *Brittanic* had strongly cautioned us about leaving the ship as the city was still besieged by the closing days of the Spanish Civil War, but Sara had been sick for two days from the storm rocking the boat, and she insisted she needed some time on land to steady herself.

Lights ahead shone through half-curtained windows. The sign above the door read *Bar Marcella*, and we ducked in quickly out of the rain. The place was nearly full. All the seats along the ornate bar on the far wall were taken. As we took off our wet coats, I saw a single table at the back with four chairs and led my wife through the crowd.

No one paid us much notice, and we took our seats, hanging our wet clothes on a coat stand beside the table. A young woman came up, looking quite flustered and tired.

"Hola, que quieres beber?"

"Beer and wine?" I asked.

"Absinthe!" she said impatiently.

I shook my head, knowing we didn't need the numbing effects of the strong liqueur, particularly Sara, who had worked hard over the years to overcome her issues with drugs and alcohol. "Vino blanco," I said, motioning for one, "tea for my wife and a menu," I continued, not knowing the words in Spanish.

The woman rushed away without acknowledging our order. I turned to Sara. "Are you feeling any better?"

She took a deep breath and wiped strands of wet hair away from her face. "I still feel like the ground is moving under me. I can't believe we still have the crossing to Miami to come."

"The captain said a break in the weather is coming soon."

Sara and I had been married a little over ten years. We lived in New York and, during parts of the year, in our old beach house in Grayton Beach along the northern Gulf Coast of Florida, where we had first met in 1925. Sara's mother, Lila, Had run a small hotel there in the village until her death that year in the wake of a killer hurricane that swept through the area.

I had taken refuge in what was then a friend's old beach cottage to get away from the betrayal and corruption of my family and their illicit bootlegging business, leaving Atlanta and finding myself in the midst of the lives of Lila and Sara Dalton and Sara's blind and extremely gifted daughter, Melanee. Sara had been away in New Orleans when I first arrived, but returned to care for her daughter, escaping the dangers and excess of life with a Cajun club owner in the old city.

When Sara was on the brink of returning to New Orleans and leaving her daughter again, I made one of the most difficult choices of my life and broke off a relationship with a woman in New York who I had met when my first novel was published. I felt for young Melanee's sake that I needed to stay with her and her mother and try to bring some sense of normalcy and stability to their lives.

We were married later that year, and with Melanee's bright spirit and my own persistent presence in her life, Sara had managed, for the most part, to escape her demons, and we had lived a full and comfortable life since as I pursued my writing career.

Melanee had moved with us to New York where we finalized adoption proceedings to formally make her my daughter. Her innate musical skills as well as a wonderful teacher and mentor had led her to a career playing the violin with the New York Philharmonic Orchestra. She had also married recently and had a young daughter of her own. We are so proud of how she has built such a fulfilling life for herself and her family, despite the challenges of her sightless world.

I looked across the table in the old Spanish bar and took in the familiar lines of my wife's face as she surveyed the place and all the people enjoying their food and drink. I had come to truly love Sara over our years together and felt blessed that she was healthy and safe. We were even considering having a child of our own.

The server returned and placed the drinks down on the table along with a crumpled and damp menu. I pointed out a couple of selections of tapas, and she rushed away again.

I held my glass up to Sara's cup. "Cheers." We both took a sip.

"You're sure we're safe here?" she asked.

I nodded. "The war is winding down, and the fighting is far to the west, I'm told."

"I wouldn't care if they were dropping bombs outside," Sara said. "I needed to get off that ship! I don't think I've ever been so sick."

I hesitated to remind her of how ill she had been from the excess of drugs and drink during her siege in New Orleans, but I didn't say anything.

"Coulter? Mathew Coulter?"

I looked up in surprise at the sound of my name and the man who had just come up to our table. There was no mistaking the familiar face of one of America's most prominent writers.

He held out his hand. "Hemingway. Ernest Hemingway."

I stood to shake his hand. "Of course. Very nice to meet you. This is my wife, Sara."

Hemingway took her right hand and kissed the back of it. "You married well, Coulter." He turned back to me. "Love your last book. Wish I'd written it."

I was taken aback that this man even knew who I was, let alone praised my work. "Thank you," I managed to reply back, unsteadily. "I must say the same," I continued.

Hemingway held up a hand. "Enough of that. Let's have a drink." He turned to find the server, but she was already coming up with a glass of the pale-green Absinthe that she handed to him, taking the empty one from his hand. He raised his glass. "To the joy of finding fellow Americans here in this God-cursed place, let alone one of my favorite writers."

We tapped glasses and cups and took a drink.

Hemingway said, "What the hell are the two of you doing here? You know there's a war going on?"

I explained the unexpected layover of our cruise ship.

"You'll be okay here in the city," he said. "How long?"

"Our captain hopes for better weather in the next day or so. We need to get back to the States for our daughter's birthday in a couple of weeks, so we hope things calm down soon."

Hemingway nodded and took another drink. "Been one hell of a mess over here the past couple of years. Franco and the fascists are taking over. I love this country, but fear where she looks to be headed."

"I've read some of your posts back home," Sara said.

"The American people need to know what's going on. The Germans and Italians are in the middle of all this, backing Franco and, I'm afraid, setting the stage for more trouble across Europe."

"Let's hope not," I said.

A woman whose face seemed familiar walked up and put her hand on Hemingway's shoulder. "We need to get going."

He stood to introduce his companion. "This is Martha Gelhorn," he said. "She's been traveling and writing about the war with me."

Introductions and formalities quickly ensued, then Gelhorn said, "Really, Hem, it's late. We have to get back to the hotel."

I could tell from his expression he was tempted to send her on ahead without him, but better sense somehow prevailed. "Coulter, Sara, it's been a great pleasure." He shook both of our hands. "Keep your heads up and have a safe passage back to the States."

I stood as he walked away through the crowd.

Sara said, "That was really Ernest Hemingway."

"Yes, it was."

Chapter Two

Pawleys Island, South Carolina. Present day.

It was a gray morning along the Carolina coast. Heavy clouds from a storm the previous night had not cleared. A small break in the cover a few miles out allowed the morning sun to shine through in a brilliant dagger of light piercing down into the Atlantic. The wind pushed in hard from the east, the last remnants of the storm. Sea birds floated high on the currents, looking down for their next meal.

Hanna Walsh felt her heart beating hard, her breath coming in labored gasps as she neared the end of her morning run. She had never been an active jogger; in fact, she had quite despised even the thought of it. But a recent visit with her doctor and a few more pounds showing up on the bathroom scale had convinced her she needed to start getting more active.

Alex had agreed to start running with her in the mornings. They had begun slowly, running and walking a mile or two, then a bit further each week. They were up to five miles now, usually three days per week.

She was running alone today because Alex had an early meeting down at the sheriff's department. There seemed to be many more meetings those days since he had been asked to fill in for Sheriff Pepper Stokes who was still recovering from a stroke.

As acting sheriff for the past couple of months, Alex was starting to show the strain of the administrative burden and ultimate responsibility for everything that occurred in the department. *Maybe it's my imagination,* Hanna thought, *but there seems to be more gray suddenly along the edges of Alex's dark, bushy hair.*

She could see her family's old beach house coming up to the left through the dunes and beach scrub. She looked at her new GPS running watch and frowned that her time was not improving.

She slowed to a walk and started to catch her breath. *I thought this was supposed to start getting easier!*

When she was out in front of the house, she took off her shoes and socks and waded out into the cool Atlantic. She bent down and scooped two handfuls of water to splash on her face. The salt taste hung on her lips as she took another scoop, running her wet hands through her sweat-soaked hair.

She stood looking out across the vast expanse of ocean, only a single sailboat out on the horizon. A dolphin surfaced not twenty yards away, swerving in her direction now, its gray sides shimmering in the morning light. She made eye contact with the magnificent creature for just a moment, then backed up onto the shore.

When she tuned, she was surprised to come face to face with her next-door neighbor, Quinn Burke. "Oh, good morning!" Hanna said, a little irritated the woman had invaded her quiet morning space.

"Hanna, my God, I thought that was a shark out there!" Quinn replied, a sincerely concerned look on her face.

Hanna laughed. "If it was a shark, I would have been running for shore, trust me. How are you, Quinn?"

The woman had moved in next door nearly a year ago with her two little yappy Yorkshire Terriers. She was an acclaimed novelist and had a manner that was beyond "quirky", bordering on bizarre, Hanna often thought. They'd had their issues in the past, particularly during the time shortly after she had moved to the beach here on Pawleys Island, when she had become the prime suspect in the murder of Alex's ex-wife down the beach. She was eventually cleared of the charges, but it had set a difficult tone for their relationship, further challenged by Quinn's obvious attraction to Alex.

Quinn pulled her close and hugged her, brushing her cheek with a light kiss. "I'm fine, dear," she replied, apparently not concerned with Hanna's sweaty body and clothes from her run. Her short, bobbed hair was dyed a new color of silver and blue Hanna hadn't seen before. "I saw you running up the beach from my deck and wanted to catch you."

"What's up?"

"I'm hosting a dinner party this Friday night. I know it's a little last minute, but I'm seeing this guy I'm actually quite crazy about, and I'd like him to meet some of my friends out here."

Hanna thought for a moment about their weekend calendar and couldn't think of any conflicts. "I'll need to check with Alex when he gets back tonight, but I think we're clear."

"Oh, terrific!" Quinn gushed. "I was hoping you two could come. I've invited Sheila Graham, Alex's partner over at the department, and a man down the beach I think she'd enjoy meeting."

"Playing matchmaker?" Hanna teased. She knew Quinn and Deputy Graham had become friends.

"Us girls have to look out for each other."

"So, who's this new guy you're seeing?" Hanna asked.

Quinn hesitated. "Now, don't get the wrong idea."

"About what?"

"Well, Carlos is a fighter . . ."

"A what?" Hanna replied, her eyes wide in astonishment.

"Mixed martial arts. He's a professional fighter. You know, you've seen it on TV."

"Well, actually not, but what an interesting way to make a living."

"He's very good . . . former world champion apparently."

"Where did you meet this guy?"

"I've been working out down at the gym off the island a few days a week and met Carlos there about a month ago. He started helping me with my weight training."

"You're doing weight training?"

"And you're running now?" Quinn shot back. "What's gotten in to the two of us!"

They both laughed.

Hanna said, "I'm pretty sure we can make dinner. I'll check with Alex tonight and let you know." Her thoughts drifted back to the day that Quinn had saved Alex's life. She shuddered when she let herself imagine what might have happened that day if Quinn hadn't driven by Alex confronting Beau Richards.

"Please, I hope you can come. I really want you to meet Carlos and help break the ice a little with Sheila and this guy I'm setting her up with."

"Sounds like an interesting evening. How's the new book coming?"

"Just sent the manuscript off to my agent for a first look. By the time it comes back from her and all the editors and proofreaders at my publisher, I'm sure I won't even recognize the story."

Hanna shook her head, having no idea what was involved in actually getting a book finished and out to the public. "I did read your first novel a couple of months ago. Very well done. Love the ending . . . a little twisted, but fitting for the story, I thought."

"Thank you," Quinn replied. "I wrote that so long ago, I'm not sure I even remember how it ended. Would you like to read a draft of this new book? I have a list of fifty or so advance readers I always send my books out to."

"I would like that, yes," Hanna said.

"I'll email you a copy to download to your computer. I will warn you, it's a little darker than the early book I wrote all those years ago. If you thought that story was twisted, hold on to your hat!"

Hanna suddenly regretted her offer to read the manuscript, not sure entirely what she was getting herself into.

Quinn said, "If you don't like it, if it's not your thing, just put it aside. No problem."

"Like I said, I really enjoyed your book. Can't wait to see this latest effort."

"I'll get it over to you later today." She turned to leave as her two dogs were making a fuss up on her deck. "Let me know about Saturday."

Hanna watched her neighbor walk up across the beach to her house. *Can't wait to meet the fighter!* she thought.

Chapter Three

Grayton Beach, Florida. 1939.

Our passage to Miami was uneventful, and we took the long train ride up the state of Florida through Orlando and Tallahassee, and then across the Panhandle to Panama City.

Our friends, Jimmy and Rebecca Headley, met us at the train station with their car. I had bought Jimmy's family's beach cottage in Grayton Beach some years ago. His prominent family in Atlanta had another home in South Florida they preferred in the cooler months. Jimmy ran one of the family businesses in Atlanta now, but spent considerable time on the coast.

Jimmy had met and married Rebecca during my first vigil down there in the twenties. She was the daughter of the Bidwells who ran the General Store in nearby Point Washington. Her father had passed away recently. Her mother still ran the store, and her brother had renovated and run Lila Dalton's old hotel in Grayton Beach.

We all exchanged hugs as we came down from the train car. Then, our lovely daughter, Melanee, stepped forward from the crowd, and we both pulled her into our arms.

"Welcome home, world travelers!" she said, as she stepped back holding her mother's hand. "We were a little worried when we got word your ship had been delayed in Spain."

Sara said, "We were fine, and your father made a new friend. I'll tell you about it later."

Melanee had been born blind at birth, but had more than overcome her sightless challenges to lead a very full and vibrant life. She also possessed an uncanny sixth sense that continues to surprise us all.

"Where's the little one?" Sara asked.

"Mrs. Bidwell and Robert offered to watch her," Melanee said. "We thought it would be too hot in the car." Robert Crowell was Melanee's husband, another member of the orchestra in New York.

"Can't wait to see that little rascal," Sara replied. "Is she really three already?"

"Going on thirteen!" Melanee replied in exasperation.

"I'm so excited to see her," Sara said, hugging her daughter again, holding her hand as we began walking away, Jimmy and I trying to manage all the bags.

We were walking behind the women when Jimmy said, "An old friend is waiting to see you when we get out to the beach."

"Who is that?"

"Louise Palumbo."

I looked over at him in surprise. The woman was the wife of the New Jersey gangster Willy Palumbo, who I had forged a friendship and unholy alliance with back during my early days in Grayton Beach. Willy and his wife, Louise, had also sought refuge in the little out-of-the-way beach town when his relationship with the crime families to the north had soured.

When both my brother and father had passed away in Atlanta and the family business was left in a precarious position that I wanted no part of, Willy offered to take the reins of the sprawling and illicit liquor business and financially support my mother and sister in the process. He had made good on that promise in the ensuing years, though I chose to refuse any monetary gain from this new business alliance.

"Why in the world would Louise be back down here?" I asked.

"She and Willy have been living over in Miami, as you know. They're having a bit of a difficult time, it seems."

"Why am I not surprised?" The relationship had always been on the edge of calamity from the time I first met them at Lila's hotel back in 1925. Louise even had a brief fling with a local man who ended up in the morgue, though no charges were ever brought against Willy or his big bodyguard, Anthony.

"She's here with one of their sons, Paolo. Wait till you meet him!"

"I haven't spoken to Willy in years," I said, thinking back on our days together in Grayton Beach. "He's reached out a couple of times, but I've tried to keep my distance."

"Wisely so," Jimmy replied.

The car ride west along the coast through heavy pine forests and then down along the glorious white sand beaches leading out to the narrow and rutted road to Grayton Beach was always a glorious journey. As we approached the little town, I thought back to my first day there in 1925, when my car got hopelessly stuck in the loose sand. Rebecca Bidwell had come up on horseback to give me a ride into town. It was the day I had first met Melanee and her grandmother, Lila. Melanee was twelve at the time, as I recall.

The old water tower loomed above the live oak and pines as we drove into town. Weather-worn beach cottages were tucked back in the shadows. Turning left at the beach road, we approached the Beach Hotel on the left, a small, white two-story structure with just ten rooms, and a large veranda along the front. Across the street was the more recently built General Store.

The town seemed abandoned, but it was likely just the midday heat that was keeping everyone inside. Ahead, I saw our own beach cottage nestled in the dunes on the shore of Grayton Lake that ran out into the Gulf of Mexico. The small cottage, built up on pilings, had nearly been destroyed with me in it during the 1925 hurricane. Rebecca's brother, Jonas, and I had worked on the repairs, and it now sat as if it had been there for decades.

Jimmy pulled the car up into the sand drive next to the cottage, and we all got out. Melanee came around the car, and I reached for her hand. "I'm sorry we missed your birthday," I said. "We couldn't get the captain to go any faster across the Atlantic."

"It's okay," she said, pulling me into her arms in a tight hug. "The Headleys and Robert are planning a big dinner and celebration tonight down at the pavilion on the beach. I told them not to fuss, but they insisted."

A twenty-fifth birthday is a big deal," I said. "I'm so glad everyone could arrange to come back to Florida to celebrate."

Sara came up and put her arms around both of us. "I just love it when we're all back down here together," she said, kissing the top of her daughter's head.

I thought back to less pleasant times when Sara's struggles had nearly cost her daughter's life, but quickly pushed those thoughts aside.

The sky was a brilliant blue above, high wispy clouds to the west, the sand, blinding white, leading out to the Gulf which shimmered emerald green and blue. White-capped waves rolled up on shore in the breeze from the southwest. It was a marvelous day, one to embrace and not dwell on the past, I thought to myself, as we pulled out bags to take inside.

Chapter Four

Georgetown, South Carolina. Present day.

The May heat was stifling, even this early, as Alex Frank walked from the parking lot to the Georgetown County Sheriff's Department office where he had a meeting with the new county prosecutor. Even the low cloud cover from the past night's storms couldn't offer relief from the oppressive heat and humidity.

He'd watched Hanna sleeping for a few moments before he left at 7:00 a.m. to get down to the office in time. Seeing her face calm, lost in the comfort of sleep, her hair tousled across the pillow, her breathing even and unhurried, gave him great peace as he considered how much she had been through since their time together. He felt guilty for not being able to stay for their morning run which had become a nice addition to their lives, certainly a healthier effort than their not-so-healthy selections of food and drink.

As he made his way to his office at the back of the building, he nodded to a few other early arrivals and night-shift staff. Deputy Sheila Graham was already at her desk and on the telephone. She tipped her head and smiled as he passed. He noticed his administrative assistant, Kay, had not arrived yet as he surveyed her always-tidy desk and work area.

He turned on the light in his office and closed the door behind him. A wall of windows let him look out over the large room of cubicles. The nameplate of Sheriff Pepper Stokes was still on the center of the desk. He hadn't seen the need to remove it. He knew it was a temporary assignment and truly hoped his boss would be back to work soon. He had visited Pepper the previous day. He was home now, slowly recovering from a devastating stroke that had left him still confined to a wheelchair and struggling to speak, though his recovery progress was noticeable, and Alex had been encouraged after his visit.

He sorted through a few message slips that Kay had left for him. His old friend and colleague, Will Foster, from the Charleston FBI office had called late yesterday. Alex had been out on a call and had not returned to the office. Foster hadn't tried to reach his cell, so he assumed it wasn't urgent and pushed it aside with the other messages. He saw that his voicemail light was blinking on his desk phone, so he lifted the receiver and pressed the button for his calls. The first was from Foster.

"Alex, we need your help following up on a lead up that way on a fentanyl smuggling operation. Call when you get a minute."

Alex listened to two more messages, then hung up the phone. He thought about Foster's call. The rise in fentanyl-related overdoses and related crimes was more than alarming. The prescription drug fentanyl had long been used as a potent opioid pain killer. The illegally made version was an extremely dangerous and often deadly drug now accounting for tens of thousands of deaths across the country. It was reportedly fifty times stronger than heroin and one hundred times stronger than morphine. Mexican drug cartels were profiting handsomely from the illegal trade, and even in South Carolina, far from the Mexican border, it was becoming a major threat.

Just three days ago, he had responded to a call at a family's home near Dugganville. Their seventeen-year-old son had been found unresponsive in his room. When Alex arrived, the paramedics had been unable to revive the boy and were loading him into the ambulance to take him down to the emergency room. They shook their heads when Alex asked if there was any hope.

He looked at his watch. It was 7:25, and his appointment with the new prosecutor, Marjorie Willett, was set for 7:30. He had a long relationship with Willett going back to his days in the Charleston Police Department when she served in the DA's office there. She was known as a tough, no-nonsense prosecutor who won the majority of her cases, on occasion with questionable legal maneuvers.

Alex recalled one particular case where he had arrested a young man on murder charges related to a gang shootout in the city. As the investigation continued, Alex became less certain they had the right suspect. At trial, Alex tried to cite new evidence that implicated two other men in the shooting, but Willett blocked him and the defense attorneys at every turn. The suspect was ultimately convicted and sentenced to twenty-five years to life at the sentencing hearing.

That trial had been over five years ago. The man was still in prison, his lawyers continuing to press for his release on appeal. Alex had been called back on two occasions to testify, but Willett and her team had built a nearly impenetrable wall of guilt, and he saw little hope for the man's release.

He looked up and saw Willett standing at his door. He rose and motioned for her to come in. He came around the desk and shook her hand, offering her a seat at his round conference table in the corner. She was a tall and stout woman, nearing six feet in height. Her gray hair was cut short, framing a pale face with little or no makeup. She wore a simple blue pant suit with a white blouse buttoned at the neck. There was no wedding ring on her left hand, though Alex thought he remembered she had been married back in Charleston.

"How are you, Alex?" she asked, arranging several file folders in front of her on the table.

"Fine, Marjorie. You getting settled in over at your new office?" He chose not to bring up the Charleston murder case and start their new relationship off on the wrong foot.

She nodded, then said, "You've had quite a professional journey since our days back in Charleston. The FBI stint and now the Sheriff's Office. What's next? DEA? CIA?"

Alex smiled. "I'm quite happy right here," he said. "Now, what can I help you with?"

She opened one of the files in front of her and slid a report across the table to him. "The state police arrested this guy two days ago during a traffic stop out on I-95, a little north of here."

Alex scanned the report. A man named Miguel Juarez was taken into custody for possession of a large quantity of illegal drugs, including heroin and fentanyl found in his trunk. "Who is he connected with?" he asked.

"He's not talking. A slick lawyer from Atlanta flew in to represent him," Willett replied.

"Atlanta? Must be a valuable asset for somebody."

"Indeed."

"So, how can we help?"

"Juarez lives in a trailer park outside of Dugganville. The state cops want to turn this over to the locals, in this case, your department."

"Okay," Alex said, "what else do you have on this guy?"

Willett pushed over the file with several other documents that Alex looked through. The past arrest sheet was alarming;

drugs, assault, check fraud. "Surprised I haven't heard of this guy before."

"Looks like most of these offenses date back to before you went to work for Stokes."

"Right. So, where is he now?"

"He's being held in Charleston, but they're having him transferred up here this morning. It's our case now," Willett said, a wry smile on her face. "Look forward to working with you again, sheriff."

Alex let the smug response slide. "Who are you going to assign to this?"

"I'll be handling it myself."

"Get me the attorney's name, and I'll have my wife reach out to her father's law firm in Atlanta to get a rundown on this guy."

"And how is Hanna?"

"She's good. Working for a small firm off the island."

"I'm sure she misses her legal clinic back in Charleston," Willett said. "She was doing some good work down there."

"Thank you, I'll tell her you mentioned that," Alex replied, surprised at the woman's gracious comment.

Willett passed over another file. "Here's the rundown on the attorney and notes from the initial interrogation." She stood, indicating her desire to end the meeting. "I want to be closely involved with this case, Alex. Let me know when you plan to have your first go round with this guy."

"Will do," Alex replied, standing and reaching across the table to shake her hand. "I have a call to return to Will Foster at the FBI office. He wants to talk about a fentanyl case. May be related?"

"Not sure," Willett said, looking at her watch. "Let me know what Foster's got. I need to get over to my office. I have little doubt this guy has ties to one of the cartels. We need to shut this down, Alex."

He nodded and then led her to the door. "I'll let you know when we're going to sit down with Juarez this afternoon."

Chapter Five

Grayton Beach, Florida. 1939.

The covered pavilion in the dunes looking out over the beach and Gulf of Mexico had also been destroyed during the hurricane. Jonas Bidwell had rebuilt it several years later, after the hotel had been restored and re-opened. It had always been a vibrant center of activity for hotel guests and town residents.

As the light faded early in the March evening, Sara and I walked down through the sand to join the others. We could see people gathering around a bar set up in one corner. Round tables set for dinner covered most of the wooden deck of the pavilion, only a small space at the far end for a band and room to dance. The band was already playing soft music, two men and a woman with drums and two guitars. The woman sang a ballad I was unfamiliar with, her voice drifting on the breeze off the water.

My new son-in-law, Robert, came up to us and welcomed us back. In his arms he held our granddaughter, Helen. She giggled as we both kissed her on the cheek. Her curly red hair bounced as she struggled to get down. Robert finally let her down, and she reached for Sara's hand.

"Grandma, come with me. I want to show you where we're sitting."

Sara excused the two of them and followed after her little treasure.

Robert said, "I'm glad you're both back safe. That was quite a journey."

"Sorry we're a few days late. The weather just wouldn't cooperate."

"Not a problem. We held off the celebration when we heard about your delays."

"How's our Melanee?" I asked.

"She's doing so well, even with all the ups and downs of raising a three-year-old. Our nanny helps so that we can both keep working."

"I can't wait to see the latest performance when we all get back to New York."

Robert looked back across the crowd. Melanee had joined her mother and daughter, and they were sharing appetizers from a tray one of the servers had offered. "The new season starts next month. Melanee has a marvelous violin solo in one of the pieces. It's breathtaking, really."

"I can't wait."

"I met your old friend."

"Who is that?" I asked.

He looked over toward the bar. Louise Palumbo was standing there with a young man who I assumed to be their son, Paolo. They both had drinks and were talking with Jonas Bidwell. She was a striking woman, her thick black hair showing only traces of early gray piled high around her face, featuring the elegant lines of her Italian descent. We made eye contact, and she excused herself and started our way.

She greeted me with a big smile and hug. She smelled of lavender and wine, and her long dress was a brilliant green, shimmering in the lights along the beams of the pavilion above.

"Welcome home, Mathew," she said, her brown eyes glistening and moist.

"It does feel like home, doesn't it?" I said, taking her free hand in mine. "And how is Willy?" I asked, quickly regretting bringing up something that would surely spoil the bright mood of the moment.

She didn't falter and just shook her head slowly. "You know Willy, always so much drama."

I smiled and nodded. "And Anthony is still watching his back?"

"Never out of sight, I'm afraid."

Robert excused himself to join his family.

I said, "Forgive me, but I understand the two of you may be having some issues."

"You've been talking to Jimmy."

I nodded again.

"I unloaded on him the other night after a little too much wine at the hotel. It's always something with my husband. He's got his mind set on going back north to patch things up with the families. They're barely tolerating him being away in Florida, but I'm afraid of what might happen if he goes back."

"I'm sorry he's not here. We really need to catch up."

"He's actually coming in tomorrow," she replied. "He called the hotel earlier. He wanted to be here tonight for Melanee's party, but something came up. I can only imagine."

I had mixed feelings about the arrival of the old gangster. He and I had become quite close those many years ago, but there was always the threat of chaos and danger when he was around. He seemed to attract it like flies on dead fish.

Later, after dinner, I asked my daughter to dance, and we moved slowly to the music, my one leg still stiff from an injury in the French countryside during the war. My thoughts turned for a moment to a nurse named Celeste who had helped me recover in the hospital in Paris. I remembered the joy of new love blossoming and the heartbreak when I had to leave her.

Melanee moved far more gracefully than I to the music. I squeezed her close and said, "Happy birthday, dear."

"Thanks, Papa." She looked up at me with her sightless gaze. "You know, I've been looking for our old friend, Champ, the mockingbird."

I chuckled, remembering the little rascal that used to mooch crackers from us on the porch of the cottage. "I don't know how long mockingbirds live. I wouldn't be surprised to have him show up any time." We named him Champ because he was always quite successful in fighting off the other birds to get the most crackers.

"How did mother do on the long trip?" she asked. She was always concerned about her mother's mental and physical health after all the mishaps during her younger years.

"She did fine," I said. "A little seasick in rough seas off the coast of Spain, but otherwise, we had a marvelous time. It was quite interesting to show her Paris after not having been back since the war. And you'll never guess who we met when we got blown ashore in the storm off Barcelona."

"She already told me!" Melanee gushed. "I can't believe Ernest Hemingway knew you and likes your books."

"I never asked because we were together such a short time, but I assume he recognized me from the back cover photo of me on my books, or maybe he saw some of the press about our book tour over there."

"Well, anyway, you must be very proud."

"It was quite an experience. I wish we'd had more time," I replied.

"Are you working on another book?" she asked.

"Yes, I started it on the ship over to Europe. It's a sequel to the last."

"You'll read it to me early?" she asked excitedly.

"I always do."

A commotion on the other side of the dance floor took our attention. Jimmy Headley and Paolo Palumbo were having words that appeared to be less than friendly.

"Excuse me a minute, honey." I escorted my daughter back to our table then made my way through the dance crowd to my friend arguing with the Palumbo boy. Rebecca was standing off to the side, an embarrassed frown on her face.

I stepped between the two men and put my hands on their chests to hold them apart. "Gentlemen, please. This is my daughter's birthday."

"Get your hand off me!" Palumbo hissed.

I stepped back. "Jimmy, what's going on?"

"Little Palumbo here is getting a little too handsy with my wife. He cut in to dance with Rebecca, and I had to rescue her."

"You call me that again," Palumbo said in his heavy Jersey accent, "I'll take your head off." He looked like a far younger version of his father, slimmer certainly, but a middle that was expanding quickly, his hair black and combed back wet.

Louise Palumbo came up and pushed her son away from the confrontation. "That's enough, Paolo! I think you need to call it a night. I'll see you back at the hotel."

He looked back at his mother for a moment, then pointed at Jimmy. "This isn't over!" Then, he turned and stormed away.

Louise turned to both of us and reached for Rebecca's hand. "I'm sorry. My son has had a little too much to drink tonight. He'll be better in the morning."

Jimmy said, "I think it will be better for all involved if he gets back to Miami as soon as possible."

Rebecca came close and hugged her husband. "I'm sorry—"

Jimmy cut her off. "You have nothing to be sorry about. I saw the whole thing."

Louise said, "I'm so sorry, dear. It won't happen again. She looked at the retreating form of her son walking up through the dunes into town. "I should get back." She turned to me and said, "I hope we didn't spoil Melanee's party."

"She'll be fine," I said.

"Good night, then." She turned and started back to the hotel.

Jimmy said, "I'm really sorry, Mathew. I just couldn't—"

I raised a hand. "It's okay. Let's get back to the celebration."

Jimmy nodded and took his wife's hand, leading her back to the dance floor.

I glanced over at our table. Melanee was in deep conversation with Jonas Bidwell. Sara was staring back at me, a concerned look on her face. I gave her what I hoped was a reassuring nod.

I couldn't help but remember a similar night, back in 1925, when Paolo Palumbo's father, Willy, got in a similar, but far more violent, scuffle with a young man who was making inappropriate moves on his wife, Louise. *Like I said, chaos and danger usually follow the Palumbos.*

Chapter Six

Pawleys Island, South Carolina. Present day.

Hanna hung up the phone in her office at the law firm as she finished a conference call with another attorney up in Greenville on a custody case she was handling for a local woman. Her phone immediately buzzed from the receptionist out front.

"Do you have time to see someone?"

"Who is it?"

"Young woman who needs help with a divorce."

Hanna looked at the calendar on her phone. "I have twenty minutes. Bring her back, please."

The receptionist ushered in a young Hispanic woman who introduced herself as Helena. As the door closed, Hanna joined the woman at her conference table.

"How can we help you, Helena?" She was a short woman, barely reaching five feet. She was dressed simply in faded jeans and a black t-shirt. Her long black hair was held up in a loose bun on the top of her head. Hanna noticed a thin gold band on her ring finger.

"My husband has been arrested . . . again," she began with a heavy accent. He's a very bad man, Ms. Walsh. I need to be rid of him."

"Please call me Hanna."

The woman nodded.

"What was he arrested for?"

27

"He is running drugs again."

"Again?" Hanna asked.

"He's been arrested several times."

"And where is he now?"

"In Charleston. He called me last night. He was picked up by the police and is being held in Charleston. I hope they never let him out!"

"Do you have children, Helena?"

"Yes, we have three daughters. I'm afraid for them, Hanna. He is very rough with them . . . and with me."

"He hurts you and the children?"

Helena nodded and looked down.

"And where are your daughters?"

"My mother is watching them this morning."

"Does your husband know you want a divorce?" Hanna watched the panic come across the woman's face.

She shook her head. "No, I'm afraid to tell him. I'm afraid of what he might do."

Hanna handed her a new client form to fill out and watched as she wrote her full name on the first line, *Helena Juarez*. While the woman was filling out the information, Hanna explained how she would handle the case and what the fees would be.

"The money is not a problem," Helena replied, looking up. "My husband makes a lot of money. I've set some aside. I knew I would eventually have to get away."

Alex watched as the transfer was made to take Miguel Juarez into custody. He was processed and then led away to a holding cell. Juarez was a shorter, very thickly built man. The dark skin on his face was framed with jet-black hair pulled back in a short ponytail. The two officers from the state police signed all the paperwork and left.

Sheila Graham came up as they were leaving. "Who's our new house guest?" she asked.

Alex filled her in on the arrest of Juarez as they walked together back to his office. She sat across from him at his desk. He said, "We need to go out to his house and see what we can find before we sit down with this guy. His attorney will be here around noon."

"Okay, what have we got on him so far?" Graham asked.

He handed her the files. As she started to look at the documents, his cellphone buzzed. "It's Hanna," he said, looking at the call screen.

Graham stood to leave. "I'll look through this."

He nodded as he took the call. "Good morning. Sorry I missed our run."

"I thought we were starting to get in shape," he heard Hanna say. "Thought I was going to die the last mile this morning."

"We need to keep at it. I'm feeling better a little at a time."

"Not soon enough for me!"

"What's up?"

"Sorry to bother you, but do you have a Miguel Juarez in custody?"

"Just took him in a little while ago. Transferred up from Charleston. Why?"

"I had his wife in here a few minutes ago. She wants to file for divorce."

"Really? Did you learn anything about Juarez?"

"Only that she's afraid for herself and her three daughters. She knows he's been arrested again and wants out. Do you think he'll get released on bail?"

"Not sure yet. He's got a hot-shot attorney from Atlanta representing him."

"Sounds mob-related," Hanna said.

"Mexican cartel, we think. This lawyer is named Rick Guidall. Can you check with your contacts at your father's firm in Atlanta and see what they know about this guy?"

"I've got another meeting in a minute, but I'll get a call out to them before lunch."

"Thank you," Alex replied. "Sheila and I are headed over to his house to see what we can learn before we talk with him this afternoon. Do you think the wife is going home now?"

"I think so. Her mother is there watching the children."

"Okay," he replied. "I'll let you know if we learn anything."

"By the way, your favorite neighbor stopped me on the beach this morning."

Alex turned to look out the window in exasperation. "What does Quinn want now?"

"She invited us to dinner Friday night—"

"No!" he said, quickly cutting her off.

"She wants us to meet her new boyfriend."

"We're busy!"

"No we're not," Hanna said. "And she's invited Sheila and a guy she wants her to meet."

"Do you really want to get in the middle of all this? I just saw Sheila, and she didn't mention any of this."

"We can talk about it tonight."

He could hear the frustration in her voice. "Look, I'm sorry, but this woman is nothing but trouble."

"She saved your life, Alex."

"Don't remind me."

The mobile home park was a mile off Highway 17, on a road just south of the Dugganville turnoff. Alex turned his pickup truck at the entrance. Sheila Graham was in the passenger seat. The park looked generally well kept. He navigated his way through the narrow drive, finding the Juarez home at the back. There was a late-model Buick in the drive. He parked the truck behind it, and they both got out.

Before they reached the front door, it opened, and a short Hispanic woman came out of the small front porch. "Can I help you?" she asked in a heavy Spanish accent.

"Are you Helena?" Alex asked.

She nodded, looking both of them in the department uniforms. "Is this about my husband?"

"Yes, can we have a word with you, please?" he asked.

"I don't want to upset my children. Can we talk out here?" She came down the steps and led them over to her car.

"Of course," Alex said. "You may know, we have your husband in custody for drug-related charges."

"Yes, he called me last night."

"Your husband has quite a long criminal record, Mrs. Juarez," Graham said.

"I am well aware. I am seeking a divorce. We have had enough."

An older woman came out on the porch and asked something in Spanish. Helena Juarez answered, and the woman went back inside. "That is my mother. She lives with us and helps watch the children when I'm at work."

"Do you know who your husband is working for?" Alex asked.

"I have nothing to say."

"If you're leaving him, ma'am," Sheila began, "why won't you help us with the investigation?"

"My husband works for some very bad people," Helena said, softly. "I don't want my family to get into any trouble with them."

"All we need is a name," Alex said. "This won't come back on you."

"Of course it will!" she replied angrily. "These people have no souls. They won't hesitate to kill us all."

Alex looked over at Graham who raised an eyebrow. Turning back to the woman, he said, "We can offer you and your family protection if you'll help us."

She started shaking her head and walking back to the steps. "There is no hiding from these people! You must leave. If they see you here we are all in danger." She hurried inside, slamming the door behind her.

"I guess I can't blame her," Graham said.

"Right," Alex replied, thinking about how sad it was that this woman and her family were in such a bad situation. "There's an office up front. Let's go see what they know about this guy."

The trailer park manager was an elderly man, likely in his eighties. He could barely stand from his desk when they first came into the office. "What can I do for you, officers?" he said in a frail voice.

Alex introduced the two of them and then said, "We have one of your residents, Miguel Juarez, in custody."

"What has he done now?" was the quick response. "Tried to get the scumbag and his family throw'd out a dozen times."

"Why is that?" Graham asked.

"You name it. He's not paying his rent on time. He's a danger to everyone else who lives here. Can't believe his sweet wife and kids are still livin' there with him."

Alex said, "Are you aware of any of his known associates or friends that might be coming around?"

"You tryin' to get me kilt, officer?"

"Just need a name, sir," Alex said.

The old man looked around the room, gathering his thoughts.

"Why are you afraid of this guy?" Graham asked.

"Ain't no secret they work for the cartels," he shot back.

"Who is *they*?" Alex asked.

"Juarez and his buddy who lives two doors down."

"A name, please," Alex repeated.

"Pays his rent in cash, when he bothers to pay. Let me check the file."

The man went back to his desk, sitting down and sorting through some files in the side drawer. He pulled one out and read from one of the documents, "Goes by Hernandez, Rios Hernandez, though I doubt that's his real name."

"Anything else on him?" Alex asked.

"No prior address. Just a cellphone number. Didn't have no social security number when we got the rental application from him. Probably an illegal, like most of 'em."

They got the address of the man's trailer and thanked the manager for his help.

As they were leaving, the old man said, "You find me strung up by my toes and gutted, you know the damn cartel got wind of me helpin' y'all."

Alex nodded, and they went out the door.

No one was home at the Hernandez trailer, and they were driving back to the department when Graham said, "I'll do a little digging when we get back and see what we've got on file with any drug cartel activity here in the county."

Alex said, "I thought Xander Lacroix and the Dellahousayes before him had the drug trade under control around here. With all of them gone now, not surprised one of the cartels would move in to take over the action."

"Still can't believe Lacroix got taken out," Graham said. "And still no leads on who killed him."

"Not that I've heard. Good riddance," Alex said, thinking back on all the bad blood between the two of them.

Chapter Seven

Grayton Beach, Florida. 1939.

I sat with my wife in my lap on the front porch of the old cottage. We were buried in the warmth of a blanket in an old Adirondack chair. The stars above sparkled bright in a dark, clear sky with just the sliver of a new moon.

Melanee and her family had turned in earlier and were asleep in the guest room.

"Why do we ever go back to New York?" Sara whispered.

"If Melanee wasn't there, I'm not sure we would," I said. "My publisher doesn't care where my next book is written, as long as I get it done."

"Let's not rush back."

"Agreed."

I looked out to the south at the calm waters of the Gulf aglow in the night sky beyond the long stretch of beach. "How about a walk? I'm nowhere near ready to fall asleep."

We put the blanket around our shoulders and walked down the steps and along the path to the beach. The scent of magnolia drifted on the air from a tree at the side of our cottage. The town was mostly dark and quiet as the hour grew late. The sand was cool on our feet as the sun's warmth faded. The waves had diminished to low swells sweeping almost silently onto the shore.

I felt the comfort of Sara's arm around my waist under the blanket and pulled her closer as a chill blew gently off the water.

"I love this place so much," Sara said. "When my mother first brought us here, I was so young I couldn't appreciate it at the time. She had this crazy idea of running the hotel, and I know she was happy here, so I have that. I always regret how much trouble and pain I brought to her."

"I don't want you to dwell on that," I said, softly. "We're beyond that now, and we're here in this lovely place together with our amazing daughter and so many friends."

She turned to face me and lifted up onto her toes, kissing me full and long on the mouth. "I love you, Mathew Coulter."

"I love you, too."

"I don't know where I'd be today without you. I'm not sure I'd still be alive, and where would Melanee be? I just can't bring myself to think about how badly things might have gone."

I kissed her again. "I told you, we're beyond all that."

She took my hand and pulled me down on the sand beside her. The blanket fell to the side. We sat together looking out at the magnificent water and beach stretching as far as we could see in both directions. I watched her lay back in the soft light and then pull me down to her. We kissed again, and she buried her face in the nook of my chin and shoulder.

Later, we gathered our clothes and dressed before walking barefoot out into the shallows, the cool water sweeping up to our knees. We stood there together for some time, holding hands and letting the sounds and smells of the place wash over us and comfort us.

In the morning, I woke early as usual and started coffee on the stove. When it was ready, I took a steaming cup and our blanket out onto the porch and settled into one of the old, worn chairs.

The sun was coming up beyond the dunes to the east, glowing red and hot in the coming morning. A bank of dark purple clouds drifted low, far offshore. The shapes and colors of the other cottages and buildings in Grayton Beach began to reveal themselves in the new light of day. A lone figure walked a big dog down at the end of the road.

I was startled when a black and white bird landed on the porch rail and squawked for attention.

"You're kidding me!" I said in response. I was tempted to go wake my daughter, but it was much too early. "How are you, Champ?"

The bird chirped back some unintelligible bird message and hopped up and down the rail. I had no idea if it was the same bird, but it certainly looked and acted like Champ. *How long do these little rascals live?*

"So, you want some breakfast?"

This seemed to get the pesky fellow more excited.

"Don't go away." I went back in and, as quietly as I could, looked through the few cabinets in the kitchen. I did, indeed, find a box half full of stale crackers and went back outside.

Champ was waiting impatiently for me, jumping precariously around on the wooden rail. I broke a cracker up into smaller pieces and spread them to the side, then sat back and watched the little glutton feast away. It was as if he hadn't eaten for days.

I heard the door open beside me and turned to see Melanee coming out in her pajamas. I'm sure she sensed the presence of our old friend in her innately surprising way.

"Champ! I knew you'd be back," she gushed as she felt her way over beside me.

I pulled her down on my leg. Our bird friend jumped around in excitement and squawked for more crackers. I handed one to Melanee, and she held it out. Champ scooted over and took it from her hand, then proceeded to peck it into pieces to munch down.

"I wonder where Maggie is? She must be nearby."

Melanee had named Champ's companion after my sister. I looked around in the trees but didn't see any other feathery creatures about. "It's been a long time, honey. I'm not sure this is really Champ. It might be one of his babies, for all we know."

"No, I'm sure this is Champ," she said, a bright smile on her face.

Sara came out and joined us, sleep still etched on her face. "Oh, you two! I can't believe you've found your old friend."

I gathered the two women in the world most dear to me around, and we enjoyed that early morning with our little beggar friend.

Later that morning, I was working at the small table in the cottage. Sara and Melanee were down at the beach with the rest of the family. I heard a car pull up and went to the door. I wasn't surprised to see my old friend and foe, Willy Palumbo, get out of the long black sedan. His bodyguard, Anthony, was getting out on the driver's side.

Palumbo had aged visibly since I'd seen him over ten years earlier. He had put even more weight on, but his face was gaunt, his hair nearly all gray.

"Coulter!" he yelled out as he came up the steps precariously and pulled me into a tight bear hug.

"How you doing, Willy?"

"Never been better, Mathew. You look great, son! Been reading all your books. You're a big star."

"Not really, but it's a living," I replied, stepping back. The ever-silent Anthony loomed ominously at the bottom of the steps, expressionless and seemingly looking straight through me. "What brings you to Grayton Beach again, Willy? Saw Louise and your son last night down at the pavilion."

"Yeah, yeah, heard it was little Melanee's birthday. Sorry I missed it."

"She's not so little anymore."

"Right, right. Can't wait to see her and Sara."

"So, why are you here?"

"Me and Louise come over every now and then from Miami for a little R&R. The Bidwell kid has done a nice job with the old hotel since we lost Lila back in the storm in '25."

"Yes, he has," I replied. "So, just a little vacation, then?"

"Yeah, we'll be here a few days. Catch up on some rest. Maybe get a fishing charter out of Destin. Want to come along?"

"Not much of a fisherman, Willy."

"Look, you're probably working, so I'll let you go, but let's get together for dinner tonight over at the hotel. Can you and the family join us?"

"I don't think we have any plans."

"Your mom and sister doing good?" he asked as he turned to go back down the steps, knowing full well I was aware of the financial support he was still providing to both of them from the family's liquor business he had taken over.

"Last I heard, they're great. Maggie got married again."

"Yeah, I heard about that. Big oil man over in Texas."

I nodded. "Good to see you Willy." And as I said it, I cringed to think about what sort of chaos would ensue as it always did when the old gangster was around.

Chapter Eight

Pawleys Island, South Carolina. Present day.

Hanna had just finished a salad at her desk that she'd brought in for lunch. She went to the kitchen to rinse her plate and refill her water bottle. *Hydration is important.* She reminded herself of the new fitness efforts she and Alex had embarked on.

On her way back to her office, her cell rang. She checked the number, and it was identified as *Unknown*. It was a 212-area code which she thought was New York City. *Oh, what the hell,* she thought, accepting the call.

"Hello, this is Hanna."

A woman's voice replied, "Ms. Walsh, we haven't met. My name is Janet Coulter Anders. My grandfather was one of the Coulters from Atlanta. I believe your father was closely related and actually ended up inheriting the Coulter home there.

Hanna was a bit cautious as she always was on the phone with strangers, but she said, "Well, hello Janet. It's very nice to meet you, even if it's just over the phone. And yes, I grew up in the house there on West Paces Ferry."

"I understand your father passed away recently. I'm very sorry."

"Thank you, Janet. Yes, it's been very hard to get on without him."

"Again, my condolences."

"Well, thank you," Hanna said, wondering where this was going. The woman sounded older, perhaps quite a bit older.

"You may know of my grandfather who is also gone now, Mathew Coulter."

"Yes, I've read some of his books. He was a great writer."

"Yes, I have to agree with you."

Hanna said, "It looks like you're calling from New York."

"Yes, I live there with my husband, but we come south quite often to our family's beach cottage in North Florida."

"In Grayton Beach? I visited there when I was a kid. Beautiful little town."

"Barely a town, even today," Janet said, chuckling. "Just a little village of cottages. My great-grandmother owned a small hotel there when my mother was a little girl, and my grandfather bought one of the cottages there from a friend way back in the 1920s. You must wonder why I'm calling."

"It's very nice of you to reach out," Hanna replied.

"Well, I'm actually down in Grayton Beach right now with my husband. We were going through some old files and boxes in the cottage to clean some things out. We came across one of my grandfather's manuscripts that, as far as we can tell, was never published."

"How exciting!" Hanna said, genuinely enthused. "What do you plan to do with it?"

"That's why I'm calling. I read the manuscript over the past couple of days, and I can understand now why Mathew Coulter never published the book."

"And why is that?" Hanna asked.

"The woman seemed to hesitate, then said, "There is some troubling information in the book about the Coulter family."

"What type of information?"

"I'd rather not say over the phone."

"Then why are you calling, Janet?"

"I understand you live on Pawleys Island in South Carolina."

"That's right."

"We'll be leaving Grayton Beach tomorrow and driving up the coast to get back to New York. I was wondering if we could stop by to see you on the way."

"Well, of course," Hanna replied. "We'd love to see you. When do you think you'd be coming through?"

"The day after tomorrow. Friday, I guess that would be."

"That would be fine, and you must stay over at *our* beach house, at least for the night."

"That's very kind, thank you."

"Can I text the address to this phone number?" Hanna asked.

"Yes, thank you, Hanna. I'm really looking forward to meeting you."

"And my husband, Alex, will be here as well. How many of you will be coming?"

"Just my husband and me. My daughter is grown and has kids of her own in Michigan. I hope I didn't upset you about my great-grandfather's manuscript."

"No, of course not."

"I just thought before we decide what to do with it, if anything, we should share this with someone with close roots to the Coulter family."

"I'll look forward to seeing you on Friday and discussing it in more detail," Hanna said.

"Thank you, Hanna. We'll call midday and give you a better idea of when we'll be getting in."

Chapter Nine

Grayton Beach, Florida. 1939.

Sara and I walked hand in hand down the dusty road from our cottage to the Beach Hotel just a couple of blocks up on the right. Melanee followed with her husband and daughter in tow. The worn, white-washed facade of the hotel was framed by the looming green branches of live oak and tall pines. I could see Willy Palumbo sitting on the wide veranda, smoking a cigar and holding a drink in his hand. He stood when he saw us approaching.

"The Coulter Clan arrives!" he gushed, coming down the steps and wrapping first Sara and then the rest of the family in his typical overpowering bear hugs.

Sara said, "Hello, Willy. It's been too long."

"You look marvelous, Mrs. Coulter," Palumbo replied, and then turned to Melanee. "And look who's all grown up!"

"How are you, Mr. Palumbo?" Melanee said, holding her daughter's hand.

"I'm just great, dear! Please call me Willy," he said, kneeling down. "And who is this?"

"This is my daughter, Janet. And I'd like you to meet my husband, Robert."

Palumbo tried to reach out to little Janet, but she slid behind her mother's legs to hide. He stood and shook Robert's hand. "How grand to have you all here after all these years.

Seems like just yesterday, Melanee was this fascinating little girl who kept us all up late playing the piano inside and singing with her mother here. I hope you'll do a song or two for us tonight!"

"We'll see," Sara said.

"Shall we head in?" I suggested.

Inside, a long table had been set for our group. Louise and Paolo Palumbo joined us. Jimmy Headley and his wife, Rebecca, were already there. Drinks were served by Jonas Bidwell and his wife and small staff. Soon, we were all seated and food was starting to be served. Willy sat at one end of the table. I was at the other. He stood and held up his glass of wine.

"I would like to welcome you all back to Grayton Beach," he began. "It's been far too long. A toast to this lovely reunion of the Coulters, Headleys, Bidwells, and the Palumbos!" He held his glass high, and everyone around the table acknowledged his toast and raised their glasses.

I felt I needed to add something, so I stood as well. "Thank you, Willy. It really is great to see you and your family again, and to have us all here in Lila's hotel. Can we raise a glass to our dear, departed Lila who brought us all together here so many years ago."

Again, everyone raised their glasses to toast Sara's mother, Melanee's grandmother, who we had so tragically lost in the big hurricane that nearly destroyed the hotel in 1925. I looked down at Sara and she had tears in her eyes. I put my arm around her shoulders and kissed the top of her head before I took my seat again.

The dinner was a wonderful assortment of local seafood and vegetables from the Bidwells' garden over in Point Washington. Jonas and his wife were great hosts, and the conversation was a seemingly endless series of stories about all our times there in Grayton Beach—only the happier times. None of us wanted to revisit the darker events that we all kept in the back of our minds.

Partway through the meal, I looked over at the front door out to the veranda and saw the big hulk of Anthony, Palumbo's bodyguard, standing watch, as always. I also noticed that Willy's son, Paolo, was the only person at the table obviously not enjoying himself. His glum expression was clear for all to see, and it occurred to me it would have been better if he had passed on the occasion. Louise Palumbo, on the other hand, was certainly enjoying herself, and I was pleased to see that she and Willy were clearly having a great time together.

After dinner and a dessert of home-baked pies and ice cream the Bidwells had brought from their store, everyone insisted that Sara and Melanee sing for us all. Sara was, at first, reluctant to get up, but Melanee was more than willing and reached for her mother's hand to be led over to the piano at the back of the room. Sara had traveled with a band as a young woman and had a lovely voice, but rarely sang those days. Her days as a performer were marred by addiction and trauma, and she tried her best to distance herself from those troubling times.

Memories flooded back to me of similar nights there at the hotel when Melanee was a little girl and her voice and talent on the piano lifted all our spirits. She sat down at the piano and Sara stood to the side. Melanee played a few notes to limber up her fingers and then she leaned in to her mother to whisper the song she wanted to sing.

Within moments, we were all captured by the beautiful melody being played on the piano and the stunning harmony of mother and daughter. When they finished, they were rewarded with a standing ovation from all at the table and demands for another song.

They performed two more songs before everyone rose to signal the end of the dinner. I went over and hugged my wife and daughter and thanked them for bringing such joy to the evening. Melanee's sightless eyes were filled with tears as I'm sure she was thinking back to evenings there those many years ago when her grandmother was still with us. Sara was crying, too, as we all made our way out onto the veranda to say our goodnights.

Willy was encouraging everyone to stay for another drink, but it was late, and all begged off and started back home, except me, after Willy insisted I stay. He had something he needed to share with me.

I told Sara that I would be along soon and joined Willy back on the veranda where we settled into two chairs, looking across the street at the newer General Store. Willy called inside for Jonas to bring out two glasses of bourbon which were soon delivered. Willy offered me a cigar. I passed and watched as he lit his. He raised his glass to mine.

"Great evening, Coulter!"

"Yes, it was." We clinked our glasses and both took a drink. I noticed Anthony standing by Palumbo's big car down on the road, watching us closely. "Does he ever rest?" I asked.

"Never," Palumbo replied. "That's why I'm still alive."

I looked over at the old gangster and could see in his expression that he wasn't kidding.

Palumbo took a long pull on the cigar and then let the smoke out in a slow exhale. Then, he leaned in closer and said, "There's something I need to share with you, Coulter."

"And what is that?"

"You and I haven't caught up in a long time," he began.

I didn't respond.

"I asked about your mother and sister earlier," he continued.

I nodded.

"You know I'm still honoring our agreement to take care of them. They get a check every month, a very generous check with their share of the profits from your father's business. Of course, it's all legal now—the liquor business, I mean. And, it's grown considerably since those earlier days."

"I'm grateful, Willy, and I know my mother and Maggie are as well."

"And you've never taken a penny," he said, staring hard at me.

"I never wanted anything from my father's business. You know that."

"You never wanted anything from me, you mean."

I sat back, surprised at his sudden accusation, but knowing full well that he was right.

He continued. "You've never forgiven me for what I did to take advantage of you with that girl over in Panama City."

I remembered back to a woman named Eleanor who I had grown very close to before meeting Sara, only to find that it had all been set up by Palumbo to ingratiate himself with me and get closer to my family's business. Our unholy alliance to protect my mother and sister after my father's passing was still a compromise that haunted many of my sleepless nights.

"Willy, that was a long time ago, but you're right, that will always be between us."

"So, you don't think I've earned your forgiveness?" he pressed.

I took a sip of my drink and scratched my head, considering my response. Finally, I said, "Let's just consider us even and leave it at that."

He looked back at me with a hard, cold expression in the dim light from inside. Then, he reached over with his glass and touched mine. "Even."

We both drank.

"There's something else, Coulter."

Of course, I thought to myself.

"You know that I'm not always on the best terms with the families back north. That's why I first came down here all those years ago."

I was well aware that the mob bosses back in New York and New Jersey had serious issues with Palumbo, and I assumed that was why he was still living in Miami. "And that's why Anthony is so jumpy?"

"He's always jumpy."

"So, what's going on?" I asked.

He scratched at his chin and took another drink before continuing. "I was never upfront with the families about my agreement with your family."

"What do you mean?"

"They had no idea I was skimming off money to send to your mother and sister."

I was truly shocked. "After all this time?"

"Well . . ."

"But now they know?"

He nodded.

"So, why are you telling me this?"

"It's my problem, Coulter. But I thought you should know. If anything happens, I may not be able to continue to honor our agreement."

I sat and considered the implications of what he was telling me. Frankly, my mother and certainly my sister were well enough off financially that it shouldn't be an issue if Palumbo's money was suddenly cut off.

"What do you mean, if anything *happens*?" I asked. "Is that why you're back over here? Your *friends* in New York are looking for you?"

"I'll be fine, Coulter. I just thought you should know."

I nodded, continuing to think through what all of it was leading to. "Do I need to let my family know about this?"

"Not yet. I'm trying to work this out."

I hesitated, then said, "Okay. I appreciate you sharing this with me. I assume there's nothing I can do to help."

"No, it's best you stay as far away as possible."

And I intended to do just that.

Chapter Ten

Georgetown, South Carolina. Present day.

The accused drug runner, Miguel Juarez, sat at the metal table in the interrogation room with his attorney from Atlanta, Rick Guidall, a man of middle age, immaculately groomed and dressed in a gray well-cut suit and red silk tie. Alex walked into the room with Deputy Sheila Graham and sat across from them.

Before he could begin the interrogation, Guidall stood and said, "I insist my client be released immediately. He was stopped and searched illegally. He's being held without bond which is totally unjustified."

Alex held up his hand. "Please take a seat, counselor. None of that is going to happen. Your client was found with enough heroin and fentanyl in his car to kill ten thousand of our citizens. He has an arrest record as long as this table and is clearly a flight risk. There is a preliminary hearing set for tomorrow morning, and we'll let you take all of this up with the judge, but for now, Mr. Juarez will be staying right here."

The door behind them opened, and Alex turned to see the county prosecutor, Marjorie Willett, coming in to join them. She introduced herself and sat down next to Graham.

Alex said, "We were just explaining to Mr. Juarez and his counsel that there is a hearing scheduled for tomorrow to consider bail and to set a court date for the charges filed." Guidall started to protest again, but Alex stopped him. "As I said, we will let the judge review your concerns tomorrow."

"In the meantime," Willett began, "Mr. Juarez needs to understand the seriousness of the charges against him. He is facing years, perhaps decades, behind bars. The epidemic of fentanyl and heroin deaths among our citizens is horrific, and it needs to stop. We need to send a clear signal that there will be severe consequences for being a part of this plaque sweeping our country."

The defense lawyer did not respond. Juarez sat there with a totally distracted look on his face.

Willett continued. "Mr. Guidall, we know that your client is not acting alone in this distribution network. If we were to get some cooperation in identifying and shutting down the key players in this operation, we could look much more favorably on his situation."

Guidall didn't hesitate. "That's not going to happen, ma'am!"

Juarez seemed suddenly interested and didn't appear to agree with his attorney. He leaned over and whispered in the lawyer's ear. Guidall answered back quietly, and Juarez sat back in his chair.

Guidall continued. "We have nothing more to say here today. We'll take all of this up with the judge in the morning."

Alex said, "Mr. Juarez, do you have anything to say for yourself?"

Juarez looked to his lawyer who shook his head.

"I asked you a question, Miguel," Alex pressed.

"We're done here!" Guidall said, standing up and lifting his client by the arm to do the same.

Alex turned to Graham. "Get him back to his cell."

The deputy left the room with the prisoner.

Willett said, "Mr. Guidall, we will find out who you're working for."

"I work for my client, Mr. Juarez, ma'am."

"Yeah, right," she replied. "See you in court, counselor." She turned to Alex. "Can I see you in your office, please?"

Marjorie Willett sat across the desk from Alex. She slid her reading glasses up on top of her head and said, "What did you learn out at the Juarez residence?"

"We spoke with his wife. She is afraid and won't cooperate. She was actually in my wife's law office earlier today to begin divorce proceedings."

"Afraid of her husband or the cartels?"

"Both, and we learned from the trailer park manager that Juarez has a coworker living out there, but he was not around. His name is Rios Hernandez. We're trying to track him down."

Willett said, "I've spoken with the judge. He'll listen to what the defense has to say tomorrow, but he's not inclined to let this guy back on the streets."

"Looks like we'll have a tough time cutting a deal with Juarez with his lawyer obviously protecting whoever is upstream on this drug pipeline."

His cellphone buzzed and he saw that it was Hanna. "Let me take this. I might have more on this attorney. "Hey, I'm here with the county prosecutor. Anything on our Atlanta attorney?" He listened as Hanna relayed what she had learned from her contact at the Moss Kramer law firm in Atlanta, where her father used to be the managing partner. "Okay, thanks. I'll call you later."

He ended the call and turned to Willett. "Our man works for one of the biggest firms in Atlanta. Our source has no idea who, or even if, one of their clients is behind trying to protect

Juarez, but they did share that this law firm is well known for taking on big, deep-pocket clients that no other firm will touch."

"Like the mob . . . or the cartels," Willett added.

Alex said, "Why don't I get Foster and the FBI involved and suggest their Atlanta Bureau take a closer look at this law firm. He left me a message earlier about a lead on this fentanyl gang."

"Good idea."

"How's it going?" Will Foster said when he took Alex's call.

"Okay, Will. Sorry I didn't get back to you earlier. We're up to our necks in a drug running case up here. Just took custody of a guy the state cops picked up out on 95 with a trunk-load of heroin and fentanyl."

"That's why I was calling. Your guy is Juarez, right?"

"Yeah. He's lawyered up with a suit out of Atlanta who we think is working for one of the cartels."

"Guidall, right?"

"You know this guy?"

"We've been on him and this law firm for about six months. They are definitely working for one of the biggest cartels running drugs through the border at Mexico with distribution across the country, including here in South Carolina."

"We have a lead on another guy who supposedly works with Juarez, a Rios Hernandez. We haven't been able to find him, yet. How can we help each other, Will?"

"Let me see what we have on Hernandez. I was calling you to see if we can come up and take a crack at Juarez."

"Of course. We're holding him without bail until his preliminary hearing tomorrow morning."

"Sharron and I can come up later this afternoon. Maybe by four?"

Sharron Fairfield was a field agent out of the Charleston office who Alex had worked with during his stint with the FBI. She had also shown some personal interest in Alex, much to Hanna's dismay, before they were married, but Alex had quickly shut that down. "I'll be here. We'll let the attorney know you're coming."

"Don't give him too much notice."

Alex looked up when his wife walked into his office. "Well, this is a nice surprise!"

"I was headed home early today because some files I needed were out at the house," Hanna began, coming around his desk to give him a hug before continuing, "but I got this call I really wanted to share with you."

"Who called?"

Hanna sat down in one of the chairs across from Alex's desk. "You know my father was related to the Coulter family in Atlanta. They were notorious for controlling the liquor trade in the South, even during Prohibition."

"Right, I remember talking to your father about it when we were visiting over there a couple of years ago."

"And the Coulters owned the Buckhead house that Allen inherited, where I grew up."

"Right, just a little 15,000-square-foot starter home on twenty acres," he said with a wry grin.

Hanna laughed. "Well, I got a call this afternoon from a woman who is the great-granddaughter of the Coulters who headed up the family business back in the 1920s. His son, Mathew, became a pretty famous writer. I shared one of his books with you a while back."

"I remember. Haven't read it yet."

"I know. It's not a spy thriller!" she teased.

"So, why did she call?"

"Her name is Janet Coulter Anders. She must be in her seventies or eighties. She and her husband are visiting their family's beach house down on the Gulf in Florida. Her grandfather, Mathew the writer, bought it back in the twenties, and it's still in the family. She found an old manuscript that Mathew wrote but apparently never published."

"And why is that?" Alex asked.

"She thinks there are some revelations about the Coulter family that would be concerning to us surviving family members."

"Seriously? Because they were bootleggers?"

"Apparently, more than that. She didn't want to discuss it over the phone. They're coming through South Carolina on Friday for a visit to talk about it with me."

"Interesting."

"Very. I've always wanted to get back over to Grayton Beach to visit the Coulter cottage again. My father took us when we were in grade school, but I've never been back. It's a beautiful place."

"I'll look forward to meeting her."

"And Saturday night, we have this dinner next door with Quinn."

"Do we really have to go?" he pleaded.

"I told you Sheila is coming."

"I mentioned it to her earlier today, and she wasn't too thrilled about this blind date, but she couldn't figure a way to get out of it, either."

"I think it will be fun," Hanna said. "Sheila's blind date and Quinn's new professional fighter boyfriend."

"You think that's fun? Sounds like a disaster to me!"

Hanna stood to leave. "Let's make the most of it. I was going to pick up some burritos on the way home for dinner. Sound good?"

"And dirty rice and beans?"

"Got it."

Alex came around and hugged her again. "Wish you would stop by more often."

"Don't want to interrupt the busy Sheriff Alex Frank!"

"*Temporary* sheriff!"

"Right."

Chapter Eleven

Grayton Beach, Florida. 1939.

As usual, I woke early and left the cottage to let everyone else sleep a bit longer. I walked down the path to the beach past the pavilion and made my way through the soft white sand, still cool from the previous night. The broad expanse of the Gulf of Mexico was gray in the early morning light and glass-calm, only a few pods of bait fish rippling the surface.

As I got down to the shore, the orange sun was just above the horizon to the east, a low bank of clouds hiding the shoreline on down to Panama City. I stepped into the water with my bare feet and was surprised at the soothing warmth of the water this time of year. I was tempted to throw off my shirt and swim out but thought better of it when I considered the big sharks that liked to cruise the shoreline this time of day.

I sensed movement behind me and turned to see Willy Palumbo's son, Paolo, approaching. He was wearing dress pants and a white shirt and tie like he was ready for business. It felt terribly out of place there on that deserted beach.

He walked up and said, "Still can't understand what you all see in this nowhere place."

I let my arm span the incredible view of beach and water, the low cottages tucked up against the dunes. "Well, all of this, for starters."

He shook his head with a look of disgust. "Nothing to do. Nothing to see."

"What do you want, Paolo?"

He looked at me with a stern, steely gaze. "Your family has got us all in hot water with our connections in the North."

"Yes, your father told me last night," I replied. "And this is not my family's fault. Your father and I cut this deal years ago, and you all have made a lot of money."

"And so have your mother and sister!"

"Like I said, Paolo, what do you want?"

He didn't hesitate. "I want you to end this deal now before things get out of hand."

"That's between me and your father."

He came in and grabbed a handful of my shirt, pulling my face close to his. "Right now, it's between you and me!"

I pushed him away hard, and he lost his balance, falling down into the sand. He came up ready to swing at me, but a shout from behind stopped him.

"Paolo, that's enough!"

It was his mother, Louise.

Paolo turned and stepped away, allowing room for her to join us.

Louise looked sternly at her son. "I don't know what this is all about, but it ends now! Am I clear?"

Paolo didn't respond, but looked out across the water.

"Paolo!" she demanded.

He abruptly started walking away back toward town.

Louise reached over and took my arm. "I'm sorry. My son has inherited my husband's temper."

"Tough to go through life with so much anger," I replied.

"His brother is just the opposite, so calm and happy with his life. He's a teacher back in New York."

"Good for him." I looked again at Paolo Palumbo walking away, then out of sight through the dunes. "It sounds like Willy is in some trouble with the families after all these years of supporting my mother and sister."

"He'll work it out," she said calmly, a warm smile spreading across her face.

The stillness of the beautiful morning was split with a thunderous crack of gunfire from up in town. Both Louise and I flinched, and I pulled her down to the sand for cover.

"What the hell . . ." I said as we both tried to make sense of what was happening. "Stay here!" I demanded and got up and started running as best as I could on my bad leg up across the beach, the loose sand making it hard to gain any speed.

Then, there were four more cracks of gunfire and silence again. My first thoughts were for the safety of my family, and I was headed for our cottage when I heard another single gunshot.

As the cottage came into view, I saw Sara coming out onto the front deck. I yelled out, "Get back inside!" I watched as she hesitated, looking down the street toward the hotel, then quickly going back through the door.

I got up to the main street and looked down to the hotel. Willy Palumbo and his bodyguard, Anthony, were kneeling next to a prone body on the ground. I quickly realized it was Paolo and started running in that direction. Then, I saw another body motionless on the ground a few yards away.

I came up, breathless from the run. Willy looked up at me with a crazed expression. His son's white shirt was covered in blood, another wound leaking from his forehead. Paolo's eyes were wide open but lifeless.

The other man was laid out on his back, arms and legs askew and bloodstains seeping red through his clothes in the early morning light. A pistol was still gripped in his right hand.

"Willy . . . ?"

"They killed my boy," he said, tears forming in his eyes. "They killed my boy . . ." He had his hand on Paolo's face, stroking it as if this might revive him.

Anthony stood and walked over to the dead assassin. He nudged him with his foot to make sure he was dead. The corpse didn't move. He drew his foot back and kicked the dead man hard in the side of the head, then started surveying the perimeter to make sure there were no further threats.

I heard steps running up from behind and turned to see Louise coming up, a look of sheer terror on her face.

"No, no!" she screamed out. "Paolo!"

Willy stood and rushed toward her, stopping her before she got any closer. He wrapped her in his arms and tried to keep her from seeing the lifeless body of their son. "He's gone. He's gone . . . I'm so sorry."

Louise tore herself away and ran to her son, kneeling beside him and throwing herself across his body, her face tight against his. She was sobbing uncontrollably and uttering something I couldn't understand.

Willy came back beside me. "What happened?" I asked.

The big man took a deep breath, then said, "The bastards sent this guy to take me out. Paolo got in the way."

"Because of the money you've been sending my family?" I asked, incredulous that the mob could be so ruthless.

"It's just the latest excuse," he said, his voice weak and nearly a whisper. "I've been running a lot of their business down here in the South these past years, but they want one of their own to take over. Louise has been trying to get me to step aside, to retire. She'll never forgive me now."

We both looked down at Louise sobbing over her fallen son.

I felt a hand on my shoulder and turned to see Sara. I took her in my arms and tried to shield her from the sight of the two dead men. "Let's go back home," I said. "There's nothing we can do here."

I looked into her eyes and saw the old familiar panic and fear from years ago when violence and tragedy in this little town had nearly driven her to madness.

Chapter Twelve

Georgetown, South Carolina. Present day.

Alex looked up from the paperwork on his desk when he heard shouting outside in the squad room. He saw three men coming in from the reception area. One was holding a woman who worked the front reception desk around the neck with a semi-automatic rifle to her head. Alex slid out from behind his desk, staying low, reaching for his own weapon on his belt.

The three men were dressed in black camo, masks hiding their faces. Each had bulletproof vests on. Three deputies, including Sheila Graham, were standing at their desks, their hands in the air. All three intruders had deadly AR15 rifles.

Alex ducked low behind the half wall in his office, his gun out and ready to fire.

One of the men yelled out, "All your weapons on the floor, now!"

The deputies complied, carefully pulling out their guns and leaning down to place them on the floor.

"We want Juarez! Bring him out now!"

The woman they were holding, Joyce Hall, was hysterical and struggling to stay on her feet. She slipped from her captor's grasp and fell to the floor. He aimed the rifle at her head but didn't fire.

The man yelled in a heavy Spanish accent, "Get Juarez or she dies!"

Deputy Graham, her hands still in the air, said, "I'll go."

The leader who had been holding the woman ordered one of his men to go with her.

Alex surveyed the situation through a crack in the door. The odds were less than favorable. He could probably take the remaining two men out, but the gunfire would alert the man with Graham, and he couldn't protect her from there. He also couldn't risk the life of Joyce Hall or the other deputies. He remained crouched, ready to engage if an opportunity presented itself.

He looked at the clock. It was five after four. He pulled out his cell and texted Will Foster, who he expected would arrive any minute. *You close? We have three armed gunmen trying to break out our prisoner.*

He waited for the reply, which came fifteen seconds later. *In the parking lot. Where are you?*

My office. Can't engage.

We'll try to jump them out here, Foster wrote.

They'll have a hostage, he typed back, his hands shaking with adrenaline.

He saw the gunman come out from the back, leading Juarez. No sign of Graham. *He must have locked her in the cell,* he thought. *No way this ends well! Can't get a good shot with those vests.*

The leader yelled out, "On the floor, now!" The other deputies slowly got down. "Do not follow us or this woman dies." He reached down and pulled Joyce Hall to her feet.

"No, please," she pleaded.

He typed, *They're coming out. All have vests and ARs.*

The three men backed their way to the exit door, then raced out, the leader pulling Hall along with him.

Alex stood and rushed out into the squad room. His deputies were getting to their feet, stunned in confusion, looking to him for direction. "Get your weapon. Randy, check on Graham in the back. Walt, you come with me. Stay low and out of sight."

They went into the reception area and peered out through the window, ducking low beneath the sill. The three men were jumping into a white commercial van, still taking Hall with them.

Alex pulled his phone again and called Foster this time. "Don't engage!" he yelled when Foster came on the line. "They'll shoot the hostage."

"Can we get someone in the air to follow?" Foster asked.

Alex said, "I'm sending out an alert now." He placed the distress call to his dispatch operator, watching as the men closed the doors to the van and sped off. When they were out of the lot and far enough away, he ran outside. Foster and Fairfield came out from behind their car. The FBI man was shaking his head.

"Sorry, Alex. Nothing we could do."

"I know. I know." He thought for a moment, looking back as Graham came out of the building with the other deputies. *At least she's okay,* he thought, his mind racing with how best to respond. Finally, he said, "Will, let's follow at a distance in your unmarked car."

"Let's go!" Foster said, heading back to his car with his partner, Sharron Fairfield. She acknowledged Alex with a nod and then jumped into the back seat of their car. Alex got in next to Foster in the front.

"They headed north out of town, probably to get to 17," Alex said as Foster put the car in gear and sped out of the lot. "We need to stay well back."

They came up quickly to the intersection with Highway 17 and looked in both directions. No sign of the van.

"Which way?" Foster asked.

Alex looked both ways again. "Let's go south! I'll have units covering all routes." He got on his radio and sent out the commands. He listened as his dispatcher said the nearest helicopter was in Charleston—no use bringing it up.

Foster turned and drove fast out of town, their eyes trained ahead for any sign of the fleeing vehicle.

They were several miles out of town when a call came in on his radio. One of his patrols had found the van. He listened as the deputy relayed that the vehicle was abandoned. Joyce Hall was bound in the back with zip ties, but she appeared unhurt.

He turned to Foster. "They must have had another vehicle waiting."

Foster turned the car around, and they sped off toward the abandoned van.

When they pulled up, two other patrol cars had already arrived. A siren could be heard approaching nearby. The white van sat in the shadows to the side of an abandoned gas station on the main highway. The side door was left open. Joyce Hall was sitting in the back seat of one of the patrol cars, an officer kneeling and talking with her. An ambulance pulled up and rushed to her aid.

Alex went over and checked on her and then came back to Foster and Fairfield, who were looking over the van.

"She okay?" Foster asked.

"Really shook up, but no injuries."

"Good. This van was probably stolen. Registered to a William Loeb from Charleston. One of your deputies is trying to track him down."

Agent Fairfield said, "Hard to believe these guys would have the gall to take down a sheriff's department."

Foster said, "Just another routine day for these cartel guys."

Alex stood, shaking his head, bewildered by all that had just gone down. *Fortunately, no one was hurt,* he thought. "I'd better call this in to HQ in Charleston," he said, dreading the conversation with his boss.

Hanna handed her husband a cold beer from the refrigerator when he came through the door a little past seven. He had called her earlier to tell her about the assault on the department and to assure her everyone was okay in case she had heard anything on the news.

She watched as he held the cold bottle to the side of his face, sweat dripping down his forehead from the late afternoon heat, then took a long drink.

"I'm sorry," Hanna said. "You sure everyone's okay?"

"Yeah. Could have been a lot worse. Still can't believe we lost our suspect. Charleston is very unhappy with me."

"I can imagine, but what could you do? No idea who these guys were or where they came from?"

"No, but almost certainly they're from whatever cartel is running these drug shipments. Didn't want to risk one of their men spilling too much information."

"How about a swim to cool off?"

They both waded into the cool Atlantic, hands grasped. Hanna felt the shock of the first wave that washed up above her waist, raising up on her toes to try to get a little higher. She felt Alex release her hand and dive out into the next wave. She did the same, and the bracing water washed over her as she slid along the sandy bottom, her eyes open, the silence a welcome respite.

When she came up, they were closer to chest-deep, and she took in a big breath of fresh air. Alex came up beside her and pulled her into his arms, spinning them both so they were facing back to the shore and the old beach house up in the dunes.

"What a great way to sweep away all the craziness of a day like this," he said, then leaned in to kiss her.

She let the salty taste of his kiss linger as they lifted up on the next wave washing toward shore. A woman was walking along the beach from off to their left. She wore a long, flowing white dress, her hair a brilliant red, almost like coals in a beach fire.

"It's Amanda," she said to her husband, watching him turn in the direction of Hanna's vision of her distant great-grandmother's spirit coming toward them.

"She's so beautiful," he said as the spirit of Amanda Paltierre Atwell stopped and turned toward them, smiling in the early evening light. The woman and her family had lived in the beach house back in the 1800s. Her kind spirit had been watching over Hanna for years, and they became accustomed to her presence in their lives.

They both watched for a few moments, making no effort to move closer. Then, Amanda raised her right hand in a gesture of farewell and continued along the beach until her form slowly faded to nothingness.

Chapter Thirteen

Grayton Beach, Florida. 1939.

The sound of gunfire brought dozens of local residents out of their cottages and into the street. They stood around, whispering among themselves as they looked over the carnage that had overtaken their usually quiet little village. The two bloodied bodies still lay prone in the dusty street in front of the hotel.

I watched as Willy Palumbo struggled to comfort his wife at the loss of their son. I knew someone had surely called the Sheriff's Office and the authorities would be there soon. As I walked toward the two of them, I could see that Louise was understandably inconsolable in her grief. She tried to push Willy away.

"Leave me alone!" she wailed and then broke free and ran up the steps into the hotel.

Willy watched her disappear inside, then turned to me, tears on his cheeks, his face swollen and red.

"Willy, it's just a matter of time until the sheriff's department arrives. You need to get your story straight."

"My story?" he replied in confusion. "What the hell is my story? This asshole killed my son and tried to kill me. My bodyguard took him out before he could get to me."

I looked over at the looming Anthony standing next to Palumbo's car in front of the hotel. "Were there any witnesses?" I asked, scanning the crowd around us.

Willy looked around at the faces staring back in stunned fear and uneasiness. "I don't know. I didn't see anyone else. Maybe?"

"In the slim chance that no one has called the cops, I think I need to—or better yet, you should call."

"Me? Seriously?"

"It was self-defense, Willy. You and Anthony did nothing wrong. He was protecting you from a killer. Go call them. Tell them what happened. Cooperate with the investigation."

He looked backed at me with a confused look, shaking his head.

"Willy, go make the call."

He glanced over at the lifeless shape of his son lying in the road. Quietly, he said, "They're not done with me. They'll be back. It's not enough for them to just take my boy. They won't rest until I'm in the dirt with him."

"What are you going to do?"

He looked back at me. "The only thing they understand is strength. I can't run from this. I need to take it to them with everything I have."

"Just you and Anthony?" I said, in disbelief.

"I gotta go after them, Coulter."

"You're going to New York?"

"Miami, first, after I help my wife bury our son."

He started toward Anthony and talked to him about something I couldn't overhear. The old gangster came back and said, "You're right. I need to call the sheriff."

The funeral was two days later in the cemetery in Point Washington, a few miles inland on the Choctawhatchee Bay. The small crowd gathered around us included our daughter, Melanee, and her family, Jimmy and Rebecca Headley, and Jonas Bidwell with his family. Sara and I stood with Willy and Louise Palumbo as the service ended. She stepped forward and threw a rose on the coffin that had just been lowered into the ground.

Sara put an arm around the woman's shoulder and pulled her close, trying to offer a little comfort in a time of unimaginable sorrow.

The attendees began to drift away to return to the Bidwell's house next to their store for a small reception.

I came closer to my wife and Louise, pulling them both into my arms. "I'm so sorry for your loss."

Louise looked at me with tear-swollen eyes. "Our family has lived in the shadow of this violence for as long as I can remember."

I didn't have an answer for her. I had been too close to that shadow during my earlier years there in Grayton Beach. I had seen the best sides of Willy Palumbo and the darkest. He had, indeed, called the authorities, and after a long evening of questioning with his bodyguard, Anthony, at the local sheriff's office in Panama City, he had been released with no charges filed. Both men were also encouraged to leave town as quickly as possible.

Willy pulled me away from the women, and we walked out of earshot to a stand of trees by the road. Willy said, "Anthony, I need to leave for Miami tomorrow. We have some business there before we go to New York to take care of all of this. Louise will be safe here, but can I count on you to watch out for her?"

"Of course, Willy."

He walked back over to escort his wife to the Bidwell's house.

I assumed Willy and his bodyguard would be on a train bound for New York in a matter of days with a mission of vengeance simmering in his gut. It was hard to imagine just two men could go up against a powerful crime family on their own. But I had learned the hard way never to underestimate Willy Palumbo.

Later that evening, as the sun fell low across the water in the sky to the west, orange and hot, shimmering back across the calm sea, I walked with my daughter, Melanee, along the shore break. We had taken off our shoes and let the gentle swells wash up over our feet. In her sightless journey, I described the beauty of the sunset. It broke my heart she had never seen the glory of a sunset like this or any of the beautiful wonders of the world around us. I had never seen her dwell on her situation in any negative way. Just the opposite, she continued to surprise us with her positive, bright spirit.

As we walked along, I could sense, though, that something was indeed troubling her. Certainly, the violent shootout two days earlier had left us all stunned and uncertain.

"What is it, dear? What's troubling you?"

She stopped and turned her sightless gaze out across the Gulf of Mexico. She took a deep breath and said, "I'm very afraid for mother. I can tell she's struggling with her old demons."

I had seen it, too, those past couple of days since the shooting. Sara had withdrawn into herself, bombarded by memories of the violence and chaos that had haunted her earlier days in Grayton Beach and back in New Orleans, when she had run away with a ruthless club owner that kept her mired in addiction to drugs and alcohol.

She had battled strongly back from those darker times, but the precipice was always nearby, just a step or two away.

I tried to reassure our daughter. "She has the two us to keep her strong. We won't let anything happen to her."

She turned and fell into my arms, tears welling in her eyes. "I couldn't bear to see her get sick again," she said, sobbing now against me.

I didn't know what to say. I had the same fear and knew what a fine line stood between my wife's sobriety and a fall back to earlier addictions. Finally, I said, "We will take care of your mother. We need to be strong for her."

Sara was still sitting on the porch when we returned to the cottage. She had declined to join us on our walk and was looking out with the same distant stare as we came up the steps. Melanee sensed her mother's presence and went straight to her, leaning in to wrap her in her arms. "I love you," she whispered.

I watched as Sara pulled her closer and shut her eyes tightly, savoring the warmth of her daughter's embrace. "I love you, too, honey."

My wife turned to me as Melanee stepped back and went inside. "I want to go home, Mathew."

"Back to New York? We just got down here."

She stared back as if I should understand, and of course, I did fully understand how that place and the darker memories could easily outweigh the happier times and drag her back to a place she was deathly afraid to return to.

She had seen her mother killed there in a violent hurricane in 1925 that had devastated the little town. A man named Boudreaux from New Orleans had come for her there and taken her back to a life of addiction and fear. Later, a man named Farley came into her life as she was still struggling to recover.

When I learned of his abuse of both Sara and Melanee, I came back down from New York and confronted the man in what turned out to be a near-deadly encounter. I still had sleepless nights remembering how close I had come to killing him.

Sara was still haunted by all of this, and I truly understood the conflicts that raged within her. "I'll take you home. We can leave tomorrow."

The chirping of a mockingbird woke me the next morning. As my mind cleared, I looked out the window at the light of the new day. The bed beside me was empty. I remembered the exchange with my wife the previous night and my promise to take her back to New York that day. I also recalled my promise to Willy Palumbo to watch out for his wife, a conflict I had yet to resolve.

I dressed quickly and went out into the main room of the small cottage. Sara wasn't there and the door to Melanee and Robert's room was still closed. I went out onto the porch, expecting her to be sitting there, but only the rascal mockingbird, Champ, was prancing up and down the rail.

"Not now," I said, shooing the bird off, and then regretting my foul reaction.

I looked down the street and toward the beach but didn't see Sara. I went down the steps quickly as best I could, an old war injury leaving one of my legs nearly stiff and uncooperative. I hurried down to the hotel. Jonas was serving breakfast to several guests sitting in the dining area, but he hadn't seen Sara.

I went out and started as quickly as I could toward the beach. The soft sand made it even harder to make my way. As I passed the pavilion, I couldn't see anyone in either direction. I kept on through the low dunes and then saw a lone figure far out into the Gulf, past the first sandbar and going completely under with each new wave sweeping in.

"Sara!" I yelled out, trying to run even faster now. "Sara!"

When I got to the shoreline, I kicked off my shoes and kept running into the surf. I could only see Sara's head when a wave would lift her up. The water over fifty yards out to the sandbar was waist-deep as the tide was coming in. I struggled up onto the shallower bar, yelling again, "Sara, come back in!"

I panicked when I didn't see her on the next breaking wave. She must have been pulled under, I thought in horror as I kept pushing along and then diving into the deeper water past the sandbar to start swimming.

I came up to the surface, scanning the water for any sign of her. A wave lifted me up, and I saw nothing but the endless white-capped swells of waves come at me. "Oh God, Sara!"

I kept swimming, trying to make progress against the waves and current. The water was now about five feet deep, emerald green on the surface and clear below to the white sand bottom. A small shark swam quickly past, thankfully wanting no part of my thrashing.

Twenty yards ahead, I suddenly saw a dark form beneath the surface. I swam as fast as I could, my heart nearly beating out of my chest, my ears ringing, panic nearly overwhelming me. As I got closer, I could see that it was Sara, floating lifelessly, face down on the bottom, now in about six feet of water, her long dress and hair flowing in the push of the tide and waves.

I took as deep a breath as I could and dove down. I managed to grab one of her arms and pushed off the ocean floor to try to get us back to the surface. Kicking my legs as hard as I could, we broke above the surface, Sara's panicked face staring back at me, her eyes wide and confused. A big wave came over us and pushed us toward shore. I tried to keep her head above water, and she started retching to rid herself of the sea water she had inhaled.

My feet finally made purchase on the sandy bottom as I got us closer to the shallow sandbar. I pulled Sara up with me, now in only a few feet of water, and I held her close in my arms. Her face was puffy and red from coughing, but she seemed to have rid herself of the salt water.

"Sara . . .?" I began before she buried her face in chest.

"I'm so sorry," she said in a muffled moan. "I don't know why . . ."

"It's okay. It's okay. Let's get you up to the house."

Chapter Fourteen

Pawleys Island, South Carolina. Present day.

Hanna sat at the kitchen island with a steaming cup of coffee and her iPad in front of her. The early morning sun was filtering in through the windows along the east side of the house. She could hear the water running upstairs as Alex showered.

As promised, her neighbor, Quinn Burke, had emailed a copy of the new manuscript she had just finished and sent off to her publisher. Hanna had begun reading it the previous night before falling asleep with the light on and the tablet on her chest. Alex must have put it aside and turned off the lights, because she found it that morning on the nightstand next to her bed.

Quinn had mentioned the book was *dark*, as she described it. That was certainly an understatement. The first few chapters set up the story of a serial killer in Charleston who was targeting priests. The grisly murder described in the first chapter was more than Hanna wanted to read, and as she looked at Chapter Two on the tablet in front of her, she wasn't sure if she wanted to keep reading now. There had been enough violence and death in her own life those past years. She wasn't really excited to read about more.

She pushed the tablet aside and took a long sip from the coffee, the caffeine bracing and strong as it went down. She heard footsteps behind her and turned to see Alex coming down the steps dressed only in his plaid boxer shorts, his hair still wet from the shower.

"Coffee?" she said, rising to get another cup from the cupboard. As she reached up to get the cup, she felt him come close behind her and wrap her in his arms.

"Yes, please," he said. "How's the book?"

"Dreadful," she replied, turning to kiss him. "Good morning, deputy."

"Good morning, counselor. So, it's really that bad? I thought she was a bestselling writer."

"Oh, I'm sure she sells a lot of books. They're just not for me. Murder and mayhem in Charleston. I think we've both had enough of that."

"More than enough," he replied, going over to the coffee pot and pouring his cup full.

They both heard barking on the front deck and turned to see Quinn coming up to the glass door with both little dogs on leashes running around her legs.

"Oh, great," Alex said.

"Go get some clothes on," Hanna admonished, not wanting her neighbor to get another eyeful of her husband half dressed.

"I'll get the door," he teased.

"No, you won't!"

She pushed him toward the stairs and then went to see what Quinn was coming over again for. She opened the door and immediately stepped back as both dogs lunged at her ankles, snarling and barking.

Quinn quickly pulled them away before they could do any damage. "I'm so sorry, Hanna. They're normally so good with my women friends. Not so much men. I can't let them anywhere near my new boyfriend."

I can imagine, Hanna thought, looking down at the two little furry beasts, still snarling up at her. "What can I do for you, Quinn?"

"Headed to the store this morning for the dinner Saturday night. Wanted to get a head count. You and Alex able to join us?"

Hanna hesitated a moment, knowing how little interest Alex had in attending, but then her curiosity quickly got the best of her, wanting to meet the new professional fighter boyfriend and Sheila Graham's blind date. "We'd love to come. Sorry I didn't let you know earlier."

"Great! It's going to be fun," Quinn replied excitedly. She stood there as if she were expecting an invitation to come in for breakfast.

Hanna noticed her looking around her, probably for a glimpse of Alex in the kitchen. She had no intention of letting those two little dogs into her house.

When the invitation apparently wasn't going to come and the pause in the conversation was becoming uncomfortable, Quinn said, "Do you need anything from the store?"

"No, thank you, but what can we bring for the dinner? I'd be happy to make a salad or dessert."

"Not necessary. I already have it all planned out."

"You're sure?"

"Bring a bottle of wine. I have plenty but can there ever be enough?" she said, her face sparkling in the early morning light with a smile.

"Done. We'll see you Saturday night, then," Hanna said, stepping backward through the door to hopefully signal the conversation was over.

Quinn said, "Cocktails on the deck at six. See you then." She turned to leave, and one of the dogs took one more lunge at Hanna's ankle, missing by only inches. "I'm having these two spend the weekend at the groomers and kennel. They love it there in their little vacation suite. It has a couch and even a TV with Animal Planet playing 24/7."

Hanna couldn't help but smile and was thankful the two beasts would not be around Saturday night.

Alex looked up when the light on his desk phone lit up and buzzed. His assistant, Kay, leaned in the door.

"It's Detective Beatty from the Charleston Police Department," she said and then closed the door behind her.

He picked up the receiver and pressed the button for the call. "Nate, how you been?" He listened as his old colleague and friend informed him that his escaped prisoner had been found executed in an old warehouse district north of town earlier in the morning.

"Executed?" he asked.

"Multiple gunshots. Other wounds. Not pretty. Looks like the cartel wanted to make sure they found out how much Juarez might have divulged after he was captured, then they sent a clear message to anyone else who might think about turning on them."

"So, you're working this fentanyl drug ring now because of the homicide?" Alex asked.

"Me and a detective from Narcotics."

"Seems like everybody has a piece of this, but nothing is coordinated, as far as I can tell . . . state police, FBI, now Charleston PD and my team up here. I have to believe the DEA is involved at some level. I'm going to talk to Will Foster about taking the lead and getting everyone on the same page. Every day we wait, more people are dying."

"I hear you, friend."

Alex said, "You got anything on a Rios Hernandez? Apparently he ran with Juarez. Can't track him down yet."

"No, but let me check with the Narc guys."

"Let me know."

"You keep your head down, Alex. These boys from Mexico have no rules. They have no souls."

Hanna answered Alex's call on her cell. She was working on a motion for one of her clients and put the pen down. "Yes, you have to go to Quinn's dinner," she teased.

"It's not about that."

She could tell immediately he had his *serious* voice on. "What is it?"

"That divorce case you told me about yesterday."

"Helena Juarez?"

"She's not going to need a divorce anymore."

"What are you talking about?"

"Her husband was found dead this morning in Charleston. The cartel broke him out of our jail, took enough time to find out if he had ratted anyone out, and then killed him."

Hanna looked out the window across the marshes to the cottages she could see on Pawleys Island, her mind numb from the shock of more senseless violence. "Does she know?"

"I'm not sure. I sent Graham and another deputy out to their home to make sure she was okay, and to inform her of her husband's death if she hadn't already found out."

"From what she told me yesterday," Hanna said, "I don't think she'll be too upset about his passing."

"It was Nate Beatty who called me from Charleston PD this morning with the news about Juarez. They're involved now, too."

"And how is Nathan?"

"Busy, as always." He didn't tell her that Beatty had asked him to consider coming back to the department. They were having a hell of a time hiring, and he was surrounded by green newbies and was tired of holding their hands. "He made captain. He's running the Homicide Division now."

"That could have been you," Hanna said, remembering their early days together in Charleston. She was running her free legal clinic in the city. He was a lieutenant in the Homicide Division. She often missed her work there and on occasion let herself question her judgment in shutting the clinic down. In her heart, she knew it was the right decision at the time. *But now?* She pushed the thoughts aside.

"Nate asked me to think about coming back. They're short on cops, more experienced cops."

"And what did you say?" she asked hesitantly, concerned about losing the life they were building together out of the city.

"I told him I had a great job here and wasn't interested."

"So, you lied," she said, then regretted the comment.

"What are you talking about?"

She could tell he was surprised and upset. "Let's talk about it tonight. I just want you to be happy."

Helena Juarez had indeed been informed of her husband's demise prior to Graham arriving to deliver the news. Her neighbor, Rios Hernandez, had stopped over earlier in the morning.

Graham recounted the story to Alex as she sat across from his desk. "You would have thought I was from the Publishers Clearing House and she had just won $5,000 a week for life. She was one of the happiest widows I've ever seen."

"This Juarez was a serious dirt bag. She's much better off with him gone. Any sign of Hernandez?"

"We checked his place. No one around. None of the neighbors had seen him recently."

Alex said, "So, we have no leads, a dead suspect, a missing accomplice. I've asked Will Foster at the Bureau to try to bring all the law enforcement agencies involved in this together to see if we can't help each other out." He watched Graham's expression of doubt as she shook her head.

He continued, "I know what you're going to say. Too many turf battles. No interest in sharing."

"Exactly," Graham said, "though with a drug crisis this serious, you would think everyone would try to come together to play nice in the sandbox."

"You would think," Alex replied.

Chapter Fifteen

Grayton Beach, Florida. 1939.

Sara slept through the morning when I got her back to the cottage. I didn't tell Melanee about her mother's near-death experience, only that we had been down swimming. I *had* told her the previous evening that Sara wanted to get back to New York. She seemed to understand and thought it likely they would stay on for the rest of their planned trip.

I was walking down the road to the hotel to talk to Louise Palumbo about leaving early. As I got closer, I saw her sitting on the porch, staring out over the dunes to the beach and Gulf beyond. She barely noticed me as I came up and sat beside her.

"Louise?"

She turned and her face was flushed red from crying. I reached for her hand, and she managed a thin smile. "Is Sara okay? I saw the two of you coming back from the beach earlier."

I hesitated. Whether my wife was purposely trying to take her own life or was so distressed she just didn't know what she was doing was our private business, and I had no intention of talking to anyone else about it. "We went for a swim. She's still very upset."

Louise turned and looked back out to the beach. "I know. We spoke for a long time yesterday after the funeral. Are you going to take her back to New York?"

"As soon as she's up to it. Listen, I told Willy yesterday that I would be here for you."

"Don't worry about me," she said quickly. "You need to take care of your wife. And I'll take care of Willy. He'll understand."

I let go of her hand but leaned in closer. "Louise, can we talk some sense into him? He's going to get himself killed going up against the families."

"Don't you think I know that? It's his damn Italian pride, Mathew. This is the second time they've sent a killer after him. And now they've taken our son. He won't let that rest. He will get his revenge or die trying."

Tears welled in her eyes again. "I don't know what I'll do if I lose him, too. We've been together so long. I love him and I hate him. I don't want to be alone."

"Why don't you come back to New York with me and Sara? You can stay with your son."

She looked back at me with a confused expression, seeming to consider my offer. "When are you leaving?"

"I need to check the train schedule out of Panama City for tomorrow."

"Let me think about it," she said, reaching out now to take back my hand. "Thank you, Mathew. You're a good friend. Willy and I are lucky to have you and Sara, even though we see you so rarely. We don't have many friends."

"Please come with us. I don't want to leave you here alone."

Sara was having coffee in the kitchen with our daughter when I got back to the cottage. They both looked up when they heard me come in. My wife had changed into a dry dress, but her hair still hung limp and unstyled. She wore no makeup, and her face was pale with dark circles beneath her eyes.

"Where are Robert and Janet?" I asked, joining them at the table and pouring another cup of coffee.

Melanee replied, "He took her down to the beach to play and take a swim. They'll be back for lunch."

In her usual prescient way, Melanee knew I needed time alone with her mother. She stood and said, "Will you excuse me? I need to take a shower before they get back."

"Of course, dear," I said. I watched as she felt her way through the furniture back to her bedroom. I turned to Sara. "Did you get some sleep?"

She nodded, not volunteering anything more.

"Do you want to talk about it now?" I asked.

"Mathew . . . I'm sorry. I don't know what came over me. I was standing looking out over the ocean, and the waves kept coming at me, and I just had this overwhelming feeling I needed to be out there in the waves, like they might wash away all this sadness and loss."

I touched her arm, and she placed her other hand over mine.

"You saved my life . . . again."

"Did you say anything to Melanee?"

She shook her head. "It makes me ill that I might have hurt her so terribly with my crazy stunt."

"Do you still want to go back to New York early?" I asked.

"Yes. More so now than ever."

"I'm checking the trains again for tomorrow. I think they'll have the same afternoon trip to Atlanta. I've asked Louise to come with us. I don't want to leave her here alone. Her other son lives up there."

"Yes, I know," she replied, reaching for her cup, her hand shaking as she tried to take a sip. She grabbed it with both hands and took a long swallow.

"You'll see the doctor, then, when we get back home?" I asked. She had been seeing a therapist for nearly ten years to help her deal with her many demons.

She nodded. "Can we not tell him about this morning?"

"I think you must tell him, Sara. He can't help you if you're not completely honest with how you're feeling and acting."

"Yes, I know." She hung her head low, staring down into her lap. "I'm just so embarrassed."

"You need to talk to him about it," I said sternly.

A gust of wind blew through the palms outside the cottage, rustling over the sounds of a chorus of birds squawking among themselves and children running by in the street. I was not happy about having to leave that place early. It had always been a great sanctuary for me, from the first day I arrived, escaping the corruption and chaos of my family back in Atlanta.

Sara stood. "I need to go pack." She leaned in to kiss me before she left, closing the door to our bedroom behind her.

Confident Sara would be safe and unlikely to try to hurt herself again with her daughter present there in the cottage, I walked down to the beach to see my son-in-law, Robert, and our little granddaughter, Janet. They were sitting near the shore break working on a marvelous sandcastle, piled high with drips of wet sand.

Janet saw me and ran up the beach toward me. "Papa! You must see our castle!"

I reached down and picked her up in my arms, feeling hers wrap around my neck.

"Is mother coming down?" she asked.

"No, she's staying up at the cottage," I said. "Maybe later."

"Good morning," Robert said as I sat Janet back down beside him and joined them next to the castle. "I hear you're leaving."

"Most likely tomorrow now, if we can get a train."

"No, Papa! You can't leave!" Janet protested.

"We'll see you soon enough back in New York," I replied. "I've asked Louise Palumbo to come with us. She shouldn't be down here alone after what's happened."

"Didn't seem to stop her husband," Robert shot back.

"I know. You have to understand Willy . . . and I guess I'm not sure I ever will completely. It's in his blood to have his revenge."

"How did you ever let yourself get so close to a mobster like this guy?"

I looked closely at the face of my son-in-law. I had never told him the full story of my early days down there and the uneasy and precarious alliance I had forged with Willy Palumbo. "It's a very long story."

"He's not safe for any of us to be around," Robert said, looking down at his daughter working again, dripping wet sand to build up the turrets of their castle.

"No, you're absolutely right. It's probably best that he's gone."

Chapter Sixteen

Pawleys Island, South Carolina. Present day.

"I just want you to be completely honest with me," Hanna pleaded as she sat beside her husband in the old, weathered chairs around the fire pit in front of the beach house.

The sun was a thin sliver of orange poised to slip below the far horizon to the west. Shore birds scurried about at the water's break, looking for their last sustenance before the dark of night. The brightest of stars sparkled in the clear sky as far as the eye could see out over the Atlantic.

Alex reached for Hanna's hand, then said, "I've never been happier than during my time here with you."

"I appreciate that," Hanna replied, "but that's not what I'm asking."

"I know." He took a drink from the glass of red wine that had been resting on the arm of the chair.

"I just don't believe that working as a local cop in this sleepy little town is your life's dream."

He let her comment sink in for a moment, then said, "The Low Country has been my home as long as I can remember. A few years away in the military, but—"

"But what about your career?" Hanna pressed.

"As long as we're together, that's secondary."

"So, just admit it. You're not happy with your work."

"It's a job, Hanna!" he shot back, then became upset with himself for losing his cool with her. He felt her squeeze his hand as she smiled at him.

"I don't want to upset you," she said. "I *do* want you to be happy and fulfilled in the work that you're doing."

He considered what she said for a moment, then replied, "Law enforcement can be a grind, wherever you are, whoever you're working for."

"But the FBI was your dream."

"And I screwed it up!"

"No you didn't!"

"Hanna . . ."

"You almost got yourself killed trying to head off a deadly terrorist attack."

"That's not how the Bureau sees it." The memories of that day along Charleston Harbor made him cringe as he recalled how close he had come to death and how savage the torture at the hands of the terrorists had been. In the end, his superiors in Washington determined he had taken rogue action that could not be tolerated in the Federal Bureau of Investigation.

"You helped head off one of the most devastating environmental disasters in history," Hanna said, rising to come over and sit in his lap.

He pulled her in close and savored the warm presence of her in his arms, her hair in his face.

Close to his ear, she said, "If you want to go back to work in Charleston, I will totally understand. I know it's not the Bureau, but we'll make it work. Maybe I need to think about re-opening a law office down there."

He looked out across the grand view of the dunes and beach and ocean. "I don't want to take you away from all this. I don't want to leave . . ." She pulled back, and he looked into her hazel eyes, flecked with green. He knew he could be happy doing whatever, as long as he had this woman to come home to every night.

"If we move back to Charleston, we still have this place on the weekends," she said.

"Beatty was just making small talk. He didn't actually offer me a job."

"You know they'd take you back in an instant."

He let his random thoughts swirl through his mind . . . the Charleston Police Department versus the Georgetown County Sheriff's Office . . . so many issues to consider. Certainly the FBI was not an option any longer. He knew his boss, Pepper Stokes, would be back on the job sooner or later. A lot of the administrative burden would be lifted that he was dealing with in his temporary role as sheriff. He enjoyed the time spent with the people he worked with. The bad elements had been rooted out some time ago. But he did have to admit that he often missed the city of Charleston, the challenge of the work, and he had many good friends there as well.

"What are you thinking?" Hanna asked, bringing him back to the moment.

He smiled back at her. "I'm thinking I could stay right here for the rest of my life and die a happy man." He pulled her closer and kissed her.

Hanna pressed her face into his shoulder. He looked past her to the orange and pink glow in the western sky. *Yes, I could die a happy man.*

Chapter Seventeen

New York City, New York. 1939.

The trip back to New York with my wife and Louise Palumbo was, as always, a long and tiring journey, catching many trains headed north. The views from the train tracks were often monotonous series of farm fields, small rural towns, and the occasional larger city where the tracks ran through often blighted industrial areas. Sleep was always difficult. The food was marginal, our muscles ached from inactivity, and we were exhausted by the time we reached our final destination.

Added to all of that was the stress of Sara's fragile mental condition. She drew far within herself for much of the trip. choosing to battle her internal issues on her own without our help. She stayed in our sleeping compartment most of the time, and despite my and Louise's efforts to engage with her and offer some support, her condition actually worsened by the time we got home.

That was two weeks prior. Louise Palumbo had gone on to Long Island to stay with her surviving son. Sara and I were trying to get back to our normal routines. She did some volunteer work at a women's shelter near our home on the Upper West Side of Manhattan. I was writing again and trying to manage the business obligations of my writing career. We had converted one of the bedrooms in our apartment into my office, looking out over the Hudson River.

I also took time each morning to walk two blocks to a coffee shop where I would write in my notebook or attend to other business issues and correspondence for an hour or two. I was sitting there in a back corner booth, papers and my notebook spread out before me, a half empty cup of coffee no longer steaming.

The owner, an aging Italian immigrant who was now a proud American citizen, came by and refilled my cup. He cleared away a small plate that had the remaining crumbs from a delicious blueberry scone his wife had baked on it.

"Mr. Coulter, you work too hard!" His old country accent had faded little in his twenty years in the States.

I laughed and said, "You're the hard worker, Mr. Moretti. What, you're here at six every morning and don't close until after the dinner hour at eight?"

"My wife and son help me in the afternoons, and I have a trusted manager who covers Sunday for us."

"You're an inspiration, Mr. Moretti."

"But you have the talent, sir, to be a great writer, a gentleman of words. I am only a maker of coffee." He smiled back.

"A maker of great coffee!" I took a long sip. "Thank you, sir."

He moved on to attend to other customers.

The bell on the front door jingled, but I didn't look up as customers were coming and going all the time.

"Coulter."

I looked up at the sound of the familiar deep voice of Willy Palumbo who was now standing at my table, his big bodyguard, Anthony, a few feet behind him, taking serious note of everyone else in the shop. I wasn't overly surprised. I knew Willy was going to eventually make his way up to New York on his mission to avenge his son's murder. "Willy, sit down. How was your trip?"

He slid into the booth. Anthony took up guard against the back wall where he could see the front door and the door back to the kitchen. Palumbo said, "I may never get back to Miami. That damn train nearly kills me every trip."

I couldn't help thinking he had far greater threats looming than another train ride. "You've seen Louise?"

"Not yet. Just got into town this morning. Thank you for bringing her back with you. I owe you."

In more ways than one! I thought to myself. "How was Miami?"

"He shuffled in his seat, looking around the little shop, then leaned in and whispered, "We found the asshole who hired the hitter for the Rossi family. We took him off the board. Carmelo Rossi is a dead man!"

The last thing I needed was to hear pronouncements of murderous endeavors. I felt nervous bile rising in my gut.

"I may need some help, Coulter."

"Willy, please—"

"No, hear me out."

"How did you find me here, by the way?"

"I went to your apartment. Sara said I'd find you down here."

Moretti, the shop owner, came up. "Mr. Palumbo, it's a great honor to have you here today. Everything is on the house!"

"That's not necessary, sir, but thank you. Just a coffee, please, and one for my friend over there," Palumbo replied, nodding in the direction of Anthony.

As Moretti walked away, I said, "If your *friends* up here don't know you're back in town, they will soon. Does everyone in this town know you?"

Palumbo just shrugged. "Comes with the job."

Moretti came up with two coffees then left to go back to attend to other customers at the counter along the far wall.

Palumbo took a sip, then said, "I gotta say, Sara didn't look too good this morning. Is she okay?"

"Forgive me, but she's taking your son's death very hard. We all are, Willy, but with Sara, there were just too many bad memories down there in Grayton Beach to have another tragedy." I chose not to tell him about my wife's apparent suicide attempt.

Palumbo closed his eyes and lowered his head. Then, he looked back up at me, a fury in his glistening eyes. "These guys up here, Coulter, they'll say Paolo's death was *collateral damage*, a mistake, that they wouldn't go after family. Well, they sure as hell came after me, and Paolo tried to protect me."

"Willy, I can't tell you how sorry I am about your son. You know I lost my brother in a similar fashion when rivals tried to take down my father."

"I know, Coulter."

"Do you really think it's worth risking getting yourself killed to go after these guys?"

"It's me or them. They're not going to quit coming after me. It's business to them, and now it's personal because we took out one of their guys down in Miami."

"I don't need to know about that," I said, "but think about Louise. Do you want to leave her alone in the world, especially now that she's just lost one of her sons?"

"Coulter, I can't hide from this."

I stared back at him as he took another sip of his coffee. "I'm afraid to ask, but you said you might need some help. I appreciate what you've done for my mother and sister over the years, but I do not want to get dragged into this mob war."

Palumbo's eyes narrowed, and he leaned in. "Did I hesitate when that scumbag took Sara back to New Orleans?"

"Willy—."

"No, let me finish. Me and Anthony stepped up, and we went with you to New Orleans, and we got her back."

In my heart, I knew he would someday play that card. Without those two mobsters, my wife would likely still be back in a slimy night club in the Big Easy, hooked on drugs and alcohol and living with a very dangerous man. When I went to get her back, I had no idea we would someday be married. I went to bring her back to her daughter, Melanee, and her mother, Lila.

"Willy, I'm no good to you in something like this. I can barely walk. I've got one good leg, and I haven't had a gun in my hands since the war in France twenty years ago."

"I don't need more muscle, Mathew. I need access. I need to draw this bastard out."

"And how do you expect me to do that?" I said, trying to imagine how I could possibly help. "I don't know these people. I don't run in those circles."

"You know people who do."

Chapter Eighteen

Charleston, South Carolina. Present day.

Alex walked into the familiar lobby of the Federal Bureau of Investigation offices in Charleston a little before 10 a.m. His short stint there as a special agent had not ended well, but he still had high regard for the organization and the people who he had served with.

The receptionist looked up and smiled. "Welcome back, Alex."

"Hi, Sophie, how have you been?"

"Fine, but it's just not the same without you around here anymore."

"Thanks, that's nice of you to say. I'm here for the joint session with Will and the other law enforcement agencies."

"You know where the conference room is."

"Yes. Nice to see you."

She nodded and pressed a button to unlock the door for him.

He walked into the conference room filled with several familiar faces: Will Foster and Sharron Fairfield from the FBI, his old colleague Nate Beatty from Charleston PD, the head of the South Carolina State Police, and two faces he didn't recognize. After greeting his past acquaintances, he was introduced to a man and a woman from the Drug Enforcement Agency, better known as the DEA.

Everyone took their seats, and Foster took the lead. "I don't need to remind you all of the devastating impact the illegal smuggling and distribution of fentanyl and heroin is having on our country. Over 100,000 people died last year from fentanyl overdoses alone. Until our southern border is secured and locked down from this illegal smuggling, we need to do all we can to protect our own here in South Carolina. I know all of you are working hard to accomplish that, but we need to work together and share information if we're going to make any significant progress."

Alex watched as Foster looked around the table to see unanimous agreement with nodding heads from all attendees.

Foster continued. "The brazen assault on the Sheriff's Department in Georgetown to free Miguel Juarez is clear evidence of how ruthless this organization is and the lengths they will go to protect their franchise. Alex, can you share your experience with us?"

"Thank you, Will," Alex began. "Three armed gunmen in full technical assault gear, including bulletproof vests and AK automatic rifles, stormed our office. They held our receptionist hostage to free Juarez and then took her with them to prevent us from following too closely."

One of the DEA agents shook his head in disgust. "And you just let them get away!"

Alex was not at all surprised by the man's outburst. Though he had never met him, he was aware of the man's arrogant and uncooperative reputation.

Foster jumped in. "Brian, as you well know, Agent Fairfield and I were also there, and with the hostage situation, there was no way to safely take these guys down. It was obviously a well-planned and executed operation. They had a car planted just out of town to mask their escape. Fortunately, no one on our side was hurt or killed."

The DEA agent named Brian Twain said, "And now the prisoner and our best chance at cracking this cartel network in South Carolina is dead!"

Alex tried to remain calm, staring back at the man, then said, "We have another potential suspect, a man named Rios Hernandez. We know his place of residence but have not been able to pick him up yet."

Foster looked around the table. "Anyone else have a lead on this guy?"

All heads were shaking *no*, and no one answered.

Alex said, "I've got our department trying to find this guy. I will keep you all informed. Will, what can we do about this lawyer who came in from Atlanta?"

"Yes, we have a slick lawyer from a highly questionable law firm in Atlanta who was flown in to represent Juarez. His name is Rick Guidall. We're told that his plane has already departed for Atlanta. We have our Atlanta bureau looking into the guy and his firm. Our sources tell us the firm has ties to organized crime and likely at least one of the cartels. We're attempting to get a warrant to raid their offices and find out who they're really connected with."

Alex continued. "Our local prosecutor put a deal on the table for Juarez to name names, but Guidall totally blocked him even though it was clear Juarez wanted to cooperate."

"And now he's dead," Twain said.

"No loose ends," Nate Beatty said. "Typical."

Foster gave everyone around the table the opportunity to share any progress they were making against the drug runners. Nothing of substance was shared, which Alex had a hard time believing.

The woman from the DEA did share that there were two prisoners currently doing time in the state penitentiary for drug-related charges likely tied to the cartels, but neither had been willing to talk.

Foster said, "I think our best leads at this time are the attorney, Guidall, and this Hernandez guy that Alex is trying to locate. Agent Fairfield and I will continue to work the Guidall connection, and Alex, keep us posted on Hernandez."

Alex nodded and looked across the table at his old friend, Nate Beatty, who gave him a frustrated shrug. He let his frustration boil over and stood to say, "We're wasting our time here if you're not willing to share and cooperate."

The head of the state police glared back. "We turn over a prisoner and potential source, and he ends up dead on your watch."

Foster jumped in. "That's entirely unfair! I told you what happened."

Alex watched the state cop turn to the DEA agent and whisper something, clearly not happy with being dressed down by the FBI.

Foster said, "Let's regroup on a Zoom call on Monday afternoon. In the meantime, if no one objects, our office will be a clearing house to collect and share all new information and updates. Does that work for everyone?"

All nodded.

As they all stood to leave, Beatty said, "Alex, can I have a moment before you head back?"

"Sure."

Will Foster was the last to leave the two men alone in the conference room as everyone filed out. He turned to Alex. "Stop by to see me."

When Foster closed the door behind him, Beatty walked to the window and looked out across the view of the Charleston skyline, then said, "What a cluster."

"I had hoped everyone would see the value in working on this together."

"Too many turf issues and old rivalries," Beatty said, then returned to sit across from Alex. "How are you and Hanna doing up there?"

"We're good."

Beatty nodded and smiled. "Glad to hear that. You're a lucky man."

"More than you know."

"Look, I was serious on the phone about getting you back down here to Charleston. I've talked to the commissioner. She's fully supportive."

"Despite my unceremonious departure from the FBI?"

"That was all bullshit, Alex!" Beatty said sharply. "Still can't believe how they dumped you. That terrorist plot would have succeeded if it weren't for you. Charleston Harbor would still be an oil slick."

"I've moved on, Nate."

"But what about coming back to the department? You didn't burn any bridges leaving for the FBI. If anything, your reputation has only improved as far as our team is concerned."

"We're settled in, Nate. Hanna's got a nice practice going off the island. Pepper will be back soon, and I can get back to real cop stuff, not pushing paper."

"I get it, but—"

"But what, Nate?"

"You ever worry about waking up twenty years from now and you're still runnin' radar traps out on Highway 17?"

Alex had to admit to himself, anyway, that this was exactly what kept him up at night . . . not just writing speeding tickets and hauling in drunks, but generally, it wasn't why he signed up all those years ago for law enforcement. His work in the Homicide Department at Charleston PD was not exactly an easy go, but at least he got satisfaction in taking seriously bad people off the board. He looked up at his friend. "I appreciate what you're doing. I just don't want to put Hanna through all this again."

"All what?"

"Another change. Moving her away from a place she loves . . . that I love, frankly. There are a lot of bad memories here in Charleston." Images flashed through his mind to the day he lost his partner in a deadly shootout downtown.

"Some good memories, too, Alex."

"Don't they say, *you can't go back*?"

"Who's *they*?"

Alex knocked on Will Foster's door before he left.

Foster looked up from some papers on his desk. "Come in. Close the door." He had his suit coat off, his tie pulled loose, and his shirt sleeves rolled up to his elbows.

Alex took a seat at the desk. "Not much progress there."

Foster had a disgusted look on his face. "These petty rivalries drive me crazy. You would think with the severity of the crisis, we could all get beyond that and focus on taking down the bad guys."

"Anything more on Guidall?" Alex asked.

"A team from the FBI office in Atlanta is waiting at the terminal where his plane is coming in to have a few words with him, see if they can put some heat on him."

"The guy's pretty smooth, Will."

"Our team is trying to determine if we can get any leverage on this firm."

"Do you want me to have Hanna's contacts at her father's firm help any further?"

"Yeah, that's why I wanted to speak with you," Foster said. "Can you please ask Hanna to give us the best person or persons there at the firm that our team can meet with to try to get some more insight on Guidall's firm?"

"I'll call her on the drive back."

In his truck on the way back north, before he called Hanna, he remembered he hadn't spoken with his father in over a week. He pressed the number on his phone.

"Hey, old man," he said when Skipper Frank answered the call, his gravelly voice thicker than ever.

"How you doin', sheriff?"

"Okay, Pop."

"How's that beautiful bride of yours?"

"Terrific. Just wanted to call and say hello, see what's happening down in Islamorada."

"Out on the *Maggie Mae* actually, right now. Runnin' a charter for a bunch of rich assholes who want to catch some mahi mahi for dinner."

"I'm sure you'll get them into some good fish."

"If I don't gut 'em and throw 'em overboard for chum first!"

Alex laughed at the thought of his grumpy, irascible father having to deal with rich fishing charter clients. On his shrimp boat, the former *Maggie Mae*, he only had himself and a mate or two to deal with. He didn't have to suck up to anyone. "What's Ella up to?"

"She joined this damn cooking club. Trying to get me to eat healthy. If I have one more avocado, I don't know what I'll do!"

Alex laughed again, envisioning Ella Moore Frank trying to force salads down his old man. He was a cheeseburger-and-fries man, seven days a week, if he could get away with it.

"When you comin' down to visit?" Skipper growled. "Tarpon are runnin' good now. Get you into a hunnert pounder that'll wear you out!"

"I'd like to do that. Tough to get away right now. We got some real trouble with the cartels bringing fentanyl and heroin into the Low Country."

"Scourge across the whole damn country!"

"Sure is." He chose not to tell his father about the armed assault on his office.

"You keep your head down, son. These are some bad dudes."

"You don't have to tell me," Alex replied. "Look, I'll talk to Hanna about getting away for a long weekend on the Keys as soon as we can."

"Soon!" Skipper shot back.

"Give my best to Ella and Scotty," he said, thinking about his deceased ex-wife's son who was now living with Skipper and Ella.

"I'll do that, son. Little Scotty's becomin' a helluva fisherman."

"That's great. I'm so glad he's with you two down there."

"Truly a blessing," Skipper said. "Kid's keepin' me young."

"You take care, Pop. Talk to you soon."

Hanna picked up on the second ring. "You on your way home?" she asked.

"About halfway. Just got off the phone with the old man."

"How are those two rascals doing down there?"

"Skipper's about ready to murder a couple of drunk charter fishing clients on the *Maggie Mae*."

Hanna laughed. "Seems like he'd get along with a couple of drunks just fine."

"Not the same when you're the hired help," Alex said. "They'd like us to come down for a long weekend."

"I'd like that. Let's check our calendars tonight. How'd the meeting go?"

"Total waste of time. Old turf issues die hard. No one would share."

"Seriously?"

"Will's trying to get everyone on the same page. We'll see," he replied, changing lanes to go around a slower truck. "He'd like you to get him a name at your father's firm who their Atlanta office could work with to learn more about the rogue law firm you checked on."

"Yeah, let me think about that. I'm sure they'll cooperate. Let me make a couple of calls."

"Thanks."

"And don't forget the dinner party tonight at Quinn's."

He had tried his best to forget about it, but the thought of an evening with that crazy woman and her friends had been bugging him all week. "You're sure there's no way we can beg off?"

"Alex!"

"I'm kidding. I'll be back in the office a little after noon. You free for lunch?"

"No, I have to work through lunch today, but thanks. See you tonight, and get ready to get your party shoes on," she teased.

Chapter Nineteen

New York City, New York. 1939.

Willy Palumbo insisted he take Sara and me out to dinner that night. I suggested he'd be better off to go to Long Island to be with his wife, but he said he needed to "finish with business" first.

The three of us sat at a waterfront table at the Boathouse Restaurant in Central Park as the sun was just beginning to fall below the trees to the west. Of course, Anthony was stationed nearby, keeping a close eye on any suspicious patrons or threats to his boss.

In deference to Sara's addictions, Willy and I both ordered just water to drink. My wife ordered a cup of tea. After we had given the waiter our food orders, Willy said, "Sara, thank you for coming out tonight. I know how difficult these past couple of weeks have been, but I felt like we all needed to get out and breathe a little fresh air, take a moment to reflect on how fortunate we are to still have friends and family in our lives who love us and who will be there for us."

Sara first looked at me, a bit surprised, then turned to Willy. "I'm so sorry for your loss of Paolo. If something were to happen to Melanee, I don't know what I would do."

"Thank you, dear," Willy said. "There is no greater curse than to lose a son or daughter, to have them leave this world before you do."

I looked over at Sara and saw tears welling in her eyes. I placed my hand on top of hers and changed the direction of the conversation to try to get her mind off the death of children. "Willy, Melanee and Robert and their little girl, Janet, got back to New York today. I spoke with her earlier. They had a marvelous stay down in Grayton Beach. It's so unfortunate it's so far away. We would all love to get down there more often."

Palumbo said, "As soon as we get a few loose ends tied up here, I'll be taking Louise back down to Miami. We like to travel across state to the Gulf Coast on occasion to spend time in Grayton."

I knew exactly what loose ends Willy was referring to. I also knew he would be very fortunate to survive and ever get back to Florida. I said, "Willy, have you spoken with Louise? Is she doing okay out on the island?"

"She's okay. As good as could be expected under the circumstances. Our son and his wife and the grand kids are keeping her occupied."

Sara pushed her chair back. "Could you excuse me, please? I have to go to the washroom."

Both Willy and I stood, and he pulled back her chair.

"Thank you."

As she walked away, we sat, and Willy leaned in close across the table. "Have you taken care of it?"

He was referring to the arrangement I had reluctantly agreed to earlier at the coffee shop to secure two good seats to the next evening's New York Philharmonic performance. The orchestra, in which my daughter Melanee was a featured violinist, was welcoming the world's most popular opera singer who normally resided in Italy, but who was in the midst of a tour across the United States playing with featured orchestras in major cities.

Palumbo knew that Carmelo Rossi was a devoted fan of the symphony and an even greater fan of Leonardo Bianchi, the renowned tenor from Florence, Italy. Willy was certain that if I were able to secure two premium seats to the performance, he would be able to get them into the hands of Rossi through nefarious channels to draw him out to Midtown the following night.

Getting the tickets had not been an issue, working through my daughter and her connections with the ticket office. I had an overwhelming sense of guilt, even peripherally involving Melanee in Willy's murderous plot. She would never know the tickets were bait to lure a mobster out where Willy and his bodyguard could gun him down.

I had made other dubious decisions and compromises in my life when it came to Willy Palumbo, but this far exceeded any previous ill-fated efforts. But Willy was right when he confronted me with the ledger of debts and obligations. I did indeed owe him for helping to save Sara's life, for setting up my mother and sister in a more than comfortable life after my father and brother were killed by a rival gang during the Prohibition years in the twenties.

I had to ask myself, *When will the ledger be even? When will I be free of these onerous obligations?* I had tried to make it very clear earlier in the day with Willy at the coffee shop that this would even the score. We would both move on in our lives with no further obligations to each other.

I pulled an envelope out of my jacket pocket that held the two front-row seats to the following night's performance. I handed them across the table to Palumbo. "Please tell me you're not going to shoot him right there in the theater with my daughter fifty feet away."

Palumbo took the tickets. "Thank you, Mathew. I knew you would come through."

"This is the last time, Willy. We're clear on this?"

"All square, Mathew, and no, we'll take care of Rossi outside the theater. You got the backdoor passes, right?" He looked in the envelope.

"Yes, Rossi will be able to come through the backstage door entrance with that pass. There's a reception for the singer before the show that he's invited to attend."

"He'll never make it to his seats," Palumbo said ominously.

Sara and I had season tickets to the symphony and were planning to attend to see our daughter's latest performance. I certainly didn't tell my wife about my questionable assistance in Palumbo's vendetta.

As Sara and I walked into the theater the next night and took our seats along the balcony, looking down on the stage, I was praying that Palumbo and Anthony would take care of their business outside in the back ally before the performance began.

Members of the orchestra began filing onto the stage, including Melanee, arranging their music sheets, taking out their instruments, and beginning to warm-up. I always felt a rush of love and respect when I watched our daughter make her way out with her white cane in one hand, her violin and bow in the other. Often, another member would assist, as a fellow violinist did that evening.

The men were all dressed in black tuxedos, starched white shirts, and black bow ties. The women wore floor-length black dresses. The chaotic noise of so many different instruments playing different parts of different selections filled the concert hall. The seats were filling up quickly. All the patrons were dressed elegantly in formal attire as well, as the symphony was a favorite venue for the city's elite social crowd.

I had no idea if we would be able to hear a gun battle in the alley behind the performance hall. *Hopefully not,* I thought to myself, sweat beginning to drip down my forehead and neck, down into my shirt.

Sara turned to me and reached for my arm. "Are you okay?"

"I'm fine. Just a little warm in here," I replied. I continued to imagine the scene outside. Willy would have his assassin, Anthony, strategically positioned to take out his rival gangster before he passed through the theater entrance. Surely, Carmelo Rossi would have bodyguards of his own, possibly several.

When the conductor finally made his way out onto the stage, he was welcomed with loud applause. He turned to the crowd and took a deep bow, then shook the hand of the first-chair violinist as was customary. He rose to his position, and as he lifted his baton to begin the performance, I didn't hear gunfire, but instead, the growing cacophony of several sirens outside.

The conductor lowered his baton and turned to look offstage. There seemed to be a flurry of noise and activity. The sound of sirens grew louder, and the patrons began whispering with each other, turning in their chairs to see what was happening. The conductor raised his hands to quiet the crowd. "Ladies and gentlemen, forgive me, please, for just a moment." He walked quickly offstage to the left and then out of sight. Now, the murmur of the crowd grew and nearly drowned out the sound of the sirens outside. A few patrons stood, seemingly concerned there was a danger and that perhaps they should leave.

As total pandemonium was about to break out, the conductor came back onstage and raised his hands to again quiet the crowd. "My sincere apologies, but there is nothing to be concerned with. Shall we proceed?" he concluded with a charming smile.

The crowd slowly took their seats again, and a low rumble of applause grew until the air was filled with enthusiastic clapping. The sirens all suddenly seemed to fade out.

"Thank you," the conductor said, then turned to the orchestra, spoke a few words to the musicians that I couldn't make out, and raised his baton high. With a dramatic flourish, his hand brought the symphony to life in a glorious harmony of instruments.

I looked over at Sara who was intently watching her daughter join in the performance.

All I could think about was what had transpired in the back alley. *Who survived? Are Willy Palumbo and his trusted man, Anthony, lying dead in pools of blood, Carmelo Rossi's men standing over them?*

Or, has Willy successfully carried out his vendetta and managed to safely get away?

It was well into the performance before I was able to draw my mind back to the moment and begin enjoying the magnificent performance.

Chapter Twenty

Pawleys Island, South Carolina. Present day.

Hanna got out of her late-model Honda Accord in the parking lot of her law office after running out for a sandwich to eat at her desk. She saw the door open on a rusted Toyota sedan. A woman got out, and she immediately recognized Helena Juarez. The woman had come to see her about a divorce. Her husband was now in the morgue, another victim of the drug cartels.

"Ms. Walsh, do you have a few minutes? I'm sorry I didn't call for an appointment, but . . ."

"Helena, I'm so sorry about your husband," Hanna said.

The woman didn't respond at first, then shook her head. "I loved Miguel for many years, but he turned bad when he started working for the cartel. He changed. He was dangerous to be around. This is better for my kids."

"Okay," Hanna said tentatively, not wanting to press her.

"I really do need to speak with you," Helena said.

Hanna gestured for her to accompany her inside, and they began walking toward the front entry of the small office building. "Where are your children?" Hanna asked.

"I left them with my mother."

They were almost to the door when the sound of a loud engine roared behind them. Hanna turned to see a big white pickup truck coming quickly toward them. She grabbed Helena's arm and pulled her quickly up the steps with her as the truck came to a sudden stop just a few feet from the stairs. Both front doors flew open, and two men rushed out of the truck.

Hanna's senses were on full alert. "What are you doing?" she yelled out.

The men were Hispanic, both dressed in black jeans and boots, pastel t-shirts that fit tightly over sculpted arms and chests, ball caps pulled low over their faces. One man went straight for Helena who tried to hide behind Hanna.

"Leave her alone!" Hanna yelled again.

He grabbed the woman and pulled her down the steps toward the truck. Hanna started after them, but the second man stood in her way and held a hand up to her face. In a heavy Spanish accent, he hissed, "This is not your business. You don't want to get hurt."

Her pulse was racing, and it was all she could do not to panic. "What do you want?" she screamed as the other man pulled Helena around the far side of the truck out of sight. "Don't hurt her!"

She heard the door open behind her, and one of the other lawyers came out. "What's going on?" It was the new young attorney, David Ross, who had just joined the firm a few months earlier. "Hanna?"

Before she could respond, she saw the gun come up in the hand of the man in front of her. He pointed it at Ross and said, "Get your ass back inside!"

Ross looked over at Hanna. She nodded for him to comply, and he reluctantly backed inside.

The gunman said, "You call the cops, somebody gets hurt!"

Hanna turned back, and now the gun was pointed at her chest. She felt the rush of fear surge through her veins. From behind the truck, she heard Helena yell out, "No, please, no!"

Hanna gathered her courage and started forward. "You leave her alone!" She felt the gun now pressed against her ribs. She put her hands up and took a step back.

The other man came around the truck. "Let's go!"

The man holding the gun on Hanna smiled and pulled the gun away. "You're a lucky lady. You might not be so lucky next time."

Hanna watched them both climb up into the truck, and then it sped away. Helena was sitting on the curb, her face in her hands, crying. She rushed over to her and knelt beside her, watching the truck squeal out into traffic. She also caught the letters and numbers on the South Carolina license plate. "Are you okay?"

The woman was hysterical and couldn't answer.

"Did he hurt you?"

Helena shook her head *no*, trying to control her gasping sobs.

"What did they want?" Hanna asked.

"I must go," Helena said.

"No, come inside. We need to talk."

"I can't speak with you. They will hurt my family." She got unsteadily to her feet and started backing away to her car. "Thank you for trying to help, but I must go."

"Helena, let us help you."

"No, I can't be here." She turned and hurried to her car and then pulled out of the lot and away down the street.

"Hanna, are you okay?" came the question from David Ross behind her.

She turned to look at him, her pulse slowly returning to near normal, her body still flaring with adrenaline.

"I need to call my husband!"

"They did what?" Alex said, incredulous as he listened to Hanna begin to tell him about the incident. "First, are you okay?" he said, desperately concerned.

"I'm fine. They obviously threatened this woman to not speak with me. I have no idea what she wanted to talk to me about . . . certainly not a divorce."

"And they pulled a gun on you?" he said, trying to control his anger.

"And my colleague, David, when he came out to see what was going on."

"Did you get a good look at them? What were they driving?"

"Oh, I got a very good look, and I also have their license plate number."

Alex had the dispatcher put out an alert for the white pickup truck with the two men who had confronted Hanna and Miguel Juarez's wife. He had Sheila Graham run a check on the license plate. He looked up when she knocked on his open door.

"What've you got?" he asked.

She came up to his desk and handed him a single sheet of paper. "The truck is registered to Rios Hernandez, the neighbor and cartel sidekick of Juarez."

"Why am I not surprised? He was probably one of the three who busted Juarez out of here."

"He may be the one who killed him," Graham said. She handed him another report. "Here are the priors on Hernandez."

Alex looked down the long list of arrests, convictions, and incarcerations. "How do these guys keep getting back out on the streets?"

"Good question," Graham said as they both turned, when there was another knock on the door.

The deputy leaned in and said, "Kelly's got your truck pulled over about two miles south of town on 17."

Alex stood up and said to Graham, "Let's go." To the deputy, he said, "Tell him to not approach. These guys are both armed and dangerous. Let's get some backup out there first."

They were pulling out of the department lot in one of the patrol cruisers, Graham at the wheel, when Deputy Ross Kelly came over the radio. "Suspects are getting restless. I think they're gonna bolt."

"Don't approach. We'll be there in five minutes," Alex said. "Keep me posted."

"Roger that."

"Light it up!" Alex said to Graham.

Graham turned on the lights and siren and sped off toward Highway 17.

A minute later, Ross came back on the radio. "The driver is getting out of the truck. He's coming back. Now, here comes the other guy."

Over the radio, Alex could also hear his deputy's door opening, then, "Stop right there! Get your hands on the truck. I said, stop!"

Alex yelled into the radio receiver, "Ross, get them on the ground. We're almost there."

Then a scream of pain came over the radio.

"Ross! Ross, can you hear me?" He looked over at Graham who pushed the accelerator down even more. Multiple questions went unanswered.

They came around a bend and saw the patrol car, lights flashing about a half mile ahead on the right. There was no sign of a white pickup. As they sped closer, Alex could see Deputy Ross Kelly lying in the road in front of his cruiser.

He heard Graham say, "Ohmigod!"

They screeched to a stop in the gravel behind the other cruiser, and both got out and rushed to their colleague. Graham was closest and got there first, kneeling beside the fallen officer. "Ross, what happened? Where are you hurt?" she yelled out.

Alex came up and knelt beside her. Ross Kelly's eyes were open, but dazed. He was breathing in frantic gasps; his right leg was twitching. "Ross, what happened?" He could tell the man was trying to answer but couldn't form the words. There was no indication of blood anywhere. "It looks like they tazed him," Alex said, looking down the road, no sign of the vehicle. "Sheila, get the paramedics out here." He stood and walked around the scene. He came back and noticed that Kelly's gun was missing from its holster and nowhere to be seen around the car.

Graham pulled the cruiser into the mobile home park where both the now-deceased Miguel Juarez and Rios Hernandez lived. She pulled over and parked two streets away from Hernandez's trailer. The radio squawked, and the backup unit confirmed they were just a minute out.

"Let's wait here," Alex said from the passenger seat. He looked at his watch. It was 2:25. He looked around the clusters of old mobile homes and late-model cars parked in the drives. A thin black dog came around the trailer they were parked in front of and started barking at them.

Graham said, "Great, that's all we need."

A woman came out of the trailer and gave their car a curious look, then called the dog three times before it finally gave up ground and followed her back inside.

Alex saw the backup cruiser pull in behind them in his side mirror. They had left Deputy Ross Kelly with the paramedics. He had eventually been able to speak and sit up. He relayed that, indeed, one of the men had pulled a Taser from behind his back and put him down. Alex knew the man was lucky to be alive and only incapacitated long enough for the suspects to get away.

All four officers got out of the two cars and gathered around Alex. "Hernandez lives around that corner to the left and down two streets."

Graham showed everyone on a map on her phone.

Alex gave instructions on how they were going to approach the place. They split back into two groups and started through backyards and an ally toward Hernandez's mobile home. A few neighbors came out, and he waved them back inside as they passed.

When they were across the street, he cautiously peered around the corner of another trailer. The white pickup was parked in the gravel drive. Frankly, he was surprised the man would come back to his home after the encounter with Kelly. He must've assumed that Kelly called in his plates. *Maybe he's clearing out?* Alex thought.

Almost on cue, a man came out of the trailer and down the steps to the truck with a big black duffel bag, heavily loaded. Another man followed and closed and locked the door behind him. He also carried a large bag.

Alex whispered into his radio, "Move in, weapons out." He unclasped the holster and pulled out his semiautomatic handgun. He watched Graham do the same and nodded for her to take cover behind a car off to their left.

He came around the building and rushed to crouch behind another car parked in the street, his gun extended in the direction of the two men loading the bags in the truck. He peered over the hood of the car, aiming his weapon, and yelled out, "Both of you, on the ground, now!"

Hernandez and the other man turned in his direction but did not look surprised or concerned. Alex could see guns tucked in the waistbands of each man.

"Get down and put your guns off to the side!"

Graham and the other two deputies now made themselves visible, but still behind cover. Graham yelled out, "On the ground, now, assholes!"

Both men dropped the bags and put their hands in the air.

Alex yelled again, "Throw the guns away, and get down on the ground!" He watched as they both slowly pulled the guns from their pants, held them out to the side, and then dropped them. "Kick them away!" He watched them comply and then came out from behind the car, his weapon still pointed at Rios Hernandez. He started walking across the street toward them. "I'm not going to ask again! On the ground!"

Hernandez moved first, falling to his knees then laying out on the ground, his arms extended. His accomplice followed.

"Hook them up!" Alex yelled to his team, and he watched as they all approached, two covering, two cuffing the suspects. When they were secured, Alex said, "Graham, read them their rights."

"We ain't done nothin!" Hernandez spat out.

Alex replied, "Assaulting a police officer, suspicion of drug trafficking, suspicion of murder. Let's start there!"

Hernandez and his accomplice were booked and locked up by 6 p.m. Alex was on the phone with the county prosecutor, Marjorie Willett, to fill her in on the arrests.

"I'll be by with my team in the morning," she said. "I'm sure they'll be lawyered up by then."

"Hernandez has already made the call, I assume to the lawyer over in Atlanta who was here with Miguel Juarez."

"You on alert for another attempted jail break?" she asked.

"We're prepared," Alex replied, certain in their precautions to prevent another escape.

"Good work, sheriff. See you in the morning."

After checking with Graham again that the prisoners were secure and all his instructions had been carried out, Alex returned to his office and called Will Foster at the Charleston FBI offices.

"We've got Rios Hernandez and one other man in custody. They took down one of my deputies in a traffic stop with a Taser, but he'll be okay. I also think Hernandez confronted Hanna and Miguel Juarez's wife at her offices earlier today."

"What was that about?"

"Hanna says they're warning Juarez's widow not to talk anyone. She's coming down to ID the guy. Prosecutor's gonna be here early tomorrow, if you want to join us."

Foster hesitated, then said, "Yeah, I'll be there. They have that slimeball lawyer from Atlanta coming back?"

"I think so."

"Good. Another chance to get in this guy's face about his ties to the cartels."

Hanna came into his office about thirty minutes later. He could see the uncertainty on her face.

"Thanks for coming over. This will just take a minute. I've had Hernandez and his pal put in the interrogation room. It has a mirrored window, so they won't be able to see you."

As he came around his desk, she came up and took both of his hands, laying her face on his shoulders. "These guys really scared me. Is your deputy going to be okay?"

"Just a little shaken up . . . and embarrassed that they took him down and got away with his gun."

She stepped back. "Do you have enough to hold them?"

"Yeah, Willett from the prosecutor's office will be here in the morning. We seized two bags of weapons and drugs when we arrested them. There's enough fentanyl to kill half the county."

"Lord, when will it stop?"

"Hopefully, we can use these two to get further up the chain to the cartel network here in South Carolina."

Alex led her back down the hall to the observation window. He watched as she cautiously looked in. "They can't see you."

It just took a moment. "It's them."

"Okay, good. Let me have Graham take your statement so we have the whole encounter on record."

Chapter Twenty-one

New York City and Long Island, New York. 1939.

Willy Palumbo was alive, but barely.

Louise called me early the next morning after the symphony performance. I was sitting in my office apartment, writing. I could tell immediately she was terribly upset.

"Mathew?" She couldn't finish, her sobs overwhelming her.

"Louise, what's wrong? What happened?"

"It's Willy. He's hurt very badly."

I had to pretend I had no knowledge of her husband's planned assault on Carmelo Rossi. "Tell me what happened."

I heard her take a deep breath to calm herself. "Willy was shot three times last night by the Rossi family."

My heart started thumping in my chest, my pulse accelerating. "Three times! Is he going to be okay?"

"I don't know. Anthony brought him in late last night. He was nearly dead. One of my son's neighbors is a doctor. He came over and got Willy stabilized and patched up."

"So, what happened?" I asked, my mind playing out Palumbo's failed attack.

"All Anthony will tell me is that it was Rossi's men. He was able to get Willy into a car before they could finish him off and before the police got there."

"Oh my God!" I said, truly not surprised, trying to mask my role in this whole crazy scheme. "Can I talk to him?"

"He's heavily medicated and hasn't been able to speak yet. He has one wound in his stomach and two in his arm and shoulder. The doctor thinks we need to get him to the hospital for surgery."

"Sounds like he's right. Can you get someone out there to move him?"

Louise paused to collect herself, then said, "The doc is trying to get an ambulance to come out to the house. There's a hospital about five minutes up the road."

I was thinking to myself that Anthony should have taken Willy there directly the previous night, but he was probably more concerned with police questioning and further threats from the Rossi family. "Give me your son's address. I want to come out."

When I got to the house, Willy had already been transported to the hospital. His daughter-in-law gave me directions. She was clearly not pleased that her husband's family was involved with this kind of mob violence, though she must have known what she was getting into when she married Willy's son. I noticed a car parked across the street with two men watching me. I didn't know if they were cops or mob. I didn't wait around to find out.

Willy was awake when I went into his room. Louise was sitting in a chair beside the bed, reading a book, I assumed to calm herself and keep her mind off her husband's near-fatal encounter. Anthony was standing in the far corner, apparently unhurt from the previous night's gunplay.

Louise stood to greet me and gave me a warm hug.

"Thank you for coming," she whispered.

I looked over her shoulder at the old gangster. He managed a weak smile. I pulled myself away from his wife and stepped over to the bedside. He held his hand out and we shook, his grip weak and trembling.

"What the hell happened?" I asked.

Willy turned to his wife. "Can you give us a minute. I don't want to upset you going through this all again."

She nodded and walked out of the room and down the hall. Anthony moved to the door to stand guard against any approaching threats.

"Willy, what the hell?"

He rubbed at the heavy stubble of black beard on his face. The shoulder of his hospital gown had fallen down, and I could see the bandages from at least one of his wounds. He took a sip of water, then said, "The docs just patched up my gut. Nicked a couple organs, but I'll be alright."

"A couple organs!" I replied in disbelief.

"Yeah, I'll be okay in a few days."

"Tell me what happened last night."

He hesitated, his face tight as he turned to gaze out the window of his third-floor room, looking out over a peaceful little Long Island town. "Rossi brought even more muscle than we thought. Anthony and two of my guys did their best to create a diversion so I could get close to Rossi, but I barely had my gun out before two of his goons were on me. Anthony saved my damn life and somehow got us both out of there, I guess as the cops were coming in."

"We heard the sirens."

"Anthony left a couple of Rossi's men in pretty bad shape. I was down and out by then."

"God, Willy, I can't believe you got out of there alive. And the police haven't been out to talk to you yet?"

"Rossi won't talk to them. This is between the two of us. He's not gonna pull the cops in."

"He knows your son lives out here, right?" I asked.

"Yeah. I got some of my old guys watching the house and out in the parking lot here."

"Willy, I have to ask. There's no way Rossi knows our family was involved in getting those tickets and backdoor passes? I don't want Melanee anywhere near any of this."

"There's no problem. Trust me," the old gangster said.

I had found on many occasions that he was the last person I could trust, and yet, there I was again in another unholy and probably unhealthy alliance. All I could think was my wife would literally kill me if she knew I had even remotely involved our daughter in this scheme.

"So, what now?" I asked, not sure I really wanted to know the answer.

"I'll be back on my feet in a few days. This isn't over, Coulter. This is far from over, and Rossi knows it, too."

I got back to the apartment late in the afternoon. Sara was sitting at the kitchen table, drinking a glass of tea and reading a magazine. She looked up as I came into the room. "How are the Palumbos?" she asked.

I hadn't told her when I left that Willy had been seriously injured in the latest episode of this mob war. She thought I was just going out for a visit. "Actually, Willy had another run-in with the Rossi family."

She gazed back in alarm. "Is he okay?"

"He'll be fine."

"They tried to kill him again?" she asked.

I nodded, still thinking it best not to reveal that Willy had escalated this latest attack. I could see the fear and concern in her face.

"Mathew, you need to stay away from those people. I don't want you—"

"I'll be alright."

"No, I love Louise, but Willy is nothing but trouble. You have to promise me."

I felt guilty enough at what I'd already kept from her, I couldn't bring myself to layer on any more empty promises. "I will be careful."

Chapter Twenty-two

Pawleys Island, South Carolina. Present day.

Alex got out of the shower wrapped in a towel but still dripping as he stepped onto the tile floor of the main bath upstairs in the beach house. Hanna had showered earlier and was already dressed for the dinner at Quinn Burke's house. She had chosen a simple blue sleeveless dress cut just above the knees. She was fussing with her hair in front of the mirror at her sink. She always kept her sandy brown hair cut about shoulder-length and let it hang straight with a part that seemed to form naturally on the left side. There were times like that evening when humidity, or some other climatic force, left her hair somewhere short of what she deemed acceptable. On most occasions she was unconcerned about such things, but perhaps due to the stress of the day and her encounters with the dangerous cartel members, she found herself a bit on edge about everything.

When her husband wrapped his arms around her from behind and whispered, "You look incredible, let it go," she felt her anxiety and stress shift a major notch downward. She put her brush down on the counter and turned into him, wet or not, and gave him a warm kiss.

"Thank you," she said with a smile. "What did I do before I met you in Charleston all those years ago?"

He just shook his head and kissed her back, lingering in their embrace.

Downstairs, she was waiting for him at the kitchen island, a glass of white wine half gone in front of her. He came down the stairs dressed in a pair of plaid shorts and a white cotton shirt rolled up at the sleeves. He was barefoot as all their shoes were kept in the back hallway entrance.

"What can I get you?" she asked, lifting her glass to take another sip.

"An excuse not to go tonight?" he said, with a mocking and playful tone.

She ignored the comment and said, "Let me guess, vodka straight over ice, a twist of lemon?"

While she made the drink, she watched him checking his phone. "Everything okay?"

"So far," he replied. "I've got four extra people taking shifts through the night to make sure our prisoners stay behind bars."

"And stay alive?" she asked.

"Exactly."

"You didn't ask Sheila to work tonight, did you? She has this blind date for dinner that Quinn lined up."

"She almost begged me to stay at the department so she didn't have to go," he said with a smirk.

"Yeah, right. Can't wait to meet this guy. He lives up the beach to the north. I don't think we've met him before. And Quinn's new man, the fighter. This should be really interesting."

"That's one way of describing it!"

When they knocked on the door at Quinn's house, Hanna was pleased not to hear the incessant barking of the two little

Yorkie terror dogs. The door opened, and Quinn greeted them with a big smile and then hugs for both. Her hair was combed back wet with some product; her short dress was patterned in red and yellow circles and cut low in front, showing a bit more than Hanna thought tasteful, but she scolded herself for judging. Quinn Burke was a grown single woman and could do as she pleased.

"My two favorite neighbors!" Quinn gushed. "Come in. Come in."

"Without the dogs," Hanna said, "it's too quiet around here."

"They love the Doggie Spa. They have their own little suite, and I'm sure they're as happy as clams."

"Thank goodness," Hanna murmured under her breath.

Quinn grabbed Hanna by the arm and pulled her back into the house toward the kitchen. Alex followed behind. A short, stocky, and incredibly fit man stood at the island in a black t-shirt that must have been at least two sizes too small, his chest and arm muscles bulging and veined. He appeared to be of Hispanic origin, his brown skin even more darkly tanned as evidenced by a lighter tan line from sunglasses on each side of his face. His head was clean-shaven and shining in the low kitchen light. A small tuft of black hair grew across his lower chin. He stepped around the counter with a broad grin. "Hello, I'm Carlos. Carlos Quintano."

Hanna stepped forward first and reached to shake his hand, which he took and then pulled her in close for a welcome embrace. She stepped back. "I'm Hanna. We live next door." She nodded in the direction to the right.

Carlos said, "I feel like I already know you. Quinn just goes on and on."

"I can only imagine," Hanna replied tentatively. She watched as Alex stepped forward, offering a firm handshake. The man was about a head shorter than her husband and certainly shorter than the tall and lean Quinn Burke.

"Alex Frank."

"Hello, Alex," Carlos said. "Very nice to meet you. Sheriff Alex Frank, I understand."

"Temporary sheriff. My boss has had some health issues. I was asked to step in."

"Quinn's told me so much about your law enforcement work. Thank you for your service."

Alex seemed to hesitate, then said, "Well, thank you. I understand you're a professional fighter."

Quintano smiled, and his head kept nodding like a bobble-head doll. "Yes, yes, I'm still in the game. Getting a bit old to hang with some of these young guys coming up in my weight class. I own a small gym and training facility south of town toward Charleston to keep paying the bills in the future."

Hanna noticed that his nose was pressed broad and flat from perhaps too many blows to the face. He had a scar beneath his right eye, and his neck seemed as wide as his bald head.

Quinn stepped up. "How about a drink? I've made a pitcher of margaritas, but I can get you anything."

"Thanks, Quinn," Hanna said. "White wine, chardonnay, if you have it. Actually, I brought you a bottle." She handed it to her neighbor.

"Thank you!" Quinn replied. "Carlos, would you open this, please?" She handed him the bottle of wine and said, "Alex?"

"A margarita sounds great, thanks."

Quinn said, "Carlos brought the tequila, his favorite from his home country."

Alex said, "You're from Mexico?"

"Born there, but my folks came to the States when I was very young. They're both teachers, retiring soon, but we've been in South Carolina most of my life. Quinn tells me you grew up near here, down in Dugganville."

Alex nodded. "My father owned a shrimp boat there until recently. Me and my brother grew up on the water running shrimp with our old man. Great little town to grow up in."

"You said owned. So, he's retired . . .?"

"No, Skipper Frank will never retire. He's got a big charter fishing boat down in the Keys now, thanks to Hanna who offered it to him when her father passed away a while back and left the boat to her."

"Love to fish!" Carlos beamed. "Maybe he'll take us out sometime?"

"I'm sure we can arrange that," Hanna said.

The doorbell chimed, and Hanna expected the two dogs to come running but then remembered they were away for the night.

"I'll get it," Quinn said.

As she walked back to greet her other guests, Carlos said, "Hanna, I understand you're a lawyer. What do you practice?"

"A little bit of everything. I used to run a free legal clinic in the city in Charleston, but we live up here now at the beach, and I work for a small firm off the island."

"Well," Carlos replied, "I commend you for your work in the city. So many people go without legal counsel because they can't afford it."

"Thank you. I do miss the work at times. But that was a while ago. It's a long story."

"Perhaps over dinner?" Carlos proposed.

"Perhaps," she replied, thinking the man seemed exceptionally nice and well mannered, despite his violent occupation and tough-man exterior.

Quinn walked into the kitchen with Sheila Graham on one arm and her new date on the other, a man who looked to be maybe ten years older than Sheila, graying at the temples under his short brown hair, a pleasing tanned face on a tall, lanky frame. Apparently, Sheila had met her date for the night outside before coming in.

Quinn made the introductions, including their neighbor from up the beach who Hanna was now sure she had never met before. His name was Jeremy Day, and they learned that he owned an antique store off the island. Hanna did remember seeing the store but had never been inside.

More drinks were served, and Quinn invited them all out on the deck overlooking the beach and broad expanse of Atlantic Ocean. A fire was already burning on the grill. Quinn said, "I hope you all like fish. Carlos and I picked up these marvelous fillets at the market this afternoon."

Everyone seemed to nod in anticipation and agreement.

Quinn raised her glass. "To old friends and new. Thank you all for coming tonight."

They raised their glasses for the toast and sipped at their drinks.

The sun was still at least an hour from dipping below the far horizon and glowed hot in the late evening sky. Hanna looked to the right and saw the familiar lines of her family's old beach house, shadowed in the late sun. *What a blessing to still have this place after so many years.* She often thought about her great-grandmother, Amanda, and how different her life must have been all those years ago, before and after the Civil War; and how sad her husband, Captain Atwell, never returned from a distant battlefield in Texas at the end of the war.

Later, they were all around Quinn's long dining table, salads cleared and well into their main course of grouper, asparagus, and a fruit salad. A third bottle of wine was nearly empty, and the conversations had become louder and more animated.

Hanna was definitely feeling the effects of her fourth glass for the evening. *But who's counting?* she thought to herself. She looked across the table, and Alex seemed to be having a pleasant conversation with Sheila's date, Jeremy, she assumed about the antique business, though she was certain Alex had zero interest in antiques. Sheila and Quinn were in deep conversation about something she couldn't hear, likely their dates for the evening. To her left was Quinn's new friend, Carlos.

She put her wine glass down and turned to him. "I have to ask . . . how did you get into professional fighting?"

"Oh, it goes way back," he replied. "I wrestled in high school and college and started learning martial arts as a way to learn more technique. I really got into it and eventually earned my black belt and started competing. Then, I guess ten years ago, a promoter came up to me at one of the Taekwondo events I was at and asked if I'd be interested in training for mixed martial arts. Long story short, I really enjoyed it and started making some real money, so I left my accounting job to fight full time."

"You were an accountant?" she said in surprise.

"Tax accountant for a big firm in Charleston. Boring as hell."

Hanna laughed. "And fighting is not boring?"

"The training can be a little grueling."

Taking another sip from her wine, she said, "Again, I have to ask . . . doesn't it hurt?"

"Hurts like hell!" he said with a smile.

"So, why do you do it?"

"I've always loved to compete. Fighting is the ultimate test. Have you trained hard enough? Are your skills good enough to defeat another man who wants to take your head off?"

Hanna watched the sincerity in his face. "You obviously take your work very seriously."

"You have to if you want to survive in the cage."

"The cage?"

"The fencing that surrounds the ring looks like a cage. You and Alex should come to my next fight with Quinn next week down in the city. I assume you've never been to a match before."

"No, can't say that I have," she replied, seriously *not* interested in going to see this guy beat someone's brains in.

Quinn leaned over. "Yes, you should come, Hanna. You've never seen anything like it."

"Oh, I'm quite sure of that!"

They had ice cream sundaes on the deck later with coffee, some sitting on the outdoor furniture group, Hanna and Sheila standing at the rail looking out over the beach.

They were far enough away from the others for Hanna to whisper, "So how's the new guy?"

Sheila turned and cautiously looked over at her date, Jeremy Day, then turned back and said, "He's extremely nice."

"Yes, he seems to be."

"He's also extremely gay."

"Seriously?" Hanna said. "Does Quinn know that?"

"Not sure," Sheila said. "I mean, it's fine. I have many gay friends, men and women."

"But why would Quinn set you two up?"

Sheila shook her head. "All he said was that he and Quinn had become friends. She stops in his store quite often to furnish the place here, and they're both newer to the island and trying to make more friends."

"Okay," Hanna replied, "the more the merrier, right?"

"Right!"

As if Jeremy knew they were talking about him, he got up from his chair and headed over to join them. "Hanna, I love your house. I understand your family's had it for generations."

"Yes, the Paltierres built it some years before the Civil War."

"Looks to be in marvelous shape," he replied.

"It's had several facelifts and updates over the years."

"Do you still have any of the old vintage furniture from your ancestors?"

"Actually, there are several pieces that have survived the ages."

"I'd love to see them sometime," Jeremy said.

"Of course," Hanna replied. "I'm not really interested in selling anything."

"No, no. I'd just like to see what you have."

Hanna pulled out her phone and brought up her contacts. "Let me have your number, and I'll text you mine so we can make a time for you to come by when we have our schedules in front of us."

"Great, thank you. And you'll have to come by the store some time."

"I'll do that."

Alex came up and joined them. "Hate to be the first to leave, but I just told Quinn I have a very early morning down at the department."

"Sure," Hanna said, actually pleased that they could get home and get some rest. It had been a very long day. "Let me go thank Quinn." She saw their host walking toward her.

"Hanna, thank you so much for spending the evening with us. I hope you enjoyed meeting some new friends."

"Very much. Thanks for having us."

Quinn looked back at Carlos who was clearing the table of dessert dishes. "Isn't he the greatest?" she gushed.

Hanna wasn't entirely sure. "He seems very nice."

Chapter Twenty-three

New York City, New York. 1939.

It was three days before I heard from Willy Palumbo. It was mid-morning, and the traffic noise outside our apartment had reached a steady din. The green canopy of Central Park was framed in my window.

I picked up the phone in my den. "Hello, this is Mathew Coulter."

"Coulter, it's Willy." His voice was still weak and hoarse.

"How are you feeling?"

"Have to admit, I've been better."

"Still in the hospital?"

"No, they sprung me this morning. I'm back at my son's, but I'm not sure how long we'll be here."

"Why is that?"

There was a pause, and I heard him put the phone down and then a door close.

"Willy?"

"Sorry, it's my daughter-in-law. If Rossi doesn't kill me, she'll be next in line."

"I sensed she's not very happy about your visit when I was out there the other day."

"We're coming back into the city tonight. I've got a hotel lined up in Midtown."

"You sure you should be traveling?" I was replaying the images of him lying near death in the hospital just a few days earlier.

"I'll be alright. Listen, I just wanted to thank you for putting your neck out for me the other night. I know it was a lot to ask."

I didn't answer, thinking that he was absolutely right.

"Coulter, I got another problem."

"Willy, I'm done—"

"No, no, you've done enough. I need to talk to you about our deal with your mother and sister."

"What about it?"

"No, not on the phone. Can you meet me tonight down at the hotel?" He told me where he was staying.

My first instinct was to decline. But if it was something I needed to know about my family, I wanted to hear what he had to say.

Palumbo was sitting at a back table in The Palm Court at the Plaza Hotel. Anthony was at the next table. Both had coffees and pastries in front of them. The hotel was only a few blocks from our apartment, and I had walked over as the light faded and the day chilled.

Willy looked surprisingly well, dressed in one of his expensive suits, his hair freshly cut, his face shaven. He didn't stand as I approached and sat beside him.

"Coffee?" he offered.

"Sure." He slid an empty cup over and started to fill it for me. I saw him grimace in pain at the effort. "Here, let me get that." I took the pot and filled my cup. "Isn't this place a little too public for a man who has a mob killer after him?" I said quietly, only a couple of other patrons in the place and several tables away.

"Rossi won't make a move here. Way too many people around."

"You sure?"

"It's my business to be sure."

I glanced over at Anthony. He was scanning the room and all entry points. His face was a mask of stoic purpose. I've never seen a man more committed to his work and his boss. I sipped on my coffee, then asked, "So, what do you need to tell me?"

Palumbo lifted his cup, and his hand was shaking so badly, he gave up and put it back down on the table. "Rossi is shutting me down."

"What are you talking about?"

"He's cutting off all my distributors, intimidating all my people into leaving my organization. It's just a matter of time until I'm out of business in the South."

It was easy to see where this was headed. I said, "And you won't be able to keep up the payments to my mother and sister?"

"Coulter, I'm a man of my word, and I will make this right with your family. It just may take a little time."

"Willy, your first priority should be staying alive and keeping your family safe."

"I'm taking care of that."

"In my opinion, you should be far away from New York and the Rossi mob. They're going to be on even higher alert. You've got no chance, Willy."

"You leave that to me. I just wanted you to know there may be some delays in my commitments to your family. Can you reach out to your mother and sister and explain what's happening?"

"I just spoke with my mother in Atlanta last night. She's fine, Willy. Your support has allowed her to keep their big house and her position in Atlanta society, but she has other resources. She'll be okay. And my sister. You know she married the oilman out in Texas. She's just fine."

"I'm glad to hear that, Coulter, but I keep my commitments, and I will in this case, too."

"I appreciate that," I said, noticing again that he appeared to be in considerable pain. "Seriously, Willy, you should be on a train back to Florida to rest and recuperate. You have nothing to gain here, and everything to lose. Think about Louise."

"Mathew, there's something you need to know. There's no such thing as backing down in our business. You take the fight to your enemy as long as you have to until one of you is buried six feet down."

I was not surprised by his pronouncement. I also thought it was incredibly ignorant. I looked him directly in the eyes. "I'm sorry I can't be of more help. I *do* have to think of my family."

"Coulter, you've done more than enough over the years and put up with some things from me that I'm not proud of. I consider you one of my closest friends, Mathew."

I nodded. "As do I. I'll let my mother and sister know what's going on."

"Thank you."

I stood to leave, and again, he didn't rise from his chair. I reached for his hand. "You keep your head down. I don't want to pick up the morning paper in the next few days and see a picture of you lying in the street with more holes in you."

He managed a smile and then looked suddenly past me. I started to turn and then saw Anthony jump from his chair and rush past me, knocking me down as he bolted past. There were shouted words, and a woman screamed as two gunshots went off behind me. I looked up at Willy from the floor, and he was crouching low, his face a mask of pain.

Then, Anthony stood over me and said, "Mr. Palumbo, we gotta go." He helped his boss up out of the chair.

I got up and turned to see a young man lying on his face not ten steps away, blood running from unseen wounds onto the carpet, a gun near his right hand.

I heard Palumbo say, "Mathew, you need to get out of here, now!"

Chapter Twenty-four

Georgetown, South Carolina. Present day.

Alex looked up when the county prosecutor, Marjorie Willett, appeared in his office doorway the next morning. He could tell from her expression that her day had not gotten off to a good start.

"Morning, Marjorie. Come in." He stood to come around his desk to shake her hand. They sat across from each other at his conference table.

"Would you like some coffee?" he offered.

"No, thank you," the prosecutor said with an edge to her voice. "Let me get to the point. I just came from a breakfast meeting with the mayor and City Council. To put it mildly, they read me the riot act about this fentanyl crisis. Another teenager was rushed into the emergency room at the hospital yesterday and died a few hours later. Preliminary toxicology report shows a heavy trace of fentanyl in her system."

"Oh, no. I hadn't heard yet."

"We need to get control of this, Alex."

"Trust me, it's our highest priority. Hopefully these two guys in the back will provide some information to get us to the root of the problem."

"Don't hold your breath," Willett said. "I just saw the cartel's lawyer from Atlanta coming in."

"Will Foster from the FBI office is coming up from Charleston. Should be here any time." He saw the look of doubt on her face.

"I know you're trying to coordinate with all the other agencies across the state, Alex, but we need to focus our attention here, close to home. We can't have our kids dying like this."

Alex tried his best to control his response. "Marjorie, this is going to take a collaborative effort. This isn't just a local problem. It's a national problem, and we need to take down more than a couple of local guys. It's not going to stop the flow."

"You try to convince that group I met with this morning. Our kids are dying. Their constituents are pissed. There's an election this fall. Connect the dots!"

There was a knock at the door behind them, and Alex waved for Special Agent Will Foster to come in to join them.

Greetings aside, they all returned to their seats at the table.

Alex began, "Will, Marjorie just told me we had another fatal overdose here last night."

"I'm sorry to hear that," Foster replied.

Willett said, "Will, we need to get this under control."

"Well, these two guys in the back are likely the main local distributors now that the other dealer is dead. We can throw away the key on these two, but the cartel will just send in more resources. We need to disrupt the network at a high level."

"And how do you propose to do that?" she asked, skeptically.

Alex said, "I really doubt we're going to get much from these two this morning. The lawyer will put the fear of God into them before we even get started. Will, I really feel like we have to go after the lawyer and his firm. Any progress with the Bureau office in Atlanta?"

"They're building a case to get a warrant to raid the firm's office up there."

"How long is that going to take?" Willett asked.

"I wish I could tell you. It depends on how convincing a case they can put together to present to the judge."

Alex said, "We've got some local politicians looking for some progress."

"I understand that," Foster said. "Maybe these two local cogs in the wheel behind bars will buy us some time with your politicians, but we need to cut much deeper into the organization to seriously disrupt the flow."

"Frankly, the biggest issue is at the southern border where all this crap is coming in," Alex said. "If the federal officials and politicians could get focused on a solution down there, the product supply could be significantly diminished, with much less ever making its way to South Carolina."

"Until then," Willett cut in, "our children are dying, and no one wants to stand by to wait for Washington to get their act together."

"We're not waiting for anything!" Foster fired back. "Look, Marjorie, let's see if we can make some progress with these two grunts out back this morning, ideally to lead us at least to their contacts at the next level."

"We'll put some serious heat on them," Alex said, "and see if either one shows any sign of rolling over. I'm sure their attorney will do everything possible to prevent that, but we have to try."

When they walked into the interrogation room, Alex saw the attorney, Rick Guidall, sitting between his two clients, his expensive suit elegantly set off by a bright floral tie and starched shirt pinstriped in blue. Alex sat across from Guidall, with Foster and Willett joining him on both sides. He began, "Mr. Guidall, we have your clients under arrest for suspicion of drug trafficking, assaulting a police officer, and accessory to murder. We had another fatality yesterday from the fentanyl these two are spreading throughout our communities."

Guidall sat up tall and leaned in. "Sheriff, you have no proof of any of that. I'm prepared to file a motion for wrongful arrest, harassment, and police brutality."

"Excuse me?" Alex said. "We have body cam footage from the officer who was assaulted by these two yesterday." He looked at both of the suspects who just stared back with indifference.

Guidall said, "We'll take that up with the judge this morning at the arraignment."

Marjorie Willett couldn't contain herself. "We're prepared to not only file these charges Sheriff Frank has outlined, but we will also argue for no bail. Let me be very clear, your two clients are facing multiple charges with sentencing that could include multiple life sentences."

Alex looked at the two suspects' faces again and saw both of them show the first signs of concern.

Will Foster cleared his throat and said, "The Bureau has growing concerns with your firm's ties to the cartels that are bringing this deadly plaque to our communities."

Alex watched as Guidall sat there with a smug look on his face.

Foster continued. "I would suggest your firm and your two clients here seriously reconsider their priorities and allegiances. There is still time to get out from under this if we can see some cooperation to help bring this deadly crisis to a halt."

Guidall just smiled back.

Willett said, "We're prepared to reconsider the charges against these two men if they are willing to cooperate and help us identify the key players in the network, at least here in South Carolina."

Alex noticed the man on the left, Miguel Juarez's neighbor, Rios Hernandez, look quickly at his attorney and then lean in to whisper something to him. Guidall shook his head *no* in response and then turned back to Willett.

"I'm confident in sharing with you that neither of my clients, and certainly no one from my law firm, has anything that could possibly help you in that regard. I believe we're done here."

Alex said, "Ah no, we're just getting started."

"I've advised my clients to remain silent until the hearing, so any questions you may still have will not be addressed at this time."

Willett stood up first. "This offer to reconsider charges will be off the table before we all get to court this morning if we don't get some serious indication of cooperation."

"As I said, Ms. Willett," Guidall said, also standing, "I believe we're done here."

Alex and Foster stood. Alex went out into the hall and brought a deputy in to take the two prisoners back to their cells.

When they were alone with Guidall, Foster said, "Our Atlanta Bureau office and the U.S. Attorney's office are taking serious aim at your firm, Mr. Guidall. The clock is ticking. You would be wise to consider our appeal for cooperation. I'm sure joining your two clients in federal prison is something you would certainly prefer to avoid."

"Agent Foster," Guidall replied with a smirk across his face, "our firm represents a wide array of clients under criminal prosecution. To suggest that we're doing anything other than legally representing the best interests of our clients is offensive to me and frankly libelous. I would be very careful in the accusations you're throwing around."

Alex watched the two men stare each other down. Finally, Foster said, "See you in court, counselor."

Chapter Twenty-five

New York City, New York. 1939.

I was sitting in my accustomed spot at the coffee shop near our apartment, my notebook open in front of me, the pen lying untouched. I was not able to get the events of the past night out of my head . . . the image of the dead assassin, the horrified looks on the faces of the other patrons as I rushed out of the Plaza Hotel.

On the way home, I decided I needed to be honest with my wife about what had transpired. She would surely read about it in the paper in the morning, and I had no idea if the authorities would be searching for me as part of their investigation.

It hadn't gone well.

When I told Sara that I had agreed to meet with Palumbo again because he had news to share about his commitment to our family, she was furious with me.

"Didn't I tell you to stay away from that man?" she shouted, near hysterics knowing how close I had just come to a gang shootout. "Please promise me this will be the last time," she cried out.

I took her in my arms and held her close, feeling her tears soak the shoulder of my shirt. "I'm sorry."

"You said you'd be careful!" She pulled away. "Do you call that careful? Sitting with a gangster in a public place a few days after he's involved in a deadly attack with his rival?"

"Sara, it will be okay. I tried to convince him he needs to take Louise back to Florida."

As I sat ruminating about my relationship with Willy Palumbo and my wife's well-founded anger and frustration with me, I looked up to see a man walk into the shop. I recognized the face immediately and felt a chill rush through me. There was no mistaking Carmelo Rossi, the handsome gray-haired Italian who ran one of the most prominent crime families on the East Coast.

He was followed by two other men who stood nearby as Rossi sat down at my small table. I stared back, trying to keep from trembling.

"Mr. Coulter, good morning."

"What do you want, Rossi?" I replied, trying to muster my fake courage.

"You and I have a problem, Mr. Coulter."

"And what is that?"

"His name is Willy Palumbo."

"Why is that my problem?" I said.

Rossi chuckled. "Palumbo has been a problem for you as long as you've known him. I got the whole story."

"Like I said, what do you want?"

He leaned in and his face turned grim. "I want Palumbo's head on a spike, and you're going to help me."

I started to gather my stuff on the table and stood to leave, knowing I wasn't going to get far.

"Sit down, Coulter," Rossi hissed. The two men backing him up came closer to emphasize the need for me to comply. When a retook my seat, he said, "I know you were at the hotel with him last night and that you were out at the hospital with him a few days ago. You two are obviously staying in touch. You need to tell me where I can find him."

148

"And why would I do that?"

"You have a lovely daughter, Coulter."

My blood went cold.

"It's too bad that she's blind. I understand she's a wonderful musician. Talent runs in your family, Coulter, you being the big famous writer."

"You leave her out of this, Rossi!" I demanded, sweat suddenly dripping down my neck.

He chuckled again, then said, "Little late for that now."

"What have you done?" I wanted to reach across the table and rip his self-satisfied face off.

"Your daughter, Melanee is her name, right?"

I didn't answer, nearing panic about what he might say next.

"Your daughter will be fine . . . as long as you help us get to Palumbo."

"You've taken her?" My heart was beating out of my chest. For a brief moment, I thought of Sara and how devastating this would be for her when she found out.

"I said she'll be fine," Rossi said with a grating smirk on his face.

"Where is she?" I shouted, standing suddenly and reaching across the table to grab the gangster by his jacket lapel. Both of his men quickly subdued me and sat me back down in the chair.

The two other customers in the shop quickly gathered their things and rushed out. The proprietor went into the back, out of sight.

"Your daughter is safe and well cared for," Rossi said. "But I can't promise that will continue if you don't help us."

"You sonofabitch!" I said, seething in anger. One of his men kept a hand on my shoulder to keep me from going after him.

Rossi handed me a card with a phone number on it. "This is where you can reach me. I expect to hear from you no later than 5 p.m. today."

"Rossi—" I began in protest, but he held up a hand.

"No excuses, Coulter. 5 p.m., if you want you're lovely daughter back in one piece." He stood and followed his men out the door of the shop. I started trembling as I heard the door close, my thoughts swirling in panic for my innocent daughter, Melanee, and what this latest turmoil would do to my emotionally fragile wife. I saw a pay phone in the corner and reached into my coat pocket for the number of the hotel Palumbo had given me.

The proprietor came back out from the kitchen, and I asked him for some change for a dollar. I placed the call and heard Willy Palumbo's familiar deep voice.

"Yeah?"

"Willy," I began, "it's Mathew."

"This better be important. I've got a few issues to deal with."

I didn't know where or how to begin.

"Coulter, what is it?"

"I need to see you."

"Can it wait? What do you need?"

"Rossi just came to see me."

"What . . . where?"

"I'm here at the coffee shop down the street from our apartment."

"Let me guess. He wants you to rat me out."

"Willy, they've got Melanee!" As I said it, I felt bile rise from my gut.

"Oh, Jesus!" the old gangster said.

Chapter Twenty-six

Pawleys Island, South Carolina. Present day.

Hanna pulled her Honda into the sandy two-track drive next to the mobile home where the widow of Miguel Juarez, Helena, lived with her three children. The early morning shade from the live oak tree at the back of the property dappled the ground, and the air was still cool and comfortable through the open windows of her car.

Over coffee with Alex that morning, they had discussed the arrest of the two men who had accosted Helena the previous day at her office before being taken into custody. Helena had come to her for help, and they had been unable to even get started before the men threatened and chased her away. Alex agreed it would be safe for her to reach out to Helena. On her drive into work, she decided to go directly to her home.

She opened the car door and reached for her bag on the other seat. Before she was halfway to the steps leading up to the front door, Helena came out, a look of fear on her face.

"You can't be here!" she said in a panicked voice.

"Helena, no it's okay. Those men are in jail. They can't do anything to you now."

"The others can! They're always watching!"

"What others?" Hanna asked as she stopped at the foot of the stairs.

"I don't know, but Miguel was always concerned they were watching us."

Hanna turned and took in all the surrounding area and the road she had come in on. She didn't see anyone or anything that seemed suspicious. She turned back to Helena Juarez. "You came to see me. What can I help you with?" She watched as Helena also nervously surveyed the area.

She took a deep breath and then said, "Come in, please, just for a minute."

Inside, Hanna sat on a couch in a small living room next to the kitchen. A hallway led back to the bedrooms. The place was sparsely furnished but neatly kept and clean. Helena sat in a chair next to her.

"Will Rios and the other man stay in jail?" she asked.

Hanna said, "You know my husband is the sheriff, right?"

She nodded.

"They arrested the two on multiple charges including assaulting a police officer yesterday afternoon. I doubt very much they'll be released on bail."

This seemed to do little to calm the woman.

"What did you want to talk to me about?" Hanna asked.

She hesitated, then replied, "Miguel had his faults, but he was good with our money. He has a bank account down the road. I don't know how much money is there, but they won't let me get to it. I'm not on the account."

"Okay, I can help you with that. Did your husband have a will?"

"I don't know. I don't think so."

"With a death certificate," Hanna said, "we can begin the probate process to have your husband's assets transferred to you."

"I don't have any certificate."

"I'll reach out to the County for you. We'll have to get some documents signed, and it may take some time. I'll do what I can to speed up the process. Do you have money to live on?"

Helena shook her head. "Very little. Not even one hundred dollars. I need to get food and pay the rent and—"

"I understand. Are you sure your husband didn't leave cash anywhere in the house?"

"I've looked everywhere." She paused and wiped at tears forming in her eyes. "Ms. Walsh, I'm afraid I can't pay you, at least until I can get into our accounts."

"You don't need to worry about that. My firm lets me take cases on a pro bono basis."

"What does that mean?"

"That means you don't have to pay me. I want to help you."

"Thank you . . . thank you so much."

Hanna flinched and Helena fell to the floor when an explosion of gunfire erupted outside the front door. There were more than a dozen bursts and the sounds of metal clanging and glass breaking, then screeching tires and the roar of a car engine racing away.

Hanna crawled to the window and cautiously peered out, her heart racing hard, her hands shaking. She pulled the curtain to the side and saw her old silver Honda with multiple bullet holes along the side, the windshield and driver window shattered. The front tire was flat. There was no sign of a car or the gunman. She turned back to Helena. "Are you okay?"

There was a look of shock and fear on the woman's face. She got to her feet quickly. "My babies!" She ran off quickly down the hall and into one of the bedrooms just as a small child started to cry. She came back out holding a little girl who looked to be around two. She had her face buried in her mother's shoulder.

Hanna said, "They're gone. I think they were just trying to scare us." *It worked!* she thought to herself. "I'm calling the Sheriff's Office."

"No, please don't!" Helena pleaded. "They can't see me with the police!"

"I have to call my husband. They've destroyed my car."

Alex saw Hanna's name and number on his phone screen. They had finished up with the session with the two prisoners and their lawyer, who had just left the building. "Hey, what's up?" he said, taking the call.

Hanna said, "I'm at Helena Juarez's house."

He could hear the alarm in her voice. "What's going on?"

"Someone came by and just shot up my car."

"What! Are you alright?"

"We're fine. Just a little shaken up. I can't say as much for my car."

"Are you sure they're gone?" he asked, reaching for his car keys and heading for the door.

"The car raced away. I don't see anyone."

"Stay inside! I'll be there as soon as I can."

Out in the squad room, he saw Deputy Sheila Graham. "Can you get away? Hanna is in trouble!"

They pulled up behind the demolished silver Honda in the drive of Helena Juarez's mobile home. Alex put his truck in park and jumped out. Graham was right behind them as they pulled their weapons and began a quick search around the property. When they came back around to the front porch, Hanna was waiting for them and then she came down the steps.

Alex went over and reached for Hanna's arms, taking a quick assessment. "You're sure you're okay?"

She nodded, then looked over at her Honda. "I can't believe they destroyed my car! How many years have I had it?"

Alex had to smile. "About ten years too many."

She pulled him in close and said, "I thought for a moment they were coming after us. The gunfire was so loud. It sounded like a war outside."

"Is everyone alright inside?"

"Helena and her baby are very upset."

"Why did she come to your office yesterday?"

Alex listened as Hanna explained the financial situation Helena Juarez was facing. He looked up when she came out on the porch with the baby in her arms. Her face was streaked with tears.

Helena said, "You all really need to leave. I can't be seen with you here."

Alex reached for Hanna's hand, and together, they walked back over to the porch. He said, "Mrs. Juarez, I'm afraid this is a crime scene. I have a forensics team coming over to process the area. There may be evidence that can help us find out who these people are."

"You still have Rios and the other man in jail?" she asked.

"Yes, the judge denied bail. They'll be held in the county jail until the outcome of their trial, which could be weeks if not months away." His words did not seem to comfort her.

Hanna said, "Helena, we can get you into a woman's shelter down in Charleston where you'll be completely safe from all of this. They'll be able to feed and help take care of you and your kids while I try to get this bank situation resolved. No one can find you there."

Helena looked at her little daughter as she bounced her on her hip to try to calm her. She brushed some hair away from the girl's face, then looked back at Hanna. "Yes, please, I think we need to go."

Chapter Twenty-seven

New York City, New York. 1939.

Making my way down a back alley off West 86th, I kept a vigilant eye behind me while heading to meet Willy Palumbo. When I told him about Melanee's abduction, he insisted we meet to discuss how we should handle this, not concerned that Rossi's men would be watching me closely. He assured me they would know if any of Rossi's goons were close and would deal with it.

I had done my best to hide my route, ducking into shops and restaurants along the way, exiting out other doors. It seemed no one was following me, but I was terrified of what Rossi might do to my daughter if he detected any deception.

As I passed several large trash cans, a big arm reached out and pulled me hard through a door on the back of a tall brick building. It was Palumbo's bodyguard, Anthony.

Palumbo was standing in a dark, shadowed hallway and said, "Coulter, come with me. Anthony, take care of that guy."

"Who?" I asked.

"You've got a tail," Palumbo said. "We'll deal with it."

"Willy! You can't mess with Rossi's men. They've got Melanee."

"I told you we would deal with it," the old gangster replied. "You have to trust me."

At that point, my trust levels with Willy Palumbo were near zero.

"Anthony, take care of it," Palumbo ordered.

The big bodyguard opened the door and slipped out, closing it behind him.

"Follow me," Palumbo said, turning to walk down the hallway. He led me into what looked to be a private room at the back of a restaurant that hadn't opened for business yet.

"Sit down, Coulter. Tell me exactly what Rossi told you."

"They know I've been around you. They've apparently been watching me for days trying to get to you. They want me to hand you over to them, or else they're going to . . . Willy, they have my daughter!"

"Settle down!" he demanded. "And what's our deadline for you to serve me up to Rossi?"

I looked at my watch. It was nearing the noon hour. "He said 5:00 today." I watched as Palumbo scratched at the stubble of beard on his face. I sensed a real exhaustion in his expression.

"We need to call the police, Willy!" I blurted out.

"You think that will get Melanee back?"

"What else can we do? If the police know that Rossi has kidnapped my daughter, he can't just kill her. They'll have him up on murder charges."

"Coulter, you think Rossi doesn't have the cops on the take? They're not gonna help."

"Not the whole department!"

"Enough, that it's the last thing we should do."

I couldn't believe what I was hearing.

"Listen to me, Coulter. The only thing we can do is give Rossi exactly what he asked for."

"You're gonna give yourself up to him? He'll kill you."

"Better me than Melanee," he said.

"There has to be another way."

He stared hard at me. "Mathew, I'm sorry I got you involved in all this. It's up to me to make this right."

I listened to what he was saying, not believing he was simply going to offer himself up to his rival. I thought about Melanee being held captive somewhere there in the city, and it broke my heart to think how scared she probably was. And my wife, Sara. *What am I going to tell her? What will she do if Melanee is hurt, or worse?*

"Coulter, we're going to take care of this. I'm going to need your help, but we're gonna get your daughter back to you and Sara."

Another one of Palumbo's men stuck his head through the door. "It's time to go, boss. Anthony says it's all clear."

Chapter Twenty-eight

Pawleys Island and Georgetown, South Carolina. Present day.

Hanna had watched sadly as her car was towed away out of the mobile home park. The old car was as much a part of her life as her house and clothes. It wasn't that she couldn't afford a new car. She simply saw no reason to waste money on one when the Honda had been such a dependable mode of transportation for more years than she could remember.

Alex had given her the keys to his truck to get back to her office. He and Sheila Graham would ride back to the department in one of the other squad cars that had come out to the Juarez place.

On her way back to her office, she had called her old friend who ran the women's shelter in Charleston to confirm there was room for Helena and her children, which indeed, there was. Alex had offered to have a deputy patrol car accompany Helena down to Charleston.

As she pulled into the parking lot at the law offices, she was making mental notes of the calls she needed to make on Helena's behalf. Her cellphone buzzed and she saw Quinn Burke's name on the screen. She was tempted to let it go to voicemail, but then took the call as she walked up the steps to her office.

"Hi, Quinn. I'm a little busy right now, but—"

"Hanna, I'm glad I reached you." The two dogs were yapping in the background.

"What is it, Quinn?" She pushed through the doors and walked past the receptionist with a nod as she headed back toward her office.

"I was walking the dogs on the beach, and I saw two men sneaking around your house."

"What were they doing?" she asked, alarmed at what could possibly be going on. She sat down at her desk and placed her bag on the floor beside her.

Quinn said, "I'm up on my deck now, looking through the trees. One of them is on your front deck looking in the windows."

"Do they have work uniforms on? I don't think we were expecting any service workers out there. Alex may have arranged something."

"No, they're dressed in street clothes. I can't say for sure, but they look Mexican."

Half the day workers in the area are from Mexico, she thought. "I'm going to call Alex and have him send someone over. Be careful, and don't go over there."

"Ohmigod!" Quinn blurted out.

"What is it?"

"One of the guys just broke a window in your door and went inside."

Hanna felt a chill rush through her. "Let me call Alex! I'll call you back."

Alex answered on the second ring. "You get back to the office okay?"

She was trying to keep her voice calm. "I just got off the phone with Quinn. Someone is breaking into our house!"

"What!"

"She called when she saw two men lurking around the house, and then one of them just broke through the door on the front deck. She thinks they look Hispanic. Would these cartel guys break into our house?"

"I don't know, but I'll get our nearest patrol car over there, and I'm coming as well. I want you to stay at your office."

"Okay. Please be careful."

Alex pulled his patrol car into the drive behind the beach house. Another department car was already there with lights still flashing. He got out quickly and saw one of his deputies coming out of the back door and then down the steps toward him.

The man said, "Alex, we just cleared the whole place. Whoever was in there is gone. They messed the house up a bit. Can't tell if anything was taken."

"Okay, thanks," Alex said, rushing past and up the stairs.

He first noticed kitchen drawers pulled out and items all over the floor. Then, in the living room, cushions from chairs and the couch had been strewn about the room. Two lamps were knocked over and broken. *Hanna is gonna be sick about this,* he thought.

He rushed upstairs but didn't see anything amiss. Coming back down, he was about to call Hanna when he heard a knock at the front door. He came around a corner and saw Quinn Burke standing at the glass-paned door, her hands on her hips, her right foot tapping impatiently.

He pushed open the door. "Quinn, come in. Thank you for calling this in."

"Is everything alright?" she asked, coming in and closing the door behind her.

"Not sure yet. They certainly made a mess of the place. Almost think they were trying to send a signal."

"A signal?" Quinn asked.

"Hanna and I have both had several run-ins with a drug cartel that's operating in the area. Maybe this is their way of telling us to back off. Or, maybe they were looking for something, but I can't imagine what."

"Did Hanna tell you they looked like they were from Mexico or some Latin country?"

"Yes, she did." His phone started ringing and he looked at the screen. *Unknown Caller.*

"This is Sheriff Frank."

The voice was low, somewhat garbled. "You have something we need back, sheriff."

"Who is this?"

"I want our men released immediately."

Alex walked out on the front deck. Quinn followed with a quizzical look on her face. He said, "Who is this, and what are we talking about?"

"Rios Hernandez and the other man. I want them set free immediately."

"And why would I do that?"

There was a pause, and then the low voice said, "I don't think you want the blood of dozens of citizens on your conscience, sheriff."

"Tell me what the hell you're talking about!" He turned and saw Quinn staring back at him from the deck rail.

"Unless my men are released immediately, we have teams in place surrounding the carnival currently taking place on your lovely little Main Street of Georgetown. They are awaiting my command to unleash holy hell on the crowd. I don't think you want to be responsible for that mess, sheriff. Automatic weapons and machetes can leave such a mess."

Alex felt his heart thudding in his chest. His mouth had gone bone dry, and he couldn't swallow. "I need to get back to the department."

"I know where you are."

He looked around, wondering if the men who broke into the house were still nearby watching him.

"Make the call, sheriff!" the man demanded.

"I need to be there," Alex insisted.

"You have one hour!"

Chapter Twenty-nine

New York City, New York. 1939.

"Mathew, what's going on?" Sara asked.

I was back in the coffee shop a little past one in the afternoon. I'd used the phone there to call my wife. "I told you I'm working and probably won't be back until dinner."

"You're a bad liar, Mathew Coulter! Tell me what's going on."

My mind was racing with possible deceptions and obfuscations. Finally, I knew I had to tell her at least some of the truth. "I have to help Palumbo with something . . ."

"Mathew, I told you—!"

"Sara, please. I need to do this. I'll explain to you later."

"What if there isn't a *later*? What if he gets you killed this time?"

"I'll be okay. You don't have to worry about me." The lies were tearing me up, but I couldn't bring myself to tell her that Melanee was being held by the Rossi mob.

"Mathew, I can't take this much longer. You need to stay away from that man. Everyone around him ends up in a box!"

Of course, she is right. But what choice do I have at this point?

"Mathew, tell me what's happening," she demanded.

"I can't get into it now. I'll call you a bit later."

"When? I can't sit here all afternoon worrying about you. I'm coming down to the shop."

"No, you need to stay at home. I don't want you anywhere near this, do you hear me?"

"You're really scaring me now," she said.

"Sara, I'll call you as soon as I can. Promise me you'll stay there."

I heard the phone crash down into the cradle.

Palumbo asked me to meet him in front of the Plaza Hotel at 2:00 p.m., and he was waiting there, standing next to one of the doormen. There was no sign of Anthony or any of Palumbo's other men. He saw me walking up along Central Park South. The elegant horse-drawn carriages and their drivers were lined up on the far side of the road along the tree-lined edge of the park. I kept glancing around, expecting gunfire to break out at any moment.

Palumbo looked remarkably calm as I walked up to him. He had a hat pulled low over his face, but you would have thought he was simply waiting to go inside for dinner. He took me by the arm and pulled me over to the side of the entrance to the big hotel.

"This is gonna go down fast, Coulter. You need to keep your wits about you."

"What's happening, Willy?"

"Just do as I say."

I didn't have time to protest or demand more answers. I saw him turn when a long black car pulled up to the curb. He turned back to me. "When you have Melanee, you get inside the hotel as fast as you can. Don't look back. Take her out the north entrance. I have a man there who will get you away from here."

"They're bringing her here?" I said, as the doors to the car opened and two men got out. One turned and reached into the back seat. My heart leapt when I saw Melanee climb out of the back seat holding the man's hand.

"Don't say anything, Coulter," Palumbo demanded.

Melanee looked tired and confused, and of course she couldn't see us, but I was certain her incredible sixth sense allowed her to know what was happening.

"Go take your daughter," Palumbo said in a low voice.

I looked at him, totally bewildered. "Willy, what's going to happen?"

"Just get her out of here. My man is waiting for you."

I took a final look, firmly believing I would never see the man alive again. "Willy, thank you—"

"Just go get your daughter!" he hissed.

I left him and walked toward the car. I couldn't tell if Rossi was in it. His two men were watching me. "Melanee, it's me."

"Daddy. I knew you'd come for me."

Of course she did.

I took her hand from the grip of Rossi's man and pulled her in close. "Are you okay, honey?"

"I'm fine. Tell me what's happening."

"We have to go." I put my arm around her shoulders and led her back toward Palumbo and the steps up into the hotel. As I passed Palumbo, I saw a steely resolve on his face, as if he were prepared for his final journey. "Willy—"

"Get out of here, Coulter!"

"Mr. Palumbo?" Melanee began.

"Go, now, Coulter!"

I hurried Melanee up the steps and into the lobby of the hotel. I took one last glance back and saw Palumbo climbing into the back of Rossi's car. I couldn't help but feel a deep sadness for the loss of a man who had been at times my biggest nemesis, at others, one of my closest friends.

"Daddy, please tell me what's going on," Melanee insisted as we hurried through the big lobby of the hotel.

"I need to get you home. Everything will be okay."

We were just about to go out the side entrance to the hotel and I was looking for Palumbo's man when the sound of tires screeching and the crack of gunfire filled the air outside the hotel. One shot, two, a dozen more. I instinctively pulled my daughter to the floor and shielded her with my body. More gunfire erupted outside.

A hand grabbed my arm. "Mr. Coulter, we need to go!"

I looked up and recognized one of Palumbo's lieutenants. "What's happening?"

"I need to get you out of here, now!"

Sara was beside herself when I brought Melanee into our apartment. I watched mother and daughter hug and then both started crying. Palumbo's man stood behind me in the hall. Police sirens were blaring a few blocks away in the city.

Sara looked over Melanee's shoulder. "Mathew, what is he doing here? What's going on?"

"It's okay now." I took them both in my arms, and the three of us stood there in a tight embrace.

Sara pulled back and looked at me with a determined glare. "I want to know right now!"

"Rossi, the man who is having the fight with Willy, was using me and Melanee to get at him."

"What do you mean using Melanee?" she demanded.

"They took her this morning. They were holding her."

Sara's eyes opened wide with fear and anger. "You let them get our daughter in the middle of this?"

"I didn't let them *do* anything!" Now, I was getting angry, despite the fact that my complicit assistance in Palumbo's feud with Rossi had led to all this.

Sara turned to Melanee. "Are you okay? Did they hurt you?"

"I'm fine, mother. Where is Mr. Palumbo?"

I turned to look at our guard standing behind us. "What happened? You need to tell us."

"We need to stay here," the man said. "We'll get a call when everything is clear."

At that moment, I was certain Willy Palumbo and who knows how many others were lying dead in the street outside the Plaza Hotel.

It wasn't an hour later when the phone in the living room rang. I rushed over and picked up the receiver. "Yes?"

I couldn't believe I heard the voice of Willy Palumbo, as calm as if we were sitting on the porch of the Beach Hotel down in Grayton Beach. "Coulter, you two okay?"

"We're fine, Willy. Where are you? How are you?"

"I'm fine. Our little problem is taken care of."

Our little problem, I thought. A deadly gangster had abducted my daughter, and my friend Palumbo was the bait to get her back.

"What did you do?"

"Let's not linger on the past, Coulter. You and Melanee are safe. I'm still breathing. Rossi won't bother us anymore. Life is good."

"Rossi was in the car?" I asked.

"He's still in the car . . . with quite a few holes in him. I'll tell you about it sometime. Right now, I need to get out of town for a while. My guy's gonna stay with you and the family until this all blows over."

Chapter Thirty

Georgetown, South Carolina. Present day.

Alex raced back to the department. He had alerted Sheila Graham to the situation and had ordered her not to do anything until he got back, but to also secure the building and be prepared for another assault from the cartel.

His next call was to Will Foster's cell. The FBI took the call immediately. "What is it, Alex?"

"They've taken the whole damn town hostage!"

"What? Who?"

"Whoever is running this operation for the cartel. They've got men in place to start shooting up a family carnival here in Georgetown."

"What the hell?" Foster said. "You spoke to them?"

"They want me to release the two prisoners we interrogated this morning."

There was a pause before Foster said, "You can't do that, Alex."

"I sure as hell can," he fired back, nearly running a red light and turning on his emergency lights and siren to drive even faster.

"We need to get a negotiator involved to try to reason with this guy," Foster insisted.

"There's no time for that. They gave us a one-hour deadline twenty minutes ago."

"Alex, I'm already back in Charleston. Let me see if I can get our hostage team lined up quickly. We may have to get Atlanta involved."

"I told you, there's no time!" Alex said.

"Alex, listen to me. I know this is your town and this is happening on your watch, but you have to think clearly. You can't just let these guys go with no guarantees or commitments in place."

He let his friend's words sink in and knew he was right. "I have no way to call this guy back. The call number that came in on my cell is scrambled." He pulled into the parking lot at the department and ran inside.

"Alright," Foster said. "Let's talk this through."

His phone buzzed again as he sat down at his desk. He saw the same *Unknown Caller* message. "I think this is the guy calling now. I'll get back to you."

"Alex, wait—"

He cut off the call and accepted the other. "This is Frank."

"I'm losing my patience, Sheriff."

Alex started to respond but was cut off.

"Walk outside, Sheriff."

He did as instructed. There was a pickup truck on the street at the entrance to the department. Two men were in the cab holding automatic rifles up so he could see them. A third was standing in the bed of the truck behind a mounted machine gun.

"You have two minutes to let my men go," the voice said, "or this truck and two others take open season on the streets of your town."

Alex watched Rios Hernandez and their other captive run across the parking lot and jump into the back of the truck. It sped away toward the highway.

Into his phone he said, "You have them back. Call off your men."

"It's already done. Let me give you some advice. We're not going away. We're never going away. You need to take a step back and let us run our business, or a lot more people are going to get hurt."

"More than you're already killing with that poison you're pushing on our kids?"

There was no response. The call had ended.

One hour had gone by since the two cartel prisoners had been set free in the parking lot. Alex was sitting at his desk with his phone in front of him waiting for a callback from the prosecutor, Marjorie Willett. Every minute that went by caused him to further doubt his decision to let the men go without further guarantees.

Graham stuck her head through his door to check if there had been any updates. He shook his head *no* and she stepped away.

When his phone finally rang, he reached out quickly, only to see that it was Will Foster.

"Alex, what's happening?"

He filled the FBI man in on the latest developments.

Foster said, "You did the right thing, Alex."

"I'll probably lose my job, but that's the last of my worries."

"No one can fault you for how you handled this. I'll stand up for you if needed."

"Thanks, Will. I better get off the phone."

"Keep me posted."

The callback from Willett in the prosecutor's office went better than he had anticipated. She supported his decision and reassured him he really had no other choice. She told him she would come by his office first thing in the morning to work through how they were going to proceed against the cartel.

Alex ran up the steps to the law office. The receptionist indicated Hanna was in her office, and he hurried down the hall. She saw him come through the door and stood to greet him.

"Sorry about your car," he said.

"I've already called the Honda dealer. They have a nice replacement on the used car lot. I told him I'd stop by on the way home."

"Good," Alex said. "I wanted to tell you something before we get home."

They both sat down around her small conference table. He walked her through the entire situation with the cartel holding virtually the entire town hostage unless he released the prisoners.

When he was done, Hanna said, "I've always heard these gangs were ruthless, but this is so far beyond extreme."

"We've literally got a war on our hands."

"What are you going to do?" she asked.

"Our task force is meeting again in the morning on a big conference call. Foster is taking the lead. We need to get every law enforcement agency fully engaged and cooperating. We can't let this continue."

Hanna nodded back, then said, "This guy threatened you that more people would be hurt if you didn't stand down. What are they going to try next?"

"I don't know, but we have to take the fight to them one way or the other," he said. "There's something else. I wanted to catch you before you get home. The house is a little torn up."

"The intruders Quinn called about?"

"Yeah, nothing seems to have been taken. I think they were sending another message."

"Message received!"

Chapter Thirty-one

Long Island, New York. 1939.

Louise Palumbo sat with my wife, Sara, and me in a group of lounge chairs on the back patio of her son's house. Willy had insisted we bring Melanee and her family out on the island to stay for a few days to let things cool down for a while. I think he also wanted us to be there as much for his wife's sake as he fled town and because of the carnage he and his men had left on Fifth Avenue in Manhattan.

Louise lifted a glass of iced tea and said, "I could kill my husband for getting you all involved in this. It's not enough that our son is buried in a graveyard a thousand miles from here in Florida. Now, he's almost—"

I cut her off. "Louise, it's okay. We're okay. Willy saved Melanee's life."

Sara couldn't contain herself. "He almost got her killed first, Mathew!"

I reached for her hand to comfort her. "I know, and I'm sorry I ever got us even close to all this, but it's done now and she's safe."

Louise said, "Willy called me just before you got here."

"What did he say?" I asked, anxious to know what had happened, what the plan was going forward.

"He just told me you were coming out for a few days, that some of his men would be here to watch the house. He told me he had taken care of his problem with Rossi but had to go away for a bit. He wouldn't tell me how long, but knowing my husband, it could be quite some time. I suspect he's on his way back to Miami and will send for me in a week or two, or who knows with that man."

Sara said, "How do you live with all this?"

"For some crazy reason, I love Willy Palumbo, have since I first met him when I was a young girl in high school. Did I ever tell you how we met?"

I was glad to have the discussion turn from the events back in Manhattan. "So, he swept you off your feet. Willy is a charmer."

"No," Louise said. "It wasn't like that at all."

"Tell us," Sara said, obviously as delighted as I to shift the discussion, knowing her daughter was safe inside with her family.

"I was a senior in high school. We lived in a little town just up the road from here. I was out with a couple of my girlfriends. We were going to go to a movie and meet some boys there. A boy I had been dating had just come up to us on the street when Willy pulled up in a big shiny car and stopped at the curb. He had some other boys in the car, but they stayed there when he got out and walked up to us. He was the most handsome boy I think I had ever seen. He was also about a hundred pounds lighter than he is now and didn't have a cigar hanging out of his mouth."

"Love at first sight?" Sara asked.

"I guess it was, though that evening didn't go well at all. Willy came straight up to me like we'd known each other for years, totally ignoring my date standing beside me, and put his arm around my shoulder. He says, 'Hey beautiful. What are ya doin' tonight?' My date didn't particularly care for that and pushed Willy away. The next thing I know, the boy is lying on the sidewalk with blood pouring out of his nose."

"Why am I not surprised?" I said.

"A real charmer, alright, that Willy," Sara said, managing a smile.

Louise continued. "He called my house the next night and asked me out. It took three more phone calls before I said yes, though I knew right away I wanted to see him again. I thought my father would send me away to a convent when he found out Willy worked for the mob. I still managed to get away to see him. A year later, we were married in a big wedding out here on the island, and a year after that our first son was born."

"An American love story if ever there was one," I joked.

Sara said, "But how have you put up with this all these years?"

"I told you, I love the old bastard!" She looked back with a sly grin. "I'm so sorry you all got caught up in it, though. This is my life, and I came to terms with it years ago. But you shouldn't have to deal with the chaos of the Palumbos."

"Let me be honest," Sara said, "I hope we never have to again. I love you, Louise, but we need to stay away from all this. I'm not sure I'll ever forgive my husband for getting Melanee caught up in all of it." She looked over at me, and I knew she was telling the truth.

Chapter Thirty-two

Pawleys Island, South Carolina. Present day.

Hanna had dozed off on a cushioned lounge chair on the front deck of the beach house. The glass of wine Alex brought for her rested untouched on a side table. The sight of her trashed house had done little to improve her shaky mood after the assault at the trailer park, and she had fallen asleep almost immediately.

The sound and buzzing of her cellphone on the arm of the lounge chair woke her. She looked out over the vast panorama of beach and ocean to bring herself back from the deep sleep. It was early evening, and the day had cooled in the shadows from the house. The ocean was a flat gray as the day faded.

Alex came through the door, hearing the call, to see if she was awake. She nodded to him and picked up the phone.

"Hello, this is Hanna."

"Hi, Hanna, this is Janet Anders, your long-lost relative from Grayton Beach."

She had nearly forgotten her earlier conversation with the woman about stopping by for a visit on their way back north from Florida. "Yes, Janet, how are you?"

Alex sat beside her and gave her a quizzical look.

Janet said, "We're fine, and actually only about an hour south of Pawleys Island according to the GPS, if it's still okay to come by."

Hanna hesitated. The house was surely still a mess, and she was certainly in no mood for company. But the woman had been so kind when she had called earlier, and frankly, she was curious to hear the story about her distant relation, Mathew Coulter. "Of course," she finally replied. "You'll have to forgive us. We had a bit of an incident here earlier today, and the place is still a mess."

"Are you sure it's okay?" Janet asked.

"Absolutely." She gave her the address to plug into her GPS. "We'll see you soon."

"Who was that?" Alex asked when she ended the call.

She reminded him of the conversation about her relative from Atlanta who was a famous novelist. His granddaughter had found an old manuscript that had never been published and wanted to share something scandalous about the family in the book.

"Well, this should be interesting," he said. "You sure you're up to having company?"

"I'll be fine. Take my mind off this crazy day."

"I cleaned up inside while you were getting some rest," he said.

"Thank you. Any idea what they were after? It creeps me out to think about them rummaging through our house."

"All I can think," Alex replied, "is the cartel is sending a warning for us to back off on the investigation."

"I think we get the message," she said, shakily.

He reached for her hand. "How are you feeling?"

She picked up the glass of wine and took a sip. "Better now!"

The back doorbell rang, and Hanna left the kitchen to answer the door. Janet Anders was standing there with her husband. They both looked to be in their seventies, if not eighty, but healthy and fit. Janet was tall and lean, her gray hair cropped short and nicely styled. Her husband was just a bit taller, his face framed with short white hair and beard. Both were tanned from their time in Florida and dressed as if they'd just taken a walk on the beach in shorts and t-shirts.

Hanna reached out to hug first Janet and then her husband who was introduced as Dale. "Welcome, come in! How long have you been on the road today?" She followed them into the kitchen.

Janet said, "We left Grayton Beach this morning around nine, so it's been a full day. Traffic was brutal."

Alex came out of the kitchen and introductions were made.

"I love your home, Hanna," Janet gushed. "I understand this place has been in your family for generations."

"Since before the Civil War."

"If you're lucky," Alex said, "you'll get to meet the ghost of her great-great-grandmother, Amanda. She stops by quite often."

"Seriously?" Dale asked.

Hanna nodded. "She's been my guardian angel for years. I could have used her help today, but that's another story. Have you eaten? We put together some things to munch on. We can send for takeout if you haven't had dinner."

"No, thank you," Janet said. "We grabbed something to eat coming through Charleston. What a beautiful city. We took a little side trip through downtown."

"Did you drive down the Battery?" Hanna asked.

"Yes, we did," Dale said. "Marvelous old houses."

Alex said, "Hanna and her family used to live in one of them when she was raising her son, Jonathan."

Hanna ushered them into the kitchen, and both agreed to join her with a glass of wine. They took the food and their drinks out onto the deck.

Janet said, "Grayton Beach is lovely, but it's hard to beat this view, Hanna."

"Well, thank you. We moved up here full time from Charleston a few years ago. Not sure we'll ever leave."

They all sat in a grouping of chairs around a table where the snacks were laid out.

Hanna said, "It's so nice to meet you after all these years. I had a chance to meet your mother down in Grayton when I was a little girl. I always wished I had been able to get up to New York to hear her play with the Philharmonic."

"She was quite a talent," Janet said. "I, unfortunately, inherited very little of it."

"It's so remarkable," Hanna continued, "what a full and interesting life she led despite her sightless challenges."

Dale said, "She was quite an inspiration to all of us."

They all shared the wine and food for a while, touching on family backgrounds and histories. Alex told them about his family from nearby Dugganville.

When he finished telling about Skipper and Ella, Janet said, "With them down in Florida now, wouldn't it be fun to have a family reunion and get all of us together with our kids and grandkids down in Grayton Beach some day?"

"We'll have to try to organize that soon," Hanna said. "Sounds like a great idea!"

Janet said, "I feel badly about dropping in like this so late. You said you had an incident earlier. Is everything okay?"

Hanna said, "It's a long story, but everything is fine. You'll have to stay over tonight."

"Oh, no," Dale replied. "We planned to get a motel out by the highway somewhere to get an early start north again in the morning."

"Absolutely not," Hanna insisted. "We have lots of room here."

"Thank you," Janet said. "That's very kind of you."

"So," Hanna said, "I've been dying to hear about your grandfather's manuscript and the scandals of the Coulter side of the family."

Alex picked up a bottle of wine and filled glasses for everyone.

Janet reached down into a bag at her feet and pulled out an old brown envelope about two inches thick with paper. "There's a storage shed on the property down in Grayton Beach. It hadn't been cleaned out in years, so Dale and I started in on it on this latest trip. We found this manuscript and some other papers of my grandparents in a big box up on a high shelf. Hard to believe it survived storms and heat and humidity all these years." She pulled out the thick pile of old, yellowed typing paper and set it down on the table.

Hanna said, "I've read most if not all of Mathew Coulter's novels. Why was this one never published?"

Janet hesitated, then said, "I'm not really sure. My only guess is the information about our family in the story is a bit . . . *surprising*, I guess I should say."

"In what way?" Alex asked.

Janet said, "I've made a copy of the complete manuscript to leave with you, but let me give you a summary of what I think caused my grandfather to delay and, ultimately, never publish this book."

"Go ahead," Hanna said, leaning forward in her chair. "I can't imagine where this is headed."

"During my grandfather's early days in Grayton Beach in the 1920s, he met a man named Willy Palumbo."

Alex said, "I think I've heard of him. Wasn't he one of the prominent mob bosses in New York back during those times?"

"Yes, exactly," Janet replied. "While my grandfather was staying out at the beach cottage in 1925, he formed what turned out to be a long relationship with Mr. Palumbo."

"In what way?" Hanna asked.

"You may know that the Coulter family ran the illegal liquor trade in the South during Prohibition."

"Yes," Hanna said, "I'm well aware. It paid for the big Atlanta house my father inherited that I was raised in. My father's second wife still lives there after his recent passing."

"Yes," Janet replied. "I've met your father a couple of times. We were very sorry to hear of his passing. So, this manuscript details the growing relationship between Mathew Coulter and Willy Palumbo," she said, holding up the pages. "Initially, this included the transfer to my grandfather from Mr. Palumbo of the ownership in an illegal club in Panama City near Grayton Beach. The ownership of the club was soon transferred again to a young woman my grandfather was seeing at the time before he married my grandmother."

"I would love to know more about all of that!" Hanna replied, her interest piqued.

"It's outlined in great detail in the book," Janet said, "as well as what became of the woman after her relationship with my grandfather."

"Doesn't seem all that scandalous," Alex said.

"Well, you'll see," replied Janet. "The book goes on to tell of another arrangement made between Palumbo and Mathew Coulter related to the operation of the Coulter liquor trade. You may know that Mathew's brother was killed about that time by a rival family, and his father died soon after from complications from a stroke. Mathew apparently wanted nothing to do with the family's nefarious business and, in fact, that's why he had first taken refuge in Grayton Beach, to get away from all that in Atlanta. It seems his brother also betrayed him with a woman he had hoped to marry, which added to Mathew's estrangement from the family."

Alex said, "Sounds like this would all make for a great novel, if it wasn't all true!"

"Oh," Janet said, "it's apparently all very real."

Hanna asked, "So, what was this other agreement?"

"With both his father and brother gone, it was expected that Mathew would return to Atlanta to take over running the business. His mother and sister were not in a position to do so, apparently, and they were living quite a lavish lifestyle that needed to continue to be supported."

Alex said, "Wealthy bootleggers who also ran in the best social circles. Only during Prohibition!"

"Right," Janet continued. "And Mathew apparently cared very much for his mother and sister and wanted them to be cared for after his father's passing."

"So," Hanna said, "let me guess. Mathew asked the gangster to step in and run the family business."

"That's right. Mrs. Coulter and her daughter, Margaret, lived off the illegal profits of bootlegging during Prohibition and for many years after from the profits earned by the gangster, Willy Palumbo, running what became a legitimate liquor distribution business across the South."

"And what about Mathew?" Alex asked.

"My grandfather continued to stay away from anything to do with or profits earned by his father's business. He became a successful writer and didn't need to do so, and apparently

Michael Lindley

continued to harbor ill will for the whole operation. But that was not the end of his interactions and relationship with Palumbo, the gangster."

"There's more?" Hanna asked in astonishment.

"Yes. Years later, Palumbo got into a feud with another prominent crime family in New York. My grandfather was living in New York then pursuing his writing career. Palumbo came to him for help. It seems, reluctantly, he agreed to help, and the whole affair blossomed into quite a scandal that left several people dead."

"Oh, my goodness!" Hanna said, reaching for her wine glass. "I'm beginning to see why Mathew chose not to have this book published."

"Well," Janet replied, "there's considerably more to the story, as you'll see when you read the book."

"I can't wait!" Hanna said.

"You also may not know that after my grandmother passed away, Mathew reunited with a woman he had met and fallen in love with in France when he served in the Army there during World War I. He was badly wounded and treated at a hospital in Paris where he met this nurse named Celeste, who was assigned to care for him. Their love story is really quite sad, though, as Celeste was betrothed to a French soldier everyone thought had been killed in the war."

"But he didn't die?" Alex asked.

"No, he returned at the end of the war from a German prison camp. It was one of Mathew's many early heartbreaks, but he decided to not interfere with this woman's life and returned to America."

"But they did get back together," Janet's husband Dale offered, "many years later."

185

Janet continued. "During my grandfather's eighty-fifth birthday celebration in Grayton Beach, again, after my grandmother had passed, an unlikely visitor caught everyone by surprise."

"Celeste?" Hanna asked.

"Yes. Her husband, the French soldier, had died, and she decided to come to America to see if she could find Mathew. They lived out the rest of their lives together, well into their nineties."

"What a romantic tale!" Hanna said, truly moved by her late ancestor's story. "But Mathew's long relationship with the gangster kept him from publishing this last book?"

"So it seems," Janet said. "You'll see there are some quite shocking details of my grandfather's exploits with Willy Palumbo, the mob boss."

Hanna said, "And you think he was concerned this would taint the family legacy if it were to become public?"

"I believe so," Janet said. "It was no secret the Coulters were bootleggers during Prohibition and became very wealthy and prominent in Atlanta society as a result. But the association with the Palumbo crime family for many years after might certainly raise some eyebrows."

"Yes, I can see that," Hanna said, thinking about her stepmother, Martha, and her current place of prominence in the Atlanta social pecking order.

"Hanna, what do you think?" Alex asked.

"I was just thinking that I would have no qualms with all this becoming public, though I haven't read the whole book, obviously. But Martha, my father's surviving wife in Atlanta, may have some serious reservations about this coming out."

"Right," Janet replied. "And I really don't know of all your extended family, but this is why I wanted to share this with you before I decided what we might do with the manuscript. We certainly aren't trying to make any money off another book published by my late grandfather, but it's quite a tale that I think a lot of his readers would like to have access to."

Hanna said, "I seriously can't wait to start reading it myself. After I've gotten a better feel for all of it, I'd like to speak to my stepmother about it, if you would give me a little time."

"Of course," Janet said. "There is certainly no hurry. It's been lost in the old storage room in Grayton Beach now for decades. A little more time won't matter."

Alex said, "You will all have to excuse me. We had a bit of a thing down at my department earlier today, and I need to get back before it gets any later."

"Of course," Janet said as everyone stood.

Alex put an arm around Hanna's waist. "Are you sure you're okay? I'll try not to be long."

"I'll be fine."

Chapter Thirty-three

New York City, New York. 1939.
. . . Three weeks later.

The coffee in my mug was still steaming and the scone was half gone next to my notebook and pen when Mr. Moretti, the coffee shop owner, came over and said, "Got a call in the back for you."

"Is it my wife?"

Moretti shook his head *no* and walked back to his counter. He pointed to the door to the back. The phone was off the cradle lying on his desk. I sat down, expecting to hear the distinctive growl of Willy Palumbo, and I was right.

"Coulter, you good?"

"We're fine, Willy. Good to hear your voice. Where are you?"

"Getting ready to head out on my boat for a day of fishing on Biscayne Bay down here in Miami."

"Sounds like a good life. You left a bit of a mess up here. The headlines have been pretty sensational."

"Tell me."

"There was a gang shootout on Fifth Avenue outside the Plaza Hotel."

"Really?" Palumbo chided, and I could just see the sly grin on his face.

"The famous mob boss, Carmelo Rossi, went down in a hail of gunfire along with three of his men."

"Sad day. Sorry to hear that."

"Yeah, right. The police are looking for the assassins, but no suspects have been named yet."

"They must own as many cops as the Rossi gang," Palumbo teased.

"Seriously, Will, tell me how it went down. Your men wouldn't tell us a thing."

"Let's just say Carmelo underestimated who he was dealing with."

"Apparently," I replied. "I heard Louise was headed down to join you."

"Yeah, she got in a couple of days ago. That woman is a saint putting up with all this."

I didn't tell him about our conversation with his wife in their son's backyard. "How is this all going to shake out?" I asked. "Someone from the Rossi family will surely step up."

"Let's just say I've come to an agreement with the other families. Rossi was getting out of line. They won't be a factor anymore."

That was reassuring to hear. I was still looking over my shoulder, even a few quiet weeks after the attack. "But you're going to stay down in Florida for a while?"

"I've resumed running most of the southern operations for the families. They appreciate my connections and grasp of the situation down here."

Again, I could imagine the smirk on his face. "I'm glad you're okay, Willy. I'll never forgive you for getting my family caught up in all this, but I have myself to blame, too."

"Takes two to tango, Coulter."

"Yeah," I replied, knowing I had my own sins of complicity and ignorance to sort out. "Not sure when we'll see you again, Willy. Sara will literally shoot me if I come within a mile of you. By the way, Anthony is okay after the—?"

"He's fine. Got nicked a bit in the dust-up with Rossi and his men, but he's fine. Going fishing with me today."

"Of course he is. When was the last time he left your side?"

"Can't remember."

"You take care, Willy. And take better care of that great wife of yours."

"I'm truly blessed, Coulter."

I was walking back to my table in the coffee shop when I heard the bell ring as the door opened and my wife came in and greeted Mr. Moretti behind the counter.

"My usual," she said as she passed by and joined me at the back of the shop.

Moretti came up with her special coffee and a Danish. He always made sure he kept one for her.

"Thank you," she said.

Moretti bowed and smiled. Sara was one of his favorite customers. He seemed to barely tolerate me, maybe because I took one of his tables for much of every day and rarely ordered more than a few cups of coffee and something to snack on in the mornings.

"How's the new book coming?" Sara asked.

"I started on a new project."

"What is that? I thought you had a deadline with your publisher coming up."

"I do, and I'll deal with that, but, as I'm sure you know, there's been a lot happening the past weeks, and I have some of new material to sort through."

"You're writing about Willy?" she said in surprise.

"Actually, I started the book a long time ago after those early years with Palumbo in Grayton Beach. I put it aside some time ago. I'm not sure I want the world to know about our little story."

"I think that's very wise," my wife said, sternly.

Chapter Thirty-four

Pawleys Island, South Carolina. Present day.

Hanna was taking the last sip of her coffee and getting ready to leave for the office. Janet and her husband had left at sun-up to continue on north and home to New York. Alex had tried to get her to take the day off to rest after the stress and chaos of the previous day, but she knew she'd be better off getting back into her work and trying to forget yesterday.

She rinsed her coffee cup in the sink and was putting it in the dishwasher when her phone buzzed. She didn't recognize the local number but took the call. "Hello?"

"Hanna, this is Jeremy Day. We met at Quinn's the other night."

It was the antique shop owner who was set up with Sheila Graham for the evening, Hanna quickly recalled. "Yes, how are you?"

"Fine. Listen, I was out on the island this morning meeting with a client. I wondered if you were home and if I could stop by for a quick look at some of the old pieces in your house."

She looked at the time on her phone. She still had over an hour until her first appointment. "Are you close? I have to be at work by ten."

"I can be there in five minutes."

"Okay, I'll see you shortly."

She put the phone down and decided to brew another small pot of coffee for her guest. She thought about the short conversations she'd had with Jeremy at Quinn's dinner party. He seemed nice enough. It still was odd, she thought, that Quinn had set him up for the evening with Detective Sheila Graham. *Maybe she didn't know he's gay?*

The bell at the back door rang and she went to greet Jeremy Day. She opened the door to let him in. "Good morning." He was dressed casually in a blue golf shirt with a Nike logo and khaki slacks, leather sandals on his feet.

"Hello, Hanna. Thanks for letting me stop by on such short notice."

"Not a problem. This worked out fine. I'm not in a rush to get over to the office for a change this morning."

She was surprised to wake that morning following a good night's sleep, despite the harrowing events of the day before. The thought of it now made her shudder though, and she forced herself to focus back on her guest. "Come in. I'm making some coffee."

They had just started the tour in the dining room when she offered, "As I mentioned the other night, some of the furniture dates back to my family who first owned the house in the mid-1800s, the Paltierres."

"Yes," Jeremy said, "I've read some of the history that I found online. Amanda Paltierre is one of the ghosts that still roam the island."

"That is true. She comes to visit on many occasions."

"I'd love to meet her."

"I'm afraid that is difficult to arrange, as you can imagine."

The handsome antique collector laughed. "I understand her husband, Captain Atwell, was a war hero in one of the last battles of the Civil War."

"Yes, and unfortunately, he didn't survive that battle. Amanda had to fend for herself through the rest of the war and later when treacherous people were trying to take over the family's plantation near Georgetown."

"*Tanglewood*, correct?" he asked.

"That's right."

"I've done some work with the current owner."

"Yes, I met her a few years ago. She gave me this picture of the Paltierres that was left at the house when she bought it."

She let him take a closer look. "Amanda was quite a striking woman."

"Yes, she still is," Hanna replied with a smile.

They spent time looking at the dining room table and chairs and the long mahogany sideboard along the wall. Jeremy was very knowledgeable about the furniture and shared some information about the manufacturer from North Carolina. He pulled out the sideboard to check the markings on the back to confirm his assessment.

"As I said the other night," Hanna began as they walked into the living room, "I'm not interested in selling any of these pieces."

"No, of course. I completely understand, and I'm not here trying to convince you otherwise. I'm just a real geek about all this and love seeing new pieces in the area. Who knows, I may come across something I think might work here in your house."

Of course you will, she thought in amusement, not faulting the man for being a good businessman.

There were a few more pieces upstairs including the big carved bed in the main bedroom. When they came back down, they stopped in the kitchen at the island to finish their coffee.

Hanna said, "You may not know, but Amanda Paltierre killed a man right where you're standing."

"Seriously?" Day said in surprise.

Hanna knew it was actually her servant, but Amanda had claimed to have fired the shot to protect the woman in the racially charged era of the time. "The rogue son of her family's lawyer came here one night drunk after the war. He tried to rape her, and he lost his life as a result."

"Oh, my. There is some interesting history in these old beach houses."

"There certainly is."

"Thank you for your time," he said. "Please come by the shop soon. I'd love to show you around."

And sell me some antiques!

She had finished her second meeting when her assistant handed her a note that her husband had called.

"Just checking in to see how you're doing," Alex said when he took her call.

"Still a bit shaky. I can't get the sight of my shot-up car out of my brain."

"I feel so bad you got in the middle of all this," Alex said.

"It's not your fault, and I don't want you feeling that way. I'll be alright. Maybe another trip or two to the shrink, but—"

"I think that's a good idea," Alex said. "He seems to help you."

She wanted to talk about anything except what had happened the previous day. "We had a guest this morning after you left."

"Did Quinn come over again?"

"No, it was her new friend that she set Sheila up with for the dinner party."

"Jeremy, right?"

"Yes, he was out on the island and called to see if I could show him some of our old vintage furniture. We had a nice chat. He thinks we have some very valuable pieces. I told him again, none of it is for sale. I'm sure he would like to sell *us* more!"

"Oh, I'm sure of that."

Hanna said, "What's happening over there?"

"All hell's broken loose over the prisoner release yesterday. The City Council wants me fired. County Prosecutor Willett is beside herself trying to fend them off."

"Well," Hanna replied, "I'm a little biased. You did what you had to do with little or no time to get support from any of those people."

"I spoke with Pepper Stokes this morning."

"How is he recovering? You think he'll be back in the sheriff's chair soon?"

"I'm not sure he's in much of a hurry with this fentanyl operation causing havoc. He seems to be doing much better. He's making some calls to run interference for me."

"Good," Hanna replied. "He knows you did the right thing. Do you have anything else to go on with the drug gang?"

"We had our call with all the other agencies. Will and the FBI are doing all they can to come down on the law firm in Atlanta that's representing these local guys. We need to find out who's running the operation here in South Carolina. We got a warrant to get call records for Miguel Juarez and the two guys we had in custody yesterday. Should be getting that in later today."

"Well, good luck with that. I hope it gives you some leads. I've got Miguel's wife and baby set up with the shelter in Charleston, and I should have all the paperwork I need by the end of the day to let her get access to their bank account."

"It's good of you to help her out so much," Alex said. "Let me take you out to dinner tonight. No need to worry about cooking or cleaning up."

"It's a date," she said. "I know just the place."

Hanna's next call was to her stepmother, Martha, in Atlanta.

"Hello, dear," came the syrupy-sweet Southern-accent response to her greeting. "How are things over in the Carolinas?"

Hanna chose not to revisit the previous day's events. Instead, she said, "I have a book I want you to read."

"Well, that's awfully nice of you. What's the title? I'll pick it up down at the bookstore."

"It hasn't been published yet," Hanna replied, relishing keeping Martha off guard for just a bit longer.

"Okay . . ."

"I'm going to overnight a copy of a manuscript written by a distant relative of my father and me. His name is Mathew Coulter. He was a prominent writer in the mid-1900s. His family built the house you're living in today."

"Yes, dear. I've heard about the Coulters. Your father shared some of the history. He took some pleasure in the fact that they were liquor bootleggers back during Prohibition. Thought it added panache to the family lore," she said.

"Well, there's apparently a lot more to the story." Hanna shared the visit of her relative, Janet Anders, and her concern about her grandfather's manuscript containing damning information about the family that some may be concerned about.

Martha said, "I can't imagine what could be that bad."

"She felt she owed it to us to have a chance to review the story before she decides whether or not to contact her grandfather's old publisher. I'm going to start reading it tonight. I'm sending you a copy. You'll have it tomorrow."

"Sounds intriguing! I'll put my book aside. Thank you, Hanna, for thinking of me."

"We'll compare notes in a few days. How's that?"

"Sounds great. Give my best to Alex."

Hanna was on the deck in front of her beach house, fifty pages into Mathew Coulter's manuscript, when Alex came out. She put the pages down, held together by a large metal clip, and got up to greet him with a hug.

"Did you make any progress today?" she asked as they sat down beside each other.

Alex said, "We did get the cellphone call logs of the men we had in custody. The FBI and DEA all have copies, and their teams are doing a deep dive to see if we can identify any suspicious contacts, hopefully whoever is running this gang."

"How are they doing with the law firm in Atlanta?"

"The Atlanta Bureau office is still trying to get a judge to issue a warrant for them to pay a visit to the place. You're reading the manuscript they left with us?"

"Yes, just started a while ago. Really interesting story. Mathew Coulter was a very intriguing man. He seemed to always try to do the right thing, but circumstances kept pulling him to the dark side and decisions he would often regret."

"I'd like to read it, too," Alex said.

"I sent a copy to Martha today, then called her to let her know what was coming."

"How is your favorite stepmother?"

"Fortunately, she's my only stepmother. She seems fine and not overly concerned about whatever dirt there might be on the family in Mathew's story. We'll see. Apparently, my father was quite proud of the fact his ancestors used to run illegal whiskey."

She watched as Alex smiled back, shaking his head.

"So," he said, "where can I take you to dinner?"

"You know I always love the Tavern." Pawleys Island Tavern was one of their most frequent stops for casual outdoor dining—good food and cold beer.

"Works for me. Let me get out of this uniform."

Chapter Thirty-five

Pawleys Island, South Carolina. Present day.

Hanna and Alex had a table at the restaurant under the live oak trees, strings of lights overhead, most of the tables full at just past 7 p.m. A small blues band was playing at the far corner of the deck. They ordered drinks and were looking through the menu, though Hanna almost always ordered the Low Country po' boy sandwich with shrimp. Alex was usually more inclined to go for the grouper basket, but they both took time to consider other options as their drinks arrived.

Alex held up a cold glass of beer to Hanna's glass of a California chardonnay. "To life in the Low Country," he began. "It gets a bit crazy at times, but we still love it, right?"

"Right!" Hanna replied, clinking his glass.

Alex leaned in. "I want you to tell me if you're having any lingering issues with all that went down yesterday. Have you scheduled anything with your therapist yet?"

"Yes, I'm seeing him again next week."

"Good. I should probably join you. This is all beginning to weigh a little more heavily on me again, too."

"Let's put it aside, at least for tonight," she said, reaching over to touch his glass again.

They both took long sips from their drinks and were about to return to their menus when they heard their names yelled out from across the deck.

"Hanna, Alex, I thought that was you!"

Quinn Burke came around the table next to theirs and gave both of them a hug as they stood to greet her. "Carlos and I are sitting just around the corner there."

Hanna looked over to see if she could see Quinn's mixed martial arts fighter boyfriend, but he was out of sight behind the corner of the building.

"And how is Carlos?" Alex asked. "When's that fight coming up he told us about?"

"Next week. He's on a strict diet. No alcohol." She leaned in closer and whispered, "No sex!"

It was obvious from her breath that she was not abstaining and had probably had more than a few drinks.

Hanna laughed. "Tough to be dating a fighter?"

"It has its pluses and minuses," Quinn replied with a grin. "We'd come over to join you but looks like you two need a little time together."

Hanna was glad to hear her say that, not really relishing company.

"Say hello to Carlos," Alex said.

She blew them both air kisses and made her way back to her table.

Hanna said, "She sure keeps it interesting out here on the island."

"That's an understatement!" Alex replied.

They were well into their meals when some commotion off to Hanna's left caught their attention—loud voices, a couple of crashing sounds. Alex stood to see if he needed to go offer some assistance.

Hanna reached for his arm. "You're off duty, Sheriff. They can take care of it."

Then, she saw Quinn's boyfriend, Carlos Quintano, hurrying around from the back of the deck. He had an angry scowl on his face. They made eye contact, but he hurried by without acknowledging them.

Alex sat back down. "What was that all about?"

"Maybe I should go check on Quinn," Hanna said.

Just as she said it, her neighbor came by, her face red and stained with tears. She was holding a hand over the side of her face. Hanna stood and met her at the steps to leave the restaurant.

"Quinn, what happened? Are you okay?"

Quinn dropped her hand, and Hanna could see the red welt that was beginning to swell under her eye. "Hanna, I'm sorry. I just need to get home."

"Did he hit you?" she said, her anger rising.

"I can't talk about it right now. I'm sorry, I need to go."

Hanna watched her hurry down the steps and away through the parked cars. She went back to the table.

"What's going on?" Alex asked.

"I don't know. They must have had some kind of a fight. She's got a bruise under her eye."

"He hit her?" Alex said in surprise.

"It sure looks like it. We should check in on her when we get home."

"Maybe I need to pay Mr. Quintano a visit," Alex said.

"Let's wait till we hear what she has to say."

Hanna made her way through the tall scrub between her house and Quinn Burke's. The sun was low and the shadows deep along the narrow path. She was a little apprehensive about intruding, but felt she needed to check on her neighbor.

She was halfway up the steps to the deck in front of Quinn's cottage when the two little dogs started barking inside. "Oh, great."

There were no lights on. The dogs seemed to be upstairs. She knocked lightly on the glass-paned door. She had to knock again before a light came on in the stairwell from upstairs, and then she saw Quinn cautiously peering about the wall as she came down the steps.

I wonder if she thinks I'm her boyfriend.

Quinn came over and opened the door, seemingly relieved it was her neighbor. Her face was no longer flushed with tears, but her left eye was nearly swollen shut.

Hanna said, "I just wanted to check in on you."

"Thank you. That's so nice of you."

"What in the world happened with Carlos?"

Quinn looked down in shame, shaking her head. "Come in. I think I need another drink."

In the kitchen, Quinn pulled a half full bottle of wine out of the refrigerator and poured two glasses. She led them into the living room, and they sat in big overstuffed chairs next to each other.

"Do you even want to talk about it?" Hanna asked.

Quinn took a long drink from her wine and then a deep breath before saying, "I'm sure it's all my fault."

"Quinn, there is no excuse for hitting you!"

"I know that. I just had a little too much to drink, and I was teasing Carlos about his lifestyle choices, and I guess I pushed him a little too far."

"What could you have possibly said?"

"I don't even remember. I kept teasing him, and he just snapped. He jumped up from the table yelling at me, knocking over chairs. When I came around to apologize and try to stop him from leaving, he just lashed out at me. I've never been more stunned in my life. And then he stormed out. He hasn't called . . ."

"Quinn, I don't know this guy other than a few words at your party the other night, but this is not acceptable."

"I know. But I feel so badly that I let it get out of control."

"It's not your fault, Quinn!" Hanna insisted. "I can't tell you what to do, but I'd stay far away from this guy if I were you."

Quinn just shook her head and then took another long drink. The dogs started barking again upstairs. She finally turned to Hanna and said, "You're a good friend. Thank you for coming over."

Alex was reading in bed when she got back. "So?"

She filled him in on Quinn's tussle with her perhaps soon-to-be ex-boyfriend.

Alex listened intently, then said, "She should stay as far away from this guy as possible. I think I'll run a quick background check in the morning. See if he has any history of this sort of thing on his record."

Hanna sat beside him on the bed. "Normally, I would say it's not our place to get involved like that, but I'm a little worried about her safety."

"I'll check him out. I grabbed the old manuscript and started in on the first pages you've already read. Interesting stuff."

Hanna stood to go into the bathroom to get ready for bed. "I'll be interested to see what Martha thinks."

Chapter Thirty-six

Georgetown, South Carolina. Present day.

Alex had gone into the department early to read through the reports on the call logs from the cartel members who had been released. There were literally thousands of calls over the past few months they were looking at, but the analysts had provided a report that summarized trends, frequently called numbers, etc. In particular, they were looking for numbers that all the men may have frequently called.

There were several actually, but one caught his eye. The analysts had included the names and business names of those more frequent numbers. He picked up his desk phone and called Will Foster in Charleston. Normally, he would have called the front desk of the FBI Bureau office, but he really needed to get through to his old associate so he called him direct on his cell.

"Alex, what's the latest?"

"Just looking through the call log report summary your analysts sent over. I was going to run a check on this guy anyway because he roughed up a neighbor of ours last night, but his business, Quintano Martial Arts, and his personal cell number is all over these guys' call lists."

"What's his name?"

"Carlos Quintano. He owns this fight club business down the road and apparently is a well-regarded MMA fighter. We met him at a dinner party our neighbor threw a few nights ago."

"And he beat her up?" Will asked.

"Smacked her in the face after some argument in a restaurant last night. But what are our cartel guys doing on the line with Quintano as much as they are? Maybe they're training to be fighters, but—"

Foster said, "Let me have our guys run a sheet on him."

Hanna took her coffee out on the deck with the manuscript to keep reading. The air was cool off the ocean and the sun was barely up above the horizon in the east. She had read nearly half the book by the end of the day prior and had started in again that morning while Alex was in the shower to get into work early.

She found herself entranced with the story of Sara and Melanee and Mathew Coulter. They were all coming alive to her in Mathew's story. It was different from his typical mystery novels. This was a journal of his life, an autobiography of sorts . . . almost a confession, she thought at times.

The more she read about the little village of Grayton Beach, the more she wanted to get back down there. She was sure it had grown and lost some of its charm since she had visited so many years earlier, but Mathew's story was bringing it to life for her again.

And his cohort, the gangster, Willy Palumbo, was a fascinating character, and real at that if Mathew's accounts were to be believed, a devoted father and husband with a heart of gold, but also a ruthless mob boss who wouldn't hesitate to kill when he felt threatened.

And there was Melanee, the gifted and sightless daughter of Sara and Mathew who seemed to hold the entire family together with her love and insight.

In his story, Mathew had revealed numerous questionable decisions and compromises he had made to align himself with Palumbo for what, at the time, seemed like all the right reasons. His regrets and recriminations were clear in his recounting of the events of his life, but she couldn't help feeling a sense of compassion for the man. She actually felt some pride in knowing he had been part of her lineage.

Foster called Alex back just before ten o'clock.

"Our man, Quintano, had a troubled childhood," Foster said, reviewing the arrest record of Carlos Quintano. "Good parents and upbringing, but apparently ran in the wrong circles and made some bad decisions. Spent some time in juvenile detention on gun and drug charges. Seems to have gotten his life back on track."

"I still think we need to check him out," Alex said.

"I agree completely, but let's not spook him. If he's truly caught up with the cartel and gets wind we're on to him, he'll disappear in a minute."

Alex thought for a moment, then said, "I have a good excuse to go pay this guy a visit. He punched out my next-door neighbor, his new girlfriend, last night. I think the sheriff needs to check in on him, and we'll see where that leads."

"I agree, just tread softly on the cartel angle. We're better off putting him under surveillance and seeing where that leads. I can take care of that on our end."

"Okay," Alex agreed. "I'll head over there this morning. I'll let you know how it goes."

The Quintano Martial Arts Gym was located in a strip shopping center about five miles south of Pawleys Island on the Ocean Highway. It was flanked by an H&R Block tax office, a

Chipotle restaurant, and several other small businesses stretching out to each side.

He decided to take Deputy Sheila Graham with him to send a signal that this was an official department call and also to hopefully get under his skin a little by bringing along another friend of Quinn Burke.

They walked into the front door and were greeted by the sounds and smells of a fighting gym, men and women grunting and punching bags, lifting weights, throwing each other around on mats. There was a ring at the center of the gym that was surrounded by high mesh walls—the cage, they called it.

A young man was at the front desk dressed in tight-fitting workout clothes, incredibly fit. He looked up when they came through the door in their department uniforms, in stark contrast to all the people working out. He stood and said, "Is something wrong, officers? What can I help you with?"

Alex walked up and handed the man his card. "I'm Sheriff Alex Frank. We need to speak with your boss, Carlos. Is he available?"

He read the card and handed it back, then looked behind him to the cage. "That's him working out. He'll be done shortly. Can I get you some coffee or a water?"

"No," Alex said. "Mind if we go in and watch?"

"Not at all. Help yourself."

Graham leaned over and said, "This is like watching the *Gladiator* movie. These people are serious."

"No swords or lions, but you're right," Alex replied.

They walked through the crowd, obviously drawing stares. They found a spot off to the side of the cage and watched Carlos Quintano totally destroy whoever he was working out with. There was a referee in the ring, and he finally had to step in to pull Quintano off his opponent. As the referee knelt to assess the damage to Quintano's victim, the MMA champion came toward them and stopped for a moment when he saw them. He gathered himself quickly and grabbed a towel before leaving the cage to head over to them.

He held out his hand, sweat pouring down his face and drenching his workout clothes. "Alex, nice to see you again." He turned to Graham and shook her hand. "And Sheila, what a pleasure. What do you think of my little gym here?"

Alex said, "Carlos, we need to have a word. Is there someplace where we can talk?"

"If it's about last night . . ." he began.

Alex pointed to the back. "Can we?"

There was a small conference room next to a series of cubicles and what must have been the boss's office in the back. They all sat around the small table.

Quintano said, "Alex, I have no excuse for what happened last night at the restaurant. I called Quinn this morning to apologize. I've sent flowers. I feel terrible."

Alex let him finish, then said. "I don't know you, Carlos, but you have to tell me, do you have a habit of beating women, or is Quinn just such a pain in your ass, you had to smack her last night?" He watched the man's expression grow dark and severe.

"I told you," he began in slow, measured words, "that I was sorry. It won't happen again."

Graham said. "You hit my friend. If you weren't a professional fighter, I think I'd take your head off right now!"

Alex could tell they were pushing all the right buttons. Quintano was growing more and more agitated. He said, "Quinn can file assault charges against you. There's no excuse for what you did."

Quintano's nostrils flared, and his fists clenched on the table. "I think you need to leave . . . now!"

Alex said, "We're here to let you know that regardless of whether Quinn Burke files charges against you, you're on our radar screen now, and there better not be any other reasons for us to have to come out here."

Quintano stood up quickly. "Like I said, you need to leave."

"Graham stood and leaned in close to the man. "What, are you gonna take a swing at me, too?"

Alex stood and said, "Carlos, we know you had some trouble in your younger years. We've seen your jacket. Let's not start down the wrong road again with assaulting women." He could see the fury growing in the man's face and was preparing to fend off an attack. The veins on the man's arms pulsed as he tensed in anger.

Graham said, "Obviously, it's up to Quinn, but I'm telling her not to come within a hundred miles of you again."

Alex watched as Quintano took a deep breath. He seemed to be trying to calm himself.

"I think it's best if you both leave now. I understand why you're here. I feel terrible about what happened last night, and I'll try to make up for it with Quinn."

Graham stepped in and got in his face again. "I don't think you heard me. I don't want you anywhere near my friend again!"

Quintano huffed up and grabbed Sheila Graham by her shirt on both arms. Alex grabbed him from behind and pulled him away. The fighter turned and flared, both arms up ready to attack.

Alex crouched to defend himself and sternly said, "If you want to add assault on a police officer to your record, let's go."

Quintano stepped back and held up his hands in compliance. "Hey, look, I'm sorry. I'm just as upset as Quinn about what happened last night."

"It doesn't seem that way to me," Graham said, not backing down.

"You need to get her out of here, Alex!" Quintano said.

"Why, you afraid you're going to hit her?"

The fighter held up his hands in surrender again. "Let's just call it a day here. I get the message. I'm sorry for what happened. Sheila, I'm sorry I put hands on you."

Graham shook her head in disgust.

Alex said, "Don't give us another reason to come over here, Carlos. Am I clear?"

Quintano stared back, his hands shaking at his side.

Alex and Graham left the conference room and started down the hall to the big gym and the front of the building. They were walking through the clustered chaos of fighters working out when Alex saw a familiar face coming through the front door.

Rios Hernandez, the drug cartel lowlife they had just released the previous day, saw them and immediately turned and ran back out the door.

By the time they got outside, Hernandez was on his motorcycle and speeding out of the parking lot. Alex knew there was no way his unmarked department sedan could keep up with the high-speed cycle. He said to Graham, "Let him go. I'll call it in. Maybe one of our patrols will pick him up."

Chapter Thirty-seven

A strong breeze freshened out ahead of a thunderstorm blowing in from the southwest, the sky turning as purple as a bruise. Lightning flashed orange and hot behind the far clouds, too far yet for thunder to be heard. Birds seemed to know it was time to take refuge, and flocks of gulls and pelicans were all headed inland for shelter, riding the gusting winds. The ocean had turned a dark gun-metal gray painted with rolling, white-capped swells.

Hanna had been sitting in one of the weathered Adirondack chairs in a grouping around the fire pit down in the dunes in front of the house. The pages she had been reading from Mathew Coulter's manuscript were blowing all about in her hands, and she decided to move inside before she lost any of it. As she gathered her things and started up the stairs, she noticed a wind devil picking up sand and blowing along the shoreline to the north. Someone's beach umbrella had been swept up and tumbled along, no one in pursuit.

She pulled the door to the deck closed behind her and left the tempest of the coming storm shut outside. She heard the back door unlock and open.

Alex yelled out, "Hello?"

"I'm in the kitchen."

"Sorry I'm running late," he said, coming in and wrapping her up in his arms. "How are you doing?"

"Keeping busy keeps my mind off crazy drug gang members shooting up my car. My brain keeps telling me to just go upstairs and crawl into bed and sleep for three days to put some of this behind us. But you know me. Can't sit still if I wanted to."

"Maybe a day or two out here at the beach and *not* in your office might be a good thing," he offered.

"One day at a time. We'll see."

A loud clap of thunder echoed through the house, and the lights fluttered for a few seconds as nearby lighting must have shaken the grid somewhere.

"Is everything battened down outside?" Alex asked.

"We should bring in the cushions before they end up over on Quinn's deck."

They both rushed outside and ferried in cushions and anything else likely to blow away. The rain began slowly, large drops thudding on the deck. Within moments, the deluge began in earnest, and they hurried back inside.

Hanna looked out a rain-soaked window. The sky was so dark now it looked like night. The rain came in pelting waves across the deck, lightning flashing and thunder booming in a quick cadence. Loose branches from trees and scrub rattled against the house, waves booming onshore.

"We better turn on the radio or television in case something severe is coming," Alex said.

No sooner had he mentioned it, the emergency sirens on the island began their piercing wail. The television weather reporter stood in front of a map of the area covered in patches of red and green, a thousand little jagged checks signifying lightning strikes, a tornado warning area now covering Pawleys Island.

"Where should we take cover out here?" Alex said. "There's no basement."

"The storage room under the house has survived storms and floods and wind for 150 years."

"Let's go!"

They grabbed flashlights and some bottled waters and snacks and went to the back door to put on rain parkas. The door almost blew off the hinges when they opened it to go outside. Rain pelted their faces as they rushed down the stairs. The door to the storage room was at the back of the house and was locked. Hanna had the key on her keyring and let them in. The escape from the howling wind and rain was a welcome relief.

Alex found the light switch, and the room lit up, revealing shelves filled with boxes and tools and long forgotten things that, at some point in time, someone thought were essential to hold on to. There were folding beach chairs against one wall, and Alex pulled out two for them to sit in the middle of the room.

Hanna pulled out her phone and brought up the latest live weather report. The tornado warning was still in effect, and four funnel clouds had been reported, all headed toward the island. Everyone in the warning area was instructed to take immediate shelter.

"This could end badly," Alex said. "I need to call the department."

He checked in with the duty officer and instructed them to implement all emergency protocols which included calling all off-duty staff back to the department. "I'll be down there as soon as it looks safe to drive," Hanna heard him say.

The wind seemed to be growing in velocity, sounding like a freight train was running through the back of the property.

Alex said, "We need to get down against that wall."

They huddled together under an old tool bench.

The light suddenly went off.

"Oh great," Hanna said, pulling herself in closer to Alex.

They both jumped when something hit the outside wall, sounding like a bull had just charged the side of the house. Then, there was a loud cracking and crashing noise as apparently one of the big live oak branches had snapped under the relentless wind and fallen to the ground.

"Debris must be flying everywhere," Alex shouted over the din of the wind and the thunder outside.

Then, just as quickly as it began, the noise began to fade as the storm passed and the wind subsided.

"I'm afraid to look outside," Hanna said.

"Let's go."

They got up from the floor, and Alex pushed the door open to the back of the property. It was still dark from the clouds overhead, but the rain had subsided to a misty drizzle. There were no lights on in any of the houses to the side of them or above them on the porch. The streetlights out at the road were out. Still, in the dim light, Hanna saw palm fronds and tree limps and other debris everywhere across the back of the house.

She turned when she heard Alex say, "Are you kidding me?"

She looked over and saw that the big tree limb they had heard falling had dropped directly across the cab of his truck, leaving it cleaved nearly in two like a hot knife through butter.

"Ohmigod!" Hanna said. She looked out across the clearing behind the house and the drive out to the main road. There was debris everywhere. Surprisingly, the old servant's cabin out by the road was still standing. She still couldn't bring herself to say the *slave's* cabin, always trying to put that abhorrent chapter of her family's history aside.

Alex said, "I need to get back down to the department. Do you want to come with me? I hate to leave you here alone."

She thought about his offer for a moment and then decided she really needed to stay and assess the damage and do what she could to start the cleanup. "No, I really should stay. Who knows what the house upstairs looks like."

"Let's go check it out," Alex offered.

A quick check of the main house revealed a window in the dining room on the south side of the house had been left open and a pool of rain lay on the floor near the elegant, carved dining table she had showed Jeremy Day earlier, but it had apparently suffered no damage.

Out front, another big tree limb had broken off and fallen across the corner of the deck. There appeared to be significant damage. A quick tour of the upstairs revealed the house had not been breached on the second level.

They regrouped in the kitchen. Alex pulled her close. "How're you doing?"

"I think we were pretty lucky. I hope everyone else out here had the same luck."

They walked out to the beach and looked in both directions to assess any further damage near them on the island. Quinn Burke's house looked like it had gotten the worst of it. A portion of the roof had been torn off and lay in pieces on her deck and on the ground in front of her house.

"We better go check on her," Alex said.

They made their way through debris and up onto Quinn's deck. She came through the door to meet them, tears streaking down her face, her left eye still swollen and bruised from the assault at the restaurant.

Hanna hugged her tight. "Are you okay?"

Quinn gasped to speak through racking sobs. "I thought the whole house was coming down. I was trying to hold on to the dogs, and part of the roof collapsed down through the ceiling. It missed us by inches."

"I'm so sorry," Hanna said. "But you're okay?"

Quinn nodded and wiped at her face.

Alex said, "We need to get something over that hole in your roof. I saw some big tarps in the storage room. I'll be back."

Quinn let Hanna back inside. The house was a mess from the wind and rain that had swept in through the damaged roof. The two little terriers came running up and cowered around Quinn's feet, not barking, obviously traumatized by the fury of the storm.

Hanna wandered through the rest of the house with her neighbor to assess any further damage. Two windows had been blown out along the south side of the house, and the storm had taken its toll.

A knock on the door and voices out on the deck led both women back to the beach side of the house. Alex was there with two other neighbors. They were putting a ladder in place to go up to work on the gaping hole in the roof. Within minutes, hammers were pounding, and a big blue tarp was fixed in place to try to keep more wind and rain from coming in until a repair crew could begin work.

Hanna stood with Quinn watching the men work up on the roof. Hanna said, "You can't stay here. Please come over tonight. We've got a spare room made up."

"Thank you," Quinn said, hugging her again. "I'm sure you don't want the dogs. I'll see if the kennel is open and drop them there."

"Either way. I hope no one was hurt out here. It all came up so quickly."

The emergency horns had stopped some minutes ago, but other sirens could be heard in the distance as police and fire departments responded.

Alex came down from the roof. "I'm sorry, but I really need to get down to work. I'll take my department car. The truck is destroyed, so you'll be without transportation. Sure you don't want to come with me?"

"I'll stay here with Quinn. I've asked her to stay with us tonight."

"Okay, good."

Quinn said, "I looked out back. My car is okay if we need to go anywhere."

Alex started toward the stairs. "I'll call you as soon as I can."

An hour later, Hanna sat with her neighbor in the living room of her own house. Quinn had dropped the two dogs at the boarding kennel, and they had just settled down with a bottle of wine and two glasses. Quinn's hand was shaking as she held it up for Hanna to fill.

They both took a drink and sat back in the comfortable chairs around the old stone fireplace.

Quinn said, "Life is so precarious. One moment you're going about your normal business of the day and then within minutes, there's danger and chaos reigning down and . . ." She couldn't finish, wiping at tears forming in her eyes again.

Hanna reached for her hand, thinking she was likely still traumatized from the attack the previous night.

Quinn said, "I had just gotten off the phone with Carlos when the storm hit. He keeps calling me to apologize for last night."

"There is no excuse for what he did," Hanna said. "Do you think you can ever trust that you'll be safe around him again?"

Quinn shook her head. "It was such a surprise. I haven't known him that long, but nothing like that had ever happened before. I was beginning to think we had a pretty good thing going and then . . ."

"Quinn, when I had my legal clinic down in Charleston, I worked with a lot of women who lived with abusive men. I can tell you, it never ended well. Never."

Quinn stared back, nodding.

"As always," Quinn began, "you've been more than a friend, and thank you for being so honest with me. I know I need to break this off."

Chapter Thirty-eight

Three times on his way back to his office, Alex had to stop to help people who were cutting tree limbs to clear the road. There was devastating damage and debris everywhere, making it nearly impossible for emergency vehicles to get to people who needed their help.

He was getting updates on his radio from his teams out across the county. There had been a number of injuries reported but, fortunately, no fatalities had been called in yet. He was pulling into the parking lot at the department when his cell buzzed on the seat beside him. It was Will Foster.

"Hey, Alex. Heard you had some pretty nasty storms blow through up there. Everyone okay?"

Alex filled him in on the preliminary assessments.

Foster said, "We got a lot of rain down here in Charleston, but no twisters as far as I've heard. I wanted to let you know the Atlanta Bureau office finally got a warrant to raid the cartel's law firm over there. The attorney we've been dealing with, Rick Guidall, was not there when they went in. But he was found later in the day, slumped over the wheel of his car in a Starbucks parking lot. He had two bullet holes in the side of his head."

"Sounds like the cartel is cleaning up loose ends to me," Alex said.

"Exactly. The Atlanta team is going over the confiscated files and communications. They'll let us know if they come up with anything helpful. How did it go with the fighter?"

"We pressed him pretty hard about the assault on his girlfriend. The guy definitely has a short fuse and almost went after one of my deputies. We hadn't come across anything that directly ties him to the drug cartel, but as we were leaving, one of the perps we had just released came into the gym, saw us, and beat out fast on a motorcycle. We had no chance to chase him down, and so far none of our patrols have come across him. We're all a little wrapped up now with storm response."

"Right, understand. So, one of your drug-bust guys was there?"

"Yes, Rios Hernandez is the neighbor of the guy who was taken out by the cartel."

Foster said, "I think we have enough on this Quintano guy for you and I to pay him a visit in the morning."

"Agree."

It was past ten that night when Alex felt that he was able to call it a day and get back out to the island to check on Hanna. He pulled out onto the main road in the department vehicle he had just checked out and headed toward the highway. He was about a block down the road when he saw headlights speeding toward him from behind.

Looking up into the rear-view mirror again, he said, "What the hell?"

The approaching car didn't slow down and suddenly veered out into the next lane just before it would have run into the back of his car. He was reaching for the emergency flasher light in the glove box to put out on the roof of his unmarked car, thinking the driver would race by and he'd have to chase him down, not realizing he was speeding by a sheriff's car.

But when Alex looked back up, the car had pulled even and had slowed to Alex's speed. He watched as the passenger window slowly lowered, and then, before he could do anything to evade the attack, the muzzle of a sawed-off double-barrel shotgun appeared in the dark opening, and the first of two blasts exploded his own window into a thousand shards of glass. He ducked and veered the car hard to the right off the road, over the curb and onto the sidewalk in front of a grocery store parking lot as the second blast hit the window behind him with similar effect. Pain seared hot along the side of his face and his left shoulder from glass cuts and pellets from the shotgun shell, as he braked hard to bring the car to a stop, pulling his own weapon out as he did.

The car with his attackers stopped as well, and the reverse lights came on as it started backing up toward him. He threw open his door, broken glass clattering on the sidewalk, and quickly got out and knelt behind the cover of the door, his weapon trained on the approaching car.

It stopped about twenty yards in front of him. He quickly noted the make and model of the car but saw that the license plate was covered with tape.

No one got out. He kept his gun trained on the left side of the car, expecting his attackers to exit at any moment. He reached inside the car for the radio mic and called in his situation to the dispatcher. "This is Sheriff Frank! I'm under attack from gunmen in front of the Food Lion on Fraser!"

He was just setting the radio back on the seat when the passenger door of the car opened. He adjusted his aim, and at first, no one got out. Then, in a sudden flash of movement, a man came out, the shotgun aimed back at him. The flash of the shotgun blast forced him to duck down behind the cover of the door again, and he heard his left tire explode and felt the car lurch downward. Before the man could fire again, Alex raised up and let off three shots through his broken window. At least one caught the man in the upper body, causing him to fall back and drop the gun. He fired two more shots as the man fell back into the car, leaving the gun by the side of the road. The door was still open when the car suddenly accelerated back onto the road and sped off.

Alex stood quickly and glanced down at the flattened tire. There was no way he could pursue his attackers. He got back on the radio. "Silver Cadillac sedan, at least two men inside, armed and dangerous, headed south on Fraser toward 17. Plate number is covered. All units in the area pursue!"

He sat back inside the car, broken glass crunching on the seat under him. He pulled the rear-view mirror down so he could see his face. The left side looked like it had been shredded in a meat grinder, blood dripping from numerous small cuts. The pain still flared hot, and he laid his head back against the headrest and took in a deep breath.

Sirens could be heard far away and then closer as response units converged on his location. His last thought as the first patrol car and then an ambulance pulled up behind him was, *Hanna. I shouldn't have left her alone. Hanna!*

Her response shouldn't have surprised him.

"You're where?"

"Down at the emergency room. I'm okay. Had a little run-in with some guys out on the road coming home."

"What happened?" Hanna asked, the panic clear in her voice.

"I'll tell you when I get home. I'm okay. I want you to check all the locks, and you know where the guns are. Get one out and loaded."

"Alex! What's going on?"

"I've got a patrol car coming over to watch the house. They'll be out by the road."

"Alex?"

"I think it's these cartel guys. We've got them a little riled up."

Hanna gasped when she saw her husband come through the back door. The left side of his face was heavily bandaged. The left sleeve of his uniform shirt had been cut away, and there were more dressings on his upper arm.

She rushed over to him. "What in the world happened? Are you okay?"

He reached out for her and took her in with his right arm. "A shotgun blast took out my driver's side window. I got hit with some of the glass."

Hanna stood back, panicked and shocked. "They were trying to kill you?"

He nodded. "We've got units out looking for them. I just wanted to make sure you were safe after what happened yesterday."

"Alex, this is out of control! Who are these guys?"

Quinn came in from the front of the house. "Ohmigod!"

Alex gave her a brief explanation, then said, "Is your house secure and dry for the night?"

"I think so," Quinn replied. "Those nice neighbors came over to let us know they had done all they could to close in the roof. I'll start looking for a contractor to work on the repairs."

Hanna said, "Our deck is going to need an overhaul as well."

Quinn said, "So, these men came up in a car and just started shooting?"

"We've been investigating a drug cartel out of Mexico that's behind all the fentanyl overdoses we've been seeing. We must be getting a little too close for their liking and they're starting to strike back."

"I can't believe this is happening here in our quiet little part of the world," Quinn replied.

"It's happening everywhere, unfortunately," Alex said. "Your friend, maybe former friend now, Carlos . . ."

"What about him?"

"Have you even seen any indication he was involved in anything more than his fighting studio?"

"You think Carlos is mixed up with this cartel?"

Alex stared back hard without answering.

Finally, Quinn said, "I can't believe he's involved in something like this . . . but after last night, I'm not sure about anything."

Alex said, "Please don't say anything to him."

"I don't plan to see him again."

"Good choice," Hanna said. Then to Alex, she said, "You really think he's part of this cartel?"

"Let's just say there are some troubling connections. We're looking into it."

Chapter Thirty-nine

It was 8:30 the next morning when Alex saw Will Foster's government car pull into the parking lot at Carlos Quintano's gym. He parked next to Alex's car and got out.

"What in hell happened to you?" Foster asked, getting his first glimpse of the bandages on the side of Alex's face.

"Had a little run-in on the way home last night." He filled Foster in on the attack.

"And no sign of who was responsible?" Foster asked.

"Not yet, but not much doubt it was the cartel either trying to send me a message or take me out completely."

"You didn't get a good look at them, then?"

"No, it was dark and I couldn't go after them. They shot out one of my tires. I called it in, but no one found the car."

"You think it's the two guys we had to let go, the guys here from the gym?"

"They would be my first guess," Alex replied. "I'm pretty sure I hit one of them during the shootout last night. They dropped a gun by the side of the road when they took off, but we haven't been able to get a useful fingerprint."

"Anything more on Quintano before we go inside?"

"No. Let's push him hard this morning to see if there are any cracks in his story."

"After you," Alex said, motioning to the front door of the building.

Carlos Quintano was coaching one of his students in the cage ring when Alex and Special Agent Will Foster walked into the gym. Alex was dressed in his sheriff's uniform. Foster wore the Bureau's blue windbreaker with "FBI" stenciled in white on the chest and across the back.

Their presence drew stares from all the men and women in the gym as they approached the cage. Quintano finally noticed them and excused himself from his student. He came through the entry to the cage and met them, a look of anger on his face.

"What is this?" Quintano demanded.

Alex said, loud enough for most in the gym to hear, "This is FBI Special Agent Will Foster. We need a word, Carlos."

Back in Quintano's office, the man turned to them and said, "Was this really necessary? I'm a legitimate businessman, and now you've got all my students thinking I'm some kind of crook."

"What your students think is really the least of our concerns," Foster said. "One of those so-called students was in here yesterday. He's a member of the local organization of a drug cartel out of Mexico running drugs in the area. Specifically, fentanyl, which, as I'm sure you've heard, is a deadly drug that is killing far too many of our young people."

"Who was this man?" Quintano demanded.

Alex said, "His name is Rios Hernandez. He was coming into your gym yesterday afternoon when my deputy and I were leaving. He saw us and ran. I assume you know Hernandez."

"Yes, he's one of my better students. We're helping him train for an upcoming fight in a few weeks. I have no idea why he ran."

Foster said, "He ran because he was arrested on drug charges and assaulting a police officer. He was released in an exchange when the cartel threatened local attacks on our citizens."

"I had no idea Rios was tied up in anything like this."

Alex said, "Two other members of the cartel we've arrested, and Hernandez as well, have made numerous calls to your personal cellphone. Do you give out your personal number to all your students?"

Alex watched as Quintano began to squirm and then hesitated before he said, "You need to tell me who these other men are, but I do give out my number to my better students who I am personally training."

Alex looked over at Foster and then continued. "Do you know a lawyer from Atlanta named Rick Guidall?"

"No, I do not."

"He's the attorney for all three of these men. He was found murdered in Atlanta yesterday."

Quintano seemed to be looking for any way to get out and away from this questioning. Finally, he said, "I don't understand why you're talking to me about any of this. I have a lot of students. I—"

Alex cut him off. "How many of them are armed and dangerous members of a Mexican drug cartel?"

Quintano was getting more agitated. "I don't know! I don't do personal background checks on my students. I teach them how to fight!"

Alex and Will Foster stared back at the man, giving him an opportunity to continue.

"Do I need a lawyer?" Quintano finally said in desperation.

Foster replied, "If you think you need one. We're not here to charge you with a crime today. We simply need some answers."

"I've told you, these men are paying clients here at my gym. We help them work out and improve their fighting skills. We're not responsible for what they do when they leave the gym."

Now, Alex was getting perturbed, particularly since one of the men had likely been one who had shot at him the previous night. "So, if these guys walk in today, you'd keep taking their money and working with them?"

Quintano hesitated, rubbing his chin and then pacing around behind his desk. He turned back to Alex. "What do you want me to do?"

"First, we want to see any information they may have provided when they signed up to join your gym."

"Done."

"Next, we want you to notify us the next time you see any of them, and don't tip them off we'll be here to pay them a visit."

Again, Quintano was hesitant to reply, then said, "I'm not sure I want a drug cartel coming down on me because I ratted out some of their guys."

Foster said, "Just let us know they're here. We'll take it from there, and no one needs to know you were involved."

Alex listened, still not sure Quintano wasn't running the whole operation.

Outside at their cars, Foster said to Alex, "Any way you can get surveillance on this place? I don't trust this guy as far as I can throw him."

"We don't have that kind of staffing."

"Okay, let me see what we can do," Foster replied. "I think we're close enough to blowing this whole thing wide open that I can get some additional support from Atlanta."

"Let me know and I'll check to see what we can do on our end."

Alex said, "Anything yet from the raid on the law firm up there?"

"I have a conference call this afternoon when I get back to Charleston. I'll try to get you patched in if you're available."

"I'll make myself available."

"How's Hanna?"

"Still a bit shell-shocked. The tornado last night didn't help."

"Much damage?"

"Our house fared pretty well, but my truck and some of the neighbors weren't so lucky."

"Saw a lot of trees down and building wreckage when I was driving up this morning."

"Yeah, a lot of cleanup to be done. Fortunately, no reported fatalities."

Hanna called her office to tell them she would be working from home for the day. With Alex's truck destroyed, they hadn't had time yet to secure a second car. She was thankful for the opportunity to have some time to herself, some time for self-healing, if that was possible.

She was halfway through the coffee pot on the counter when Quinn Burke came down the stairs from the guest room. Her hair was tousled from the night's sleep, her face drawn and pale. Hanna held up an empty coffee cup and Quinn nodded.

Handing her the steaming cup, Hanna said, "Did you get any sleep at all?"

"Not really. I just kept remembering my house falling in around me. And then everything Alex told me about Carlos. I couldn't stop my brain from thinking about it. I just can't bring myself to believe he's involved with a drug cartel that's killing thousands of people with this poison."

"You're going to stay away from him, right?"

Quinn nodded. "I should get back over to the house to start cleaning up and see if I can get a contractor lined up. I'm sure everyone's phone is ringing off the hook this morning."

"Let me know if you find someone who can work on our deck, too. I'll do the same."

"Thank you for putting me up." Quinn set the coffee cup down and went over to give Hanna a tight hug. "I know we got off to a rough start when I first moved out here, but I feel so lucky to have you and Alex as neighbors."

Hanna nodded, remembering the earlier days of their relationship and some rocky times between the two of them. "Let me know if I can help with anything. I'm working here today. Just call."

"And my car is available if you need to run out. I'll probably pick the dogs up a little later after I get some cleanup done." Quinn smiled, moved in to hug and kiss Hanna on the cheek, and then hurried out the back door.

Chapter Forty

The sky had cleared from the previous night's dark fury and shined a brilliant blue with high clouds pushed into a feathered canopy above. Alex walked back into his department after their earlier confrontation with Carlos Quintano, Will Foster following.

Back in his office, Alex checked messages while Foster sat at the conference table and did the same on his cellphone. The FBI agent looked up and said, "Sharron wants us to call. They've got something on the law firm." Sharron Fairfield was another agent in the Charleston office.

Foster made the call and then placed the phone on speaker mode on the desk between them.

"What have you got, Sharron?" Foster asked.

"This law firm has clients all over the country linked to the drug trade, mostly criminal complaints against members of several drug operations both from Mexico and domestic."

Alex said, "Hell of a way to make a living."

Fairfield continued. "This Guidall, who represented the guys up your way and is now resting in the city morgue, was a senior partner in the firm. He was involved in many of the drug-related cases around the country."

"Apparently, one too many," Foster replied.

"Any other connections up this way?" Alex asked.

"We have files on the three you've arrested already. Nothing further yet."

Foster said, "Nothing on a Carlos Quintano?"

"Nothing yet."

"Thank you, Sharron," Foster said. "I know you'll keep us posted." He signed off on the call and turned to Alex. "I've got a contractor hired on to watch Quintano's gym."

"Good. I really can't spare anyone to sit over there," Alex replied. His phone buzzed and he took the call. It was one of his deputies out on patrol.

"Alex, I just did a run through the trailer park where Juarez and Hernandez live. There's a motorcycle parked outside Hernandez's trailer."

"Where are you now?"

"Just down the street from the park."

"Wait there. Let me get some additional backup and we'll be out there in fifteen minutes. Keep an eye on the trailer park entrance to make sure he doesn't take off."

"Roger that."

Alex pulled in behind the patrol car outside the trailer park with Will Foster sitting next to him, Deputy Sheila Graham following in a second car with another deputy. They all got out, and Alex gathered the team around the front of his car. He had a map of the park on his cellphone and assigned everyone their positions for the assault on Rios Hernandez's trailer.

"I'm pretty sure this is the guy who tried to take my head off last night, and probably the one who killed Miguel Juarez. Expect him to be ready for a fight."

Everyone checked their weapons and put on bulletproof vests. Graham was assigned to take the tear gas rifle.

They all walked in through alleys and backyards to move into position. Alex and Will Foster moved from cover to cover to finally get up next to Hernandez's trailer, kneeling down to the side of the front steps.

Alex yelled out, "Hernandez! This is Sheriff Alex Frank. You are completely surrounded. Throw your weapons out on the yard, and come out with your hands up where we can see them!" He could hear movement inside but there was no response. "Hernandez, I mean now!"

Again, no response.

Then, in a thunderous crash, the window above Alex's head exploded in a thousand shards of broken glass from a shotgun blast from inside. He ducked and covered his head, glass raining down all around him. Looking up, he saw the barrel of the shotgun extend out the window and fire again, striking a neighbor's car that Graham was taking cover behind.

Alex got on his radio. "Graham, you okay?" He backed away from the window toward the corner of the trailer.

"Good, sheriff!"

"Fire the gas in there!" he commanded and then watched as Graham leaned out from behind the car, kneeling and then firing the tear gas canister through the open window that had been shot out. He heard the shell explode inside, and within seconds, the gas started drifting out of the open window. He backed up even further behind the cover of a large live oak tree.

He watched as the front door to the trailer was thrown open, and then a long round of shells from an automatic rifle peppered the car Graham was behind. Everyone crouched low, their weapons trained on the front door.

There were a few moments of calm and then a lone figure ran from behind the trailer near where Will Foster had taken cover behind a storage shed. It was Hernandez, and he was sprinting to his motorcycle.

Alex didn't have a clear shot, but he watched Foster rise up and fire three shots from his pistol. Hernandez jerked and stumbled, then fell a few feet from his bike. The rifle was released from his grasp. Alex raced toward the man, his gun extended. A few feet away, Foster was coming from the other side. Alex yelled, "Hernandez! I want you face down, arms extended!"

The man lay on his side, his eyes open but dazed. He tried to move but his brain couldn't make the connections with his body. Foster moved closer and kicked the rifle further away, then pushed the man over on his belly with his foot.

Alex rushed up to assist and knelt beside Hernandez, securing cuffs on his wrists behind his back.

Graham rushed up. "I've got paramedics on the way."

Alex leaned close, his face inches from the fallen man's face. "I want names! Who are you working for?"

Hernandez tried to speak, but blood dripped from the side of his mouth and his words came up garbled and unintelligible.

Alex yelled into his ear, "Who are you working for?"

Hernandez turned his face to Alex with a grim smile. He spit out a mouthful of blood and managed to whisper, "You're a dead man! You just don't know it yet." Again, he saw the smile with blood-soaked teeth as his eyes rolled back and he lost consciousness.

Standing inside Hernandez's trailer after the gas had cleared, Alex put down his phone. Special Agent Foster ended his call, coming in from outside. Alex said, "The emergency docs have stabilized Hernandez. He's in critical condition, but they think he'll survive."

Foster said, "I just arranged for private security to put a guard outside his door."

"Good. The cartel won't hesitate to take him off the board."

"You find anything we can use?" Foster asked. Graham and the other deputy were continuing the search of the trailer as they spoke.

Alex said, "I took Hernandez's phone before the paramedics got him out of here. Can your guys get through the passcode and get this thing open?"

Foster said, "We've got the number from the call logs. I think they can do it remotely. Let me make the call." He stepped away.

Alex thought of Hanna and called her cell. "Just checking in."

Hanna said, "I'm trying to keep busy with all the work I brought home, but I'm not making much progress. Quinn headed home a while ago. She's really shaken up."

"Understandable," Alex replied. "How are you holding up?"

"Don't worry about me. I'll be okay. You've got enough to deal with."

"Nothing more important. I've got a patrol car driving by on the hour just to check on you."

"Thank you, but I'm not sure it's necessary. I've got your gun on the table beside my laptop. I know how to use it."

Alex was not reassured. "We just recaptured one of the cartel guys we had in custody . . ."

"Is he the one who shot at you last night?" Hanna said, her voice suddenly unsteady.

"Probably one of those guys," he said. "I'd feel better if you were working down here. We've got a couple of empty offices. I can come home for lunch and pick you up."

"Why not? I'll have some sandwiches made."

Chapter Forty-one

Alex brought Hanna into the department and got her settled in an office just down from his. Foster stopped him in the hall.

"Our team got us into the phone." He held it out between them. There's a text from this morning from a number we're tracing right now. It looks like there's a delivery coming in tonight."

"Where?"

Foster looked at the phone. "The message says *Usual docks at D. 11 pm.*"

"What do you think? Alex asked.

"Most likely Dugganville, wouldn't you think? Easy access up the channel from the ocean."

"It's had its share of drug traffic," Alex said, thinking about past drug busts in his old hometown. "Dewees Island is a little further south, on the coast."

"We can cover that as well," Foster said.

"Let's get two teams assembled. We really need to call in the DEA and the state police to do this right."

"Agree," Foster replied. "I'll make the calls. Our guy down at the hospital has regained consciousness. Let's get this set up for tonight and then go pay him another visit."

Alex and Foster showed their credentials to the private security guard in the hallway. Rios Hernandez lay on the hospital gurney inside, his right wrist handcuffed to a rail. His eyes were closed, and he was hooked up to a monitor and an IV drip. Bandages on his shoulder and upper chest could be seen under the hospital gown.

Alex stepped up next to the bed and fought back the urge to strangle the man who was probably the gunman who had tried to take him out the previous night. "Hernandez, wake up."

The man stirred but didn't open his eyes.

"Hernandez!" Alex said louder as he shook the arm hooked up to the rail.

Finally, his eyes fluttered open, and as his brain registered who was in the room with him, he jerked in reaction and pulled at his arm to get away, grimacing at the pain to his wounds it caused.

"Settle down," Foster said. "You're not going anywhere for a long time, except the maximum-security prison cell waiting for you down south."

The man's voice was low and raspy. "I got nothin' to say to you guys."

Alex said, "If you want any hope of seeing the outside world again, you should work with us."

"They'll kill me."

"We all die sometime, Rios," Foster said. He held up the man's cellphone. "Got a message on here there's a shipment coming in tonight."

Hernandez shook his head in defiance.

Foster continued. "We've been doing a little digging. Seems you have some family who live down in Charleston."

No response.

Foster continued. "Let me be very clear, Rios. Either you cooperate with us, or your wife and kids and your parents will be on the next bus back to the Texas border."

This got the man's attention. "What do you want?"

Foster held the phone up again. "This message about the shipment coming in tonight. How do you acknowledge it?"

Hernandez took a deep breath, then looked over at Alex, as if there were some hope for support there. Alex just stared back. He looked back to Foster. "K."

"What?" Foster asked.

"Just type the letter *K* for *Okay*. *C* means *Cancel*."

Foster looked over to Alex who nodded back. He pulled up the text screen on the phone and typed the response, *K*.

Alex said, "How many men will be coming with the drugs?"

"Two," Hernandez replied.

"What kind of boat?"

"Big cruiser . . . fifty feet. Don't know what make."

Foster said, "What kind of weapons?"

Hernandez shook his head. "You better be ready. These guys play for keeps."

"*D* is for Dugganville?" Foster asked.

Hernandez nodded in agreement.

Alex said, "Who do you work for?"

"Don't have a name. Never seen the guy. We only communicate by phone."

Alex snapped back, "I don't believe you! How is your trainer, Quintano, involved in all this?"

The man looked back, a puzzled expression on his face. "Carlos?"

Alex nodded.

"He's my fighting coach, man. Got nothing to do with this."

"You and your associates spend a lot of time on the phone with him," Foster said.

"I told you, he trains us to fight."

"Who is supposed to be at the pickup with you tonight?" Alex asked. "Juarez is dead. Where's your other buddy?"

"We always meet there. He comes up from Charleston."

They kept on and managed to get more details about the night's coming drug shipment.

Finally, Alex said, "You the two guys who blew out my windows last night?"

Hernandez smiled back. "Don't know what you're talkin' about, man."

Alex and Foster left the hospital with clear instructions to the security detail, and the next shift to come in, to not let Hernandez anywhere near a phone. They were taking every precaution to make sure whoever was bringing the drugs into Dugganville that night at 11:00 would not be tipped off.

On the way back to the department, Foster spoke on the phone with the private contractor watching Quintano and the gym, asking that they be kept abreast of his location through the rest of the day and evening.

They were pulling into the parking lot of the Sheriff's Department when Foster's phone started to chirp. It was Agent Fairfield calling from Charleston.

Foster said, "I've got you on speaker. I'm here with Alex."

Fairfield said, "Just got off a call from the Atlanta Bureau office. From the law firm records, they've identified the major drug cartel running the operation here in the South. They go by the name of Caldona. Major player globally, and have secured most of the trade in the southeast quadrant of the U.S."

"Any names of the leaders?" Alex asked.

"Only from the main operation out of Mexico City," Fairfield replied. "Still looking for the local connections."

"Okay," Foster said. "It looks like we have a shipment coming in tonight just south of here in Dugganville. Alex and I are mobilizing Drug Enforcement and the state cops. I'd like to have you come up as well."

"Will do. Anything else you need?" she asked.

"Not yet," Foster replied. "This isn't going down until 11 p.m. Why don't you wait there until early evening in case we do?" He ended the call and turned to Alex. "If we can believe Hernandez, we probably don't need to cover Dewees Island tonight, but I think we should have a skeleton crew there, too, just in case."

Alex nodded. "Let me make some more calls."

Hanna took a break from the stack of paperwork in front of her and walked out into the hallway to get a cup of water from the kitchen. She saw Alex and Will Foster and stuck her head in the door. "Any progress?"

They filled her in on the information gained from Rios Hernandez and the drug drop coming in.

"Any more indication Quinn's *former* boyfriend is involved?" she asked.

Alex said, "Hernandez denied he has any connection. I'm still not sure. We have someone watching him."

"I'm more afraid for Quinn than ever if this guy is a drug smuggler," Hanna said.

"She should keep her distance, regardless," replied Alex.

"I told her that."

Foster said, "We'll let you know if we get anything further on Quintano."

"I'm about to call it a day," Hanna said.

"Why don't you take my department car?" Alex replied. "I need to be here most of the night. This deal is coming down at eleven over in Dugganville."

"I know I don't need to say it," Hanna pleaded, "but please be careful."

He came around his desk and walked over to give her the car keys. He kissed her on the cheek. "*Careful* is my middle name."

"Yeah right."

Chapter Forty-two

Hanna drove slowly down the island road to her beach house. The damage from the storm was heartbreaking. Trees were down everywhere. Blue tarps were nailed to roofs to keep more rain out until repairs could be arranged. Debris was being piled at the street for cleanup crews. The sound of chainsaws could be heard from several directions clearing trees.

She pulled into her drive thinking they had been fortunate not to receive even more of the storm's wrath. As she parked and started to get out, she saw a salvage crew of three men working to cut up and remove the tree that had fallen on Alex's truck.

One of the men came over to confirm where they were taking everything and when the truck would be picked up. He said, "The insurance adjuster was here about an hour ago. He left some paperwork at your back door. Sounds like your husband is getting a new truck. No way they're putting that back together."

She looked at the truck. "I would hope not!" she said. "Thanks for getting out here so quickly."

"Your husband called us this morning."

"Do you work on decks? I haven't been able to find anyone yet."

"No, sorry. Tree removal and salvage is our gig."

"Okay, thank you." She was walking toward the back steps when she was startled by someone coming through the bushes from her neighbor Quinn's house. It was Carlos Quintano. She felt her skin prickle, and then anger overcame any sense of fear. She turned to him. "I don't know what you want, but you need to leave!"

He stopped a few feet away, his face a mask of mixed emotions. "I've been trying to call Quinn. She won't pick up. I thought I would come over and apologize in person, but either she's not home or just won't come to the door."

"Maybe you should take that as a sign she doesn't want to see you again." She watched as he tensed, his chest puffing up and down. One of his fists was clenching open and shut. She started backing toward her porch. "Like I said, you need to leave."

"Hanna, please, can't you talk to her? What happened the other night isn't me. I don't know what came over me."

"All I know is you don't get a second chance when you treat someone like that." Her phone rang and she looked at the screen. It was Alex and she took the call. "Hi—" Before she could say anything else, Alex cut in.

"Our guy who is watching Quintano says he's out at the island."

"He's actually right here behind our house."

"What?"

"Let me talk to him."

She handed Quintano her phone, putting it on speaker mode so she could hear. "My husband would like a word."

Alex's words echoed out. "I don't know what in the hell you think you're doing—"

Quintano cut in. "Sheriff! I'm only here asking for your wife's help in talking with Quinn Burke. I'm trying to make amends."

Alex said, "You need to get your ass out of there, now! If I ever see or hear of you within ten feet of my wife—"

"I'm leaving!" He handed the phone back to Hanna. "I'm sorry if I upset you."

"Just go!" she commanded, pointing down the drive to the road.

He turned and walked quickly away down the drive.

"Hanna?"

"He's gone."

"I'll make sure our security guy follows him off the island."

"I'll be okay." She heard dogs barking and turned to see Quinn coming through the bushes with her two little dogs on their leashes.

"Is he gone?" she asked.

Hanna nodded. To Alex, she said, "Quinn's here. I'd better go."

"Call if you need me."

"Of course." She clicked off the call.

"Hanna, I'm so sorry to get you in the middle of this. I wouldn't answer the door when I saw it was him. You were right."

The dogs were growling at her, and Quinn pulled them back a couple of steps.

Hanna said, "Let's hope we've seen the last of him."

"Let's hope. I need to walk the little monsters. Will you come over later for a glass of wine? I'll call when I get back."

Hanna hesitated. All she really wanted to do was crawl into bed and finish Mathew Coulter's manuscript. She'd given up on Quinn's new novel after only a few pages. *Much too dark!* "Sure, give me a call."

Alex drove, with Will Foster in the seat beside him, into his old hometown of Dugganville. He passed the church he'd been baptized in and attended Sunday school. The fire tower in the park loomed ahead among the tall pines. With the windows open, he could smell the scents of the Low Country marsh blowing up the river as they came along the docks and then the house he grew up in. The old shrimp boat his father had made a living on for decades was apparently out to sea with a new owner. The house seemed unchanged except for a front yard filled with young children's toys.

Memories flooded his mind as they made their way into the village on Main Street. They passed Andrew's Diner, and he saw his old friend, Lucy, tending to customers in the window, then the old hardware store his high school friend's family had run for years and the drug store where he and his brother used to sit at the counter and order ice cream sundaes. The thought of his brother made him pause, blinking hard to lose the memory of a soldier lost in another war far away.

Earlier, they had made arrangements with the law enforcement agencies participating in the night's drug bust to meet in an abandoned warehouse just down from the docks. Their cars were to be unmarked and parked inside where weapons and equipment could be unloaded. It was currently just past 8:30 p.m. The others would be arriving at 9:00.

The sun was falling low through the trees. A mist was drifting up the river as the day cooled. The air smelled of fish from the cannery and diesel fuel from the shrimp boats.

Alex pulled the car in behind the warehouse and got out to open the door left unlocked by an old acquaintance. Inside, he and Foster began pulling tables and chairs together for the meeting that would soon begin. Much of the night's plan had been discussed earlier on a conference call with the Bureau, the Drug Enforcement Agency, the South Carolina State Police, and Alex's Sheriff's Department.

He and Will sat across from each other, waiting for the others to arrive.

Alex said, "My biggest concern, as I said earlier on the call, is we take these guys down tonight and are no closer to finding the head of the snake, the people who are running the whole operation. They'll just keep coming and bringing more of this poison into our towns."

"I agree," Foster replied. "At least we can prevent more of this stuff from getting out on the street, at least until the next run."

Within the hour, all agencies were in attendance, the plans had been reviewed again in detail, all assignments given, contingencies agreed to. There were four locations near the dock that was expected to receive the drug boat where the law enforcement teams would take cover before converging to make the arrests. It was critical that no one tipped off any local cartel members before the boat arrived.

The arrest of Rios Hernandez had clearly been a problem. When his phone received the first message about the drug run, Alex had assigned one of his deputies to respond to any further texts. The man also spoke Spanish if a call happened to come in, which fortunately didn't happen. Two hours before the delivery was scheduled to occur in Dugganville, the deputy had been instructed to send another text indicating Hernandez was sick, testing positive for COVID, and wasn't coming. They were all hopeful the ruse would prove successful.

Alex was hidden inside a small outbuilding just three slips down from the targeted dock with Deputy Sheila Graham. Will Foster and his associate, Sharron Fairfield, were positioned inside a boathouse two slips down in the other direction. The DEA and state police formed a second perimeter to collect anyone trying to escape, including two marine patrols stationed just upriver.

Alex checked his watch. There were about fifteen minutes until the boat was scheduled to arrive. The sound of a car or truck engine split the quiet along the docks. A late-model white panel van pulled through the drive into the access lot along the docks and stopped at a spot next to the empty slip. He could see two men inside. Neither got out. Pulling his service weapon out, a Ruger 9mm semiautomatic pistol, he checked the clip again. Graham did the same.

The drug boat arrived ten minutes earlier than expected. The green and red navigation lights on the sides of the boat could be seen first as it rounded a bend in the river and came in toward the docks. As it got closer, overhead lights along the pier revealed a long ocean cruiser, one man on the front deck with a docking line in hand, an automatic rifle slung over his shoulder. Another man could be seen in the cabin driving the boat. There didn't appear to be a third.

Alex watched as the boat slowed and turned to start heading into the slip. The two men in the van both got out and looked around suspiciously before walking out to help the boat tie up.

It was agreed that the signal to initiate the takedown would come from Alex over the designated radio channel when the drugs were all off the boat and the delivery was complete. It was expected that the four cartel members confronted suddenly by four armed police officers ready to shoot would be enough for all to quickly surrender. If not, the contingencies included secondary cover if any gunfire ensued.

Alex felt his pulse quicken as the men got the boat tied up. He couldn't hear any conversation. None of the men seemed to be in any hurry. In fact, the boat driver came up with a bottle of some kind of liquor, and they all passed it around for a drink.

"Come on, let's go," Alex said silently to himself.

The man with the bottle went back into the cabin and came out moments later with a duffel bag that he handed to one of the men on the dock. Ten more bags were exchanged and loaded into the van. All four men gathered again on the dock and were discussing something when Alex lifted his radio mic and said, "All units, now!"

He and Graham burst out of the building with their guns out and pointed at the drug runners. Alex yelled, "Sheriff's Department! Drop your weapons and down on the ground!"

Seconds later, he heard Will Foster yell, "FBI! Everybody down," He saw Will Foster and Fairfield coming in fast from the other side.

The men looked around in surprise. Two put their hands up, the captain started backing toward the boat, and the fourth who had been on the front deck with the rifle lifted it toward Alex to fire.

"Put it down, now!" Alex yelled. He crouched low behind a boat storage box on the pier and took aim as the man's gun came into position, aimed directly at him. He was about to let off a series of shots when the crack of gunfire from the direction of the FBI agents split the night. The drug gunman lurched and then fell backward into the water.

Alex and Graham ran forward again, seeing Foster and Fairfield doing the same from the opposite direction. The other three men fell prone on the dock and held their hands out in front of them.

As the three prisoners were being cuffed, Alex walked up and down the dock with his gun pointed down to the water, looking for the other man. There was no sign until he saw the wake of a big alligator headed back across the river dragging the limp form of the man with him.

Chapter Forty-three

The prisoners were brought back to the Sheriff's Department and processed. Senior members of all four law enforcement agencies had participated in a long debrief of the takedown and had left, except for FBI Agent Will Foster. He sat in Alex's office with a cup of coffee in his hand.

Alex said, "You okay after taking that guy out tonight?"

Foster nodded. "Not the first time. Never easy, but it needed to be done. I hope the search team finds the body before that gator destroys any evidence or ID."

"The DEA guy estimates ten million dollars worth of fentanyl in that van."

Foster said, "That's enough to take out the whole damn county."

"And as I feared, these guys in the can back there look like low-level grunts. I doubt we'll get much out of them. Obviously, no sign of Quintano out there tonight."

"No, our tail says he hasn't left the gym all night."

Alex said, "I still think the guy is dirty."

"One thing I do know," Foster replied, "this bust is going to get the cartel all fired up. They lost a lot of money with those drugs off the market tonight. We can count on some kind of reaction or retribution. You need to keep your eyes open and your head down."

"Likewise."

Hanna was woken from sleep at the sound of someone downstairs. She sat up in alarm, listening carefully for another sound. Nothing. She reached for the gun on the nightstand beside the bed and loaded a round into the chamber, then pushed back the covers and got up. She walked quietly to the door. The light she had left on in the kitchen for Alex was still on, then suddenly went out.

"Alex?" she called out, hoping desperately to hear his voice.

"Hey, sorry I woke you. I'll be right up."

She lowered the gun and took a deep breath of relief. She ejected the shell in the chamber and put the gun back down, turning on the light for Alex.

He came through the door of the bedroom and said, "Sorry, I should have called, but I thought it better to let you get some sleep." He went over and held her close, then kissed her. They sat together on the bed.

He told her about the drug bust and the incredible amount of fentanyl they had seized.

"And nobody got hurt?" she asked when he had finished.

"Will had to take out one of the cartel guys. He was warned but was about to fire at us."

"So, what happens now?" she asked.

"We have three of them in custody and under heavy guard. We'll see if they're willing to give up anybody further up the chain, but I doubt it. We've also got all units of law enforcement on alert for any threats to get the prisoners back."

"And Quintano wasn't there?"

"No, but he's still under suspicion. I still can't believe he came out here today."

Hanna said, "I had a glass of wine, actually several, with Quinn earlier. She's still really upset and doesn't know what to do to get this guy to go away."

"Maybe we can encourage him. Foster and I are going to pay him a visit again in the morning." He got up, unbuttoning his uniform shirt as he walked toward the closet. "I need a quick shower. Sorry to keep you up so late."

Quinn Burke was driving her dogs to the vet's office the next morning. It was a misty, gray day, fog lying low over the marshes behind the island. She had just come across the south causeway toward the mainland when she saw Carlos Quintano's car pass her going in the opposite direction. They made quick eye contact, and she looked back in the rear-view mirror to see his brake lights come on.

Panic and fear raced through her. She pushed down hard on the accelerator. When she looked back again, his car was speeding toward her and, within moments, was right behind her. He started flashing his bright lights at her, and she could see him gesturing for her to pull over.

A traffic light ahead at the main highway with several cars in each lane turned red and she slowed, looking for any avenue of escape. There was a deep ditch to her right off the road and oncoming traffic coming up on her left. When she came to a stop behind the other cars, she looked back again, and Carlos was coming up to her window. She made sure doors were locked at the traffic light, praying it would turn.

Quintano filled the window beside her and then leaned down. "Quinn, please, I just want to talk."

She tried to ignore him, her pulse racing, both hands gripping the steering wheel hard as she watched for the light to change.

He started pounding on the top of her car. "Quinn! I'm not going to hurt you. Please pull over so we can talk."

The light changed, and as soon as the cars ahead started to move, she inched forward. Quintano walked beside her car for a few feet before she could speed up.

Pounding the roof again, he yelled out, "Quinn!" one more time before she sped away.

Alex came over the causeway heading off the island, thinking about the previous night's arrests and how he and Will Foster would follow up on that today. Ahead, he saw the light turn green, but there was a car not moving and a man going back to get inside. It was Carlos Quintano. He could see Quinn Burke's car in front, heading away.

"Oh great," he said under his breath, reaching down to engage his emergency flashers and siren.

Quintano glared back, and before he could get in the car, Alex got on the patrol car's exterior speaker and said, "Pull the car over, Carlos." He watched as the man hesitated, then got in and started forward. He put on his right turn signal and turned at the light and then pulled in the drive of a convenience store.

Alex put his car in park behind Quintano's and got out. As expected, the fighter got out with a defiant look and came quickly toward him. "Carlos, what in hell—"

Before he could finish, Quintano lashed out with a lightning-fast punch that caught him in the gut just below his rib cage. The air rushed out of his lungs, and he struggled to take a breath as his knees wobbled. The second punch came and landed square on the side of his cheek where he still had bandages from the shattered glass cuts a couple of nights earlier. He fell to his knees, struggling to get his breath.

His face only inches away, Quintano yelled, "Leave me the hell alone!" He started back toward his car and then turned, as if he wanted to inflict more damage, then thought better of it, getting into his car and speeding out into traffic.

Alex got to one knee and then managed to stand.

A woman came over, apparently seeing the attack. "Can I get some help for you?"

He shook his head, trying to recover from the blows. "No . . . no, thank you."

"I'd call the police," the woman said, "but you're the police!"

"Thank you, ma'am. I'm okay. I'll take care of this."

When he got to the department, Alex found Will Foster in the kitchen pouring some coffee.

"What in hell happened to you?" Foster said, seeing the swelling and bruises around Alex's left eye.

"Saw Quintano a little earlier than expected," Alex said. He shared what happened as they walked back to his office.

Foster sat across the desk from him. "We need to go pick him up! This is unacceptable."

Alex took a sip of his coffee and then winced at the pain searing across the side of his face. He put the cup down. "Not yet."

"What do you mean? Assaulting a police officer. We can put him away for a very long time."

"This was personal, Will. This is between him and me. I chased him off our property over the phone yesterday when he was giving Hanna a hard time about our neighbor, his former girlfriend. We've already had words about this. I'll deal with it."

"What, you're gonna go mix it up with a professional fighter?" Foster said in exasperation.

Alex took a deep breath and looked out the window, his thoughts swirling about the beating he'd just taken. He turned back to Foster. "What's more important is we nail this guy if he is truly involved with the cartel."

Hanna was working from home again, at least through the morning, her work spread out before her on the desk in her den. There was a knock at the back door. She got up, reaching for the gun on the desk. Walking into the kitchen, she could see through the window in the door that it was Quinn Burke. She opened a drawer on the island and put the gun in before going to let her in.

She could tell her neighbor was very upset as she opened the door. "Quinn, what's the matter? What happened?"

They walked back into the kitchen together, and Quinn told her about the encounter with her ex.

Hanna listened, then said, "I can't believe he's not giving up on this."

"I'm really scared, Hanna. I don't know what he might do."

"Maybe I can get Alex to talk to him again," she said, not knowing about her husband's run-in with Quintano.

"No, I don't want the two of you in the middle of this any longer. I'll talk to him . . . somewhere public where he can't do anything to me. I need to tell him this is over and to give it up."

"Are you sure?"

The parking lot of Quintano's gym was nearly full. Alex and Foster finally found a spot to pull in.

"Business is good," Foster said.

Inside, there was no sign of Quintano. They went up to the check-in desk and asked the woman there to see her boss.

"He's not here," she said, eyeing Alex's uniform warily.

"When do you expect him?" Foster asked.

The young woman, dressed in colorful workout leggings and a cropped top, muscles flaring in her arms and shoulders, said, "Never know. Don't keep his schedule."

They both put cards on the desk, and Alex said, "Tell him we were here. I expect a call."

Turning to leave, Alex stopped when Quintano came through the door. The man hesitated, then rushed at Alex.

"I thought I told you . . .!" He wrapped Alex in a tight grip and threw him up against a wall.

Foster rushed in, grabbing Quintano from behind to pull him away. "That's enough! I'm FBI!"

"I know who you are!" the fighter said, sneering back and starting to come at Foster.

Two men rushed in from the gym and both grabbed Quintano and pulled him away. He struggled to get loose, but they held him tight.

Alex walked up, pointing a finger an inch from the man's nose. "That is the last time you touch me and don't land your ass in jail!"

The fighter struggled to get free, and his face looked like a viper about to strike.

Foster moved in between the two of them. "Do we have to cuff you and take you in, or can we have a conversation?"

Quintano huffed and then shook the two men away who were holding him. "Why are you two harassing me?" he hissed.

"Let's go in the back, Carlos," Foster said.

The man seemed to have calmed some when the three of them sat around a table in a small meeting room. He held up a hand and said, "Look, I'm sorry. I've had a lot going on lately. I'm very stressed out. I'm sorry—"

"No excuses," Foster said, cutting in. "We have enough on you to put you away for a long time. You're not in the ring, Carlos. You can't keep taking swings at people, particularly a county sheriff."

Alex said, "We're not here to talk about that. We're here to see why you weren't at the drug deal we took down last night."

"What drug deal?"

"Your bosses in Mexico can't be very happy with you," Alex said.

"Where were you last night, Carlos?" Foster asked.

"I was here at the gym, working with some of my fighters. What do I have to do to convince you people I'm not in on these drug deals. Never have been. Never will be."

Alex said, "We've got three prisoners down at the jail who might say differently."

"You going to come peacefully," Foster asked, "or do we have to hook you up?"

Quintano did cooperate and sat in the back of Alex's patrol car on the way back to the department, without cuffs on.

Inside, he was sitting at the end of a conference room table when Alex and Foster came in followed by two deputies who had the three prisoners from the night before. All three were cuffed at the wrists and angles.

Alex had them sit along one side of the table. He and Foster sat on the other.

Foster said, "Carlos, you know these men, right?"

The fighter looked down the line of faces then said, "Yes, I know the man on the end, Martin. He works out at my gym. I don't know the others."

Alex said, "Martin, how long has Mr. Quintano been working with you on these drug deals?"

"I'm not talking to no one!" he said, defiantly.

Quintano stood. "This is outrageous!"

Alex stood and got in his face. Are you going to sit down and cooperate, or do we hook you up as well?"

Quintano glared back, seeming ready to lash out again. Then, he hesitated and sat back down. "I'm not talking to anyone without a lawyer here," he finally said.

"You want a lawyer?" Foster mimicked.

"Yes, you two aren't going to railroad me into this crazy scheme."

Chapter Forty-four

Hanna and Quinn were on the front deck, having a glass of iced tea and looking out over the beach and ocean. Hanna had made sandwiches and they were just finishing lunch. The earlier clouds and rain had cleared, and a glorious blue sky stretched out beyond as far as they could see. The beach was full of families and sunbathers, many splashing out in the waves.

She heard steps coming up to the deck from the beach and was surprised to see the antique dealer, Jeremy Day, walk up. She smiled as he came toward them, dressed casually in tan Bermuda shorts and a blue golf shirt with the logo of his store on the chest, one strap of a backpack over his shoulder.

Quinn said, "Jeremy, what a nice surprise."

Both women stood to meet their unexpected guest.

"Hanna, sorry. I knocked at the back door," Day said. "Thought you might be out here. Quinn, how are you?"

"Okay, thank you," Quinn said.

"What brings you out here, Jeremy?" Hanna asked.

"Had a couple of things I wanted to share with you. Could we go inside for a few minutes?"

"Sure," Hanna replied, more than a little puzzled at the sudden visit.

Day said, "Quinn, why don't you join us?"

"Okay, why not?"

Hanna led them all inside and over to the kitchen. They gathered around the big granite island. She said, "Jeremy, I told you a few days ago, I'm not really in the market to buy any more furniture." She watched as he pulled his backpack from his shoulder and reached into it. She thought he'd be pulling out some furniture t. She gasped when she saw the large silver gun in his hand.

Alex had the deputies lock Quintano in the interrogation room and return the three prisoners to their cells. Quintano had made a call to an attorney, and they were waiting to resume their *discussion*. He was looking through some messages, trying to remain calm about his encounters with the mixed martial arts fighter and possible drug chief.

Foster had been in a room down the hall making some calls, but leaned his head in the door. "A minute?" he asked.

"Yeah, come in."

"Just spoke with the detail down at the hospital watching Rios Hernandez," Foster said, taking a chair. "The hospital wants to release him. We need to bring him down to join the others."

Alex parked the cruiser in front of the emergency room entrance at the hospital and was standing at the open car door waiting for the security detail to bring Rios Hernandez out. Will Foster was standing on the other side, talking on his phone.

Hernandez came out in a wheelchair pushed by a male nurse, security trailing. His left arm was in a sling.

Alex walked up to meet them. "You missed all the excitement last night, Rios," he said. "Got a bunch of your friends down at the jail waiting for you."

The man didn't respond, glaring back.

Foster helped the security team get Hernandez in the back of the car and locked to the D-ring on the floor while Alex signed some paperwork for the nurse. He got back in the cruiser.

Foster climbed in the passenger side and looked back at Hernandez, "There's still time for you to come clean about who you're working for. We've got him waiting for you back at the station."

The man shook his head and looked out the window.

They were halfway back to the department when Alex's cell rang. He didn't recognize the number on the screen but took the call. "Sheriff Frank."

He didn't know the voice but was immediately concerned with the ominous tone. "I want you to listen very carefully, sheriff."

"Who is this?" He put the call on speaker mode and set it in the holder so Will Foster could hear.

"You have something I want, actually four things."

"And what would that be?" Alex responded, pretty certain he knew where this was headed.

"The four men you're holding down at your jail. I want them released immediately."

"And why would I do that?"

"Well, I happen to have something that I'm sure you would like in exchange. And a friend of hers as well."

Alex's senses went on full alert. "Who is this?"

"That should be the least of your worries."

He looked over at Foster who shook his head in concern. "Let me speak with my wife."

"I'm afraid that's not possible."

Alex felt his gut lurch. "Let me talk to her now!"

There was a pause on the other end.

"Listen to me," Alex shouted into the phone. "This conversation is going nowhere if you don't put her on the phone!" He could hear some muted conversation, then, "Alex?"

"Are you okay?"

Another pause, then Hanna replied, "I'm here with Quinn."

"Where are you?"

"I can't say. He has a gun to her head if I say anything."

"Who has you?"

"Alex . . ."

He could hear the fear in her voice. "What happened?" he asked.

In a low whisper, Hanna said, "We thought he was showing us some furn—"

She didn't finish, and the man came back on the line. "You have one hour to release the four men you're holding. I'm sending a van to pick them up. No one tries to stop them. No one follows."

"What about Quintano?" Alex asked.

"Quintano?" Another long pause. "He's your problem, sheriff. One hour."

The call clicked off.

They pulled into the department parking lot. He put the car in park and turned to Foster. They both shook their heads, trying to think through how to respond. He got back on his phone and called the desk inside. "Send someone out to get this prisoner."

"Yes sir, sheriff."

They both got out and walked around to the back of the car. Rios Hernandez was grinning at him when he passed the window.

Alex was trying his best to remain calm, but his heart was beating out of his chest. "There's one problem here, Will. We let these guys go, our man on the phone has no reason to let Hanna or Quinn go. He'll probably kill them so they can't ID him."

"I was thinking the same thing," Foster said. "Alex, I'm sorry—"

He cut in. "I think I know where they are."

Chapter Forty-five

The antique store sat on the end of an old strip shopping center just off Highway 17. Alex parked a block away behind another building, and he and Special Agent Will Foster got out. He opened the trunk lid, and they both reached in for assault rifles they had secured back at the department. They both had on bulletproof vests and extra ammunition on their gun belts.

Alex said, "He won't know you're with me. Hopefully, he doesn't even suspect I'm coming. I'm going in alone, at least I'll try to convince him of that."

"He may have backup," Foster said.

"I expect he does."

Alex heard Foster press the delivery doorbell in the back alley as planned. It was his signal to go through the front door. He had the assault rifle aimed in front of him. No one was visible in the display room. He moved forward slowly, looking for a door to the back. He was only a few feet into the store when he sensed a rush of motion to his side. Before he could turn, the cold steel of a pistol pressed into the side of his neck.

"Drop the gun," said a voice with a heavy Spanish accent.

Alex turned and saw a Hispanic man he didn't recognize.

"Put the gun down, now!" the man demanded, pressing the gun barrel harder into Alex's neck.

He did as he was told and knelt to lay the gun on the floor. As he came up, he heard a thud and a muted groan. The man fell to the floor beside him, and Alex turned to see Will Foster holding the butt of the gun out.

Alex whispered, "I'm going in alone. No weapons."

Foster nodded then pulled the unconscious man over behind some large furniture.

Alex walked slowly toward a door at the back of the store. He looked around one more time and couldn't see anyone else. At the door, he started to reach for the knob, then stopped. "Day, this is Alex Frank. I'm alone. I'm unarmed. We need to talk."

For a few moments, nothing happened. Then, the door slowly opened, and a long 357 magnum pistol extended out, pointed directly at his forehead. He put his hands up and stood back a step as the door opened and Jeremy Day, the antique dealer . . . and drug boss stared back over the barrel of the gun.

"Come in, sheriff."

Inside, Alex looked around a large storage room with furniture spread about, some covered, some packed for shipment. He didn't see Hanna or Quinn.

"Where is my wife?"

"I thought we had an understanding, sheriff?" Day said, lowering the gun to Alex's stomach. "My men are there to pick up your prisoners."

"And we're ready to release them. As long as I walk out of here with my wife and our friend."

"Not very smart, sheriff. I'm sure you realize I have no intention of releasing anyone."

A muted cry came from the back of the room.

"They're still alive," Day said.

"I want to see them now. I'll make the call to have your men released. We walk out. You get the hell out of here to wherever you think you can hide. My people know who you are. You're not going to kill anyone."

Day hesitated, then looked behind him when another string of muted cries came from behind them.

Alex was tempted to jump the man, but the gun came up quickly to his face again. Staring down the barrel of a gun that can take your head clean off at the neck was not something Alex had ever dealt with before, and he tried with all his will to keep his composure.

Day said, "I don't think so." He pulled back the hammer on the gun and tightened his finger across the trigger. "Goodbye, sheriff."

The explosion of the gunfire echoed through the room. Alex saw Jeremy Day's forehead explode in shards of blood and tissue as he fell back lifeless, the big 357 falling from his hands to the floor.

Alex turned as Will Foster ran up, smoke still coming from the barrel of his assault weapon, the smell of gun powder heavy in the air.

Foster said, "You okay?"

He nodded then ran to the back of the room. Hanna and Quinn were bound back to back in two chairs, their mouths covered with gags. He pulled one off of Hanna as Foster went to assist Quinn Burke.

"Ohmigod!" Hanna yelled out when she could finally speak. "What happened?"

"You're safe. Day is dead." He hugged her and kissed her hard on the lips. "Let me get you out of here."

Chapter Forty-six

Grayton Beach, Florida. Two weeks later.

The white sand was blinding and as soft as sugar under their feet. Out past the long expanse of sand and dunes, the Gulf of Mexico shone a brilliant blue and green, sparkling in the afternoon sun. Several Jeeps and four-wheel-drive trucks were backed down to the water's edge with beachgoers in chairs, wading in the light crystal-clear surf, throwing frisbees, enjoying another beautiful day along South Walton County's Emerald Coast.

Alex held Hanna's hand as they walked out toward the shoreline. Both were dressed in shorts and t-shirts, their feet bare, enjoying the warm comfort of the sand beneath them. The small village of Grayton Beach spread out behind them. Several old beach cottages that dated back over one hundred years were still nestled in the dunes. New and much larger beach homes loomed in both directions.

They had flown into Panama City Airport that morning and were picked up by Skipper Frank and his wife, Ella, who had arrived earlier and secured a rental car. More family had come as well. Hanna's stepmother, Martha, had driven down from Atlanta with a friend, and her cousin, Janet Anders, the granddaughter of the old writer, Mathew Coulter, had flown back down from New York as well.

Several days after the deadly encounter in the antique store, Alex had suggested to Hanna they get away from the Low Country and all the stress of drug runners and dangerous boyfriends. Hanna had finally offered the idea of bringing family together in this beautiful place she had longed to return to.

Surprisingly, everyone was available and jumped at the opportunity for a reunion. A large house down the beach had been found on VRBO, and they were all staying together for the four days, except Janet and her husband who were staying at the old family beach cottage.

Hanna also felt it was an opportunity for the family to come together to discuss Mathew Coulter's many secret alliances and scandals in the book he had never published.

She and Alex got down to the beach and felt the warm Gulf waters wash over their feet.

"Is this not the most beautiful beach you've ever seen?" she said.

Alex looked in both directions, Panama City far to the east and the misty horizon of Destin miles to the west, not a single high-rise condo anywhere close, only the low profiles of beautiful beach houses, meandering white dunes edged in live oak scrub, and the beautiful clear blue waters of the Gulf. He turned back to Hanna, pulled her close, and said, "If there is another, I hope to see it someday."

Skipper and Ella were waiting for them at the famous Red Bar restaurant and bar in the tiny village, sitting at an outdoor table with cold beers half gone. The place had first been a general store back in the mid-1900s and then a restaurant for many years until a fire took it to the ground a few years earlier. It had been rebuilt and restored to its original quirky beach design and was packed with locals and visitors almost every night.

Skipper rose and hugged his daughter-in-law, then signaled for the bartender to send over two more beers.

They all sat down, and Alex said, "Can't believe you two aren't down at the beach. It's incredible."

"The beer is up here at the bar, son," Skipper said, scratching at his scruffy beard and taking another sip. "We see the damn water every day down in Islamorada."

Ella said, "Haven't able to get this old coot to take a swim since I've known him."

"That's what they make boats for, woman!"

Hanna laughed and said, "Thank you for coming up for this little family thing. I hope it wasn't too much trouble."

Ella said, "Needed a break from the heat down in the Keys."

Skipper said, "Got my mate and a buddy runnin' my charters on the *Maggie Mae* for the next few days. Scotty stayed down to help. He's becoming quite a fisherman. Anyway, nice to get away. Heard you two had a tough go of it a while back."

Alex said to Hanna, "I told Pop about the drug cartel while we were checking into the house earlier."

Ella said, "How you doin', honey? Sounds like you had a rough time."

Hanna said, "Let's just say I feel a lot better knowing Alex put most of these guys away for the rest of their lives."

Later, a family dinner was spread out on the island in the kitchen of the big beach house. Everyone filled their plates and took a seat at a long dining table in a room with windows on three sides looking out to the beach. The sun was on its way to the far horizon across the water, shining orange and hot, lighting the sparse clouds pink as it fell.

Hanna lifted her wine glass and said, "Thank you all for coming. I know it was a long trip and we have very busy lives. I just thought it was time to bring as many of us together as we could. Who knows when we'll have this chance again." Martha and her friend, Lois, Janet and her husband, Dale, Skipper and Ella, and Alex beside her all raised their glasses and yelled out, "Cheers!" before taking a drink and starting in on their dinner.

A while into the meal, Janet got everyone's attention. "I know most of you have heard this story, but if you'll indulge me."

"No, please go ahead," said Hanna.

Janet began, "Many years ago, almost a hundred, I guess, my grandfather, Mathew Coulter, made his way down here to Grayton Beach. His father and family were notorious in Atlanta for controlling the liquor trade during Prohibition, and Mathew got to the point where he wanted nothing more to do with it.

"Grayton Beach was his refuge, but it wasn't long before he found himself in the middle of even more chaos and trouble. He became a reluctant friend of a ruthless gangster named Willy Palumbo who was also down here to escape. He met my grandmother, a young woman whose mother had brought them here some years earlier to run a hotel that's now the art gallery and gift store just down the road.

"My grandmother, Sara, had a daughter, Melanee, from an early relationship while she was traveling as a singer with a band across the South. Melanee, my mother, was born blind at birth, but lived a marvelous life with a sixth sense and intuition that always amazed us. Sara had many demons, and Mathew Coulter stepped up to protect her and save her. They were married and Mathew adopted Melanee, and they all lived a great life together in New York City and had many travels around the world. He became a famous and very successful author. Melanee and my father raised me in New York City, too, where she became a featured violinist with the Philharmonic Orchestra."

She stopped and took a sip of water, tears forming in her eyes. Then, she continued. "They are all gone now, but one last bit of family history remains. My grandfather's last book, untitled and unpublished, was found by Dale and me when we were here in Grayton Beach at the old family cottage several weeks ago. Mathew wrote about his long and often questionable relationship with the gangster, Willy Palumbo. He also wrote of the addictions and demons that haunted my grandmother's life before he stepped in to help her recover. There were many scandals and secrets that, in the end, I guess he decided were best kept locked away in an unpublished manuscript."

She paused again, dabbing at her eyes, and Hanna reached an arm around her shoulder to comfort her. She said, "Janet, thank you so much for sharing Mathew's story, our family's story. You know I sent a copy to Martha in Atlanta where her husband, my father, Allen Moss, was a descendant of the notorious Coulter Clan. Martha still lives in their house today and carries on the family's position in Atlanta."

Martha cleared her throat. "Janet, thank you so much for sharing your grandfather's story with us. I know Hanna was concerned I might not want some of the more controversial aspects of Mathew Coulter's life and alliances made public, that it might bring some shame or scandal to the family lineage." She paused and took a sip of her wine. "Frankly, I think just the opposite is true. I believe Mathew Coulter was a fine man, one we should all be proud of. He made some tough decisions and compromises in his life, all for what he thought was best for everyone he truly cared about, and at times, even Willy Palumbo. So, I have no reservations about any of this going public or being published. I think it's a wonderful story that needs to be told."

Janet said, "Thank you, Martha. That's so gracious of you. And Hanna, what do you think?"

Hanna looked around the table at those most dear in her life. Only her son, Jonathan, was unable to come because of demands from law school. To Janet, she said, "The story of Mathew Coulter is one we should all be proud to share." She lifted her glass for a silent toast, and all joined in.

Later, Hanna was standing on the broad deck of the house looking across the dark expanse of beach, the moon glimmering on the calm surface of the Gulf. Alex had just left her to go get ready for bed. She wanted a few more minutes alone to try to imagine the days Mathew Coulter spent there those many years earlier in a rustic old beach cottage the family still owned just down the road, far too small to accommodate the reunion she had organized.

In his story, he had described a terrible hurricane that had blown up from the south and washed through the village, leaving very little behind, even killing Sara Coulter's mother that night. Mathew had, of course, survived the deadly storm, as had the early pages of the manuscript they had all discussed earlier.

She could almost see Mathew walking down to the beach holding the hands of his new wife, Sara, and his new daughter, Melanee, all those many years ago.

She heard someone coming up behind her and turned to see Janet walk up and join her at the rail of the deck.

Janet said, "What a beautiful gathering. Thank you for bringing us all together. We'll have to do it again and try to get even more of the family to come."

"That would be nice," Hanna said. "You know, I have some interesting family secrets as well. My great-grandmother, Amanda Paltierre Atwell, lived on a tobacco plantation back during the Civil War."

"Yes, and her house that you live in out on Pawleys Island," Janet said. "A beautiful spot."

"I still see her, you know," Hanna said.

"What do you mean, dear?"

"Her spirit, her ghost, I guess. I see her often out on the island. She's there to watch over me . . . and Alex. I'm not sure where we'd be today without her with all we've been through."

Janet looked back for a moment, then said, "You know, I've never told anyone this because I didn't think they'd believe me. I was up late alone many years ago in our beach cottage down the way. Everyone else was asleep. I went out on the porch and sat in one of the old chairs, taking in the stars, enjoying a beautiful evening. A mockingbird landed on the rail and started dancing around, chirping at me like I might understand."

"A bird?" Hanna repeated.

"Yes, and then I realized someone was sitting beside me, and it was my grandfather, Mathew. He had passed away years earlier, but there he was, as real as you and me talking tonight."

"What did he say?" Hanna asked.

Janet smiled and said, "He reached out for the bird, but it scampered down the rail a few feet, still chirping back at us. My grandfather said, *His name is Champ. He loves crackers.*"

"Seriously?"

"I swear I wasn't dreaming, and I already knew about the story of Champ from my mother, but he said, *Janet, I'm sorry I can't be here with you and the family any longer. I love this place, and I love that you are all still here. Always treasure your time here. It goes far too quickly.* And then, he was gone."

Hanna reached for the old woman's hand. They were both crying now. "And you never saw him again?" she asked.

Janet shook her head, wiping at her eyes.

"You think Champ might still be around?" Hanna asked.

Janet laughed, choking back her tears.

They walked hand in hand down the quiet village street, a single streetlight ahead illuminating the old Coulter beach cottage. Hanna squeezed Janet's hand as they went through the picket fence gate and then walked together up the path and then the few steps up to the porch. The two old chairs Janet had described were still there under a window, the rail stretching down the length of the deck.

"This is where you talked to your grandfather?" Hanna whispered, knowing that Janet's husband was probably asleep inside.

Janet nodded and motioned for Hanna to join her, and they both sat down. She said, "I've decided to honor my grandfather's wishes. Some stories are best kept among family."

Hanna nodded and patted her on the arm. "Of course." When she looked up, the canopy of stars above was breathtaking, a billion shimmering lights through the palm fronds and live oak branches.

In the morning, Alex woke early, the sun just casting its first light through the blinds. He grabbed his clothes and looked down at Hanna sleeping. Her sandy brown hair covered her face, and her breathing was slow and relaxed. He had been so worried about her after all the drama and danger with the drug cartel back in Carolina. Remarkably, he thought, she had weathered all of it with a sense of determination to not let it drag her down. She had gone back to work in just a couple of days and life on Pawleys Island returned to near-normal, even with all of the clean-up from the storm.

He went down the steps to the kitchen as quietly as he could and started the coffee maker. He checked his phone for messages that may have come in late after he had gone to bed. *Nothing that can't wait*, he thought.

He did have a conference call scheduled for later in the morning with Will Foster. The FBI was wrapping up their investigation of the law firm in Atlanta that had been representing the cartel members. Indictments were pending on several senior members of the firm who had crossed the line in their representation of the gangs.

Jeremy Day, the antique trader and ruthless cartel leader in South Carolina had met a violent end at the hands of Special Agent Will Foster when they had gone in to rescue Hanna and their neighbor Quinn Burke. Other cartel members had been rounded up, arrested and were being held without bail until trial dates could be set. Hopefully, Alex thought, none of them would have any chance of being back on the street for decades.

Alex felt some sense of accomplishment in putting a serious dent in the cartel's operations in the Low Country. He also knew it was just a matter of time until the Mexican drug lords rebuilt their organizations, and the deadly flow of fentanyl would resume.

Quinn Burke's former boyfriend, Carlos Quintano, had been cleared of any dealings with the cartel, yet Alex felt there would be more issues with the violent professional fighter down the road.

He poured some coffee and took a sip from the steaming cup, then turned when he heard footsteps on the stairs. Hanna padded down the wood steps, her hair amiss and face still flushed from sleep. She had put on shorts and a hooded Duke sweatshirt. He welcomed her with a morning hug and buried his face in her hair.

"Good morning," he whispered. "You were out late. I didn't hear you come in."

Hanna pulled back and moved over to pour some coffee. "I was out with Janet. We had a great conversation about the family. I'll tell you about it."

"How about a walk? Alex suggested.

They took their coffee and made their way down through the dunes. No one else was out in the quiet little town, and they had the entire beach to themselves as they walked out to the shoreline.

The sun to the east was up above the far horizon down in Panama City, with yellow rays flaring out from behind low gray clouds. The Gulf was glass calm, not a breath of wind. Several pods of bluefish feeding on baitfish broke the still water further out and gulls hovered above them hoping for some easy scraps.

Hanna sat down on the sand, her bare feet just touching the cool water. She pulled Alex down beside her. "Do we ever have to leave this place?" she said.

"What about Pawleys Island?"

"I know, we are blessed," she said. "By the way, I got a call from my friend who runs the women's shelter in Charleston. She's been helping Helena Juarez get settled with her children. She's found a job and an apartment. The kids are going to school."

"That's great. I hope the cartel will leave her alone now that her husband is gone and out of the picture."

"Let's hope."

"Speaking of Charleston," Alex said. "Nate Beatty called me again yesterday about my old job with the Homicide Division."

"What did you tell him?"

"I thanked him and told him I was very happy with the Sheriff's Department and our life out on the island."

"Are you sure?" she asked.

"Absolutely."

She leaned over and kissed him. "I'm happy that you're happy."

He smiled back and kissed her again. "How about that walk?" he said.

They got up and started west along the shore, the sun coming up bright and hot behind them. A lone walker was coming toward them now, the first person they had seen on the beach. As he came near, Hanna thought it odd he was dressed in long pants held up by suspenders, leather shoes, and a white dress shirt open at the neck. His hair was sparse, graying and brushed back wet. He looked older, possibly in his eighties, his gait slow and guarded.

As they came up to him, she could see his face now in the morning sun. She knew the face. She had seen it on the back of many book covers.

The man smiled and said, "Thank you for being here with my Janet."

"Mr. Coulter?" she asked tentatively, reaching for Alex's hand. She looked over at Alex and when she looked back, Mathew Coulter was gone, not a sign of him in either direction.

They both stepped back from the water's edge, Alex shaking his head. "What is it with you and your ancestors?"

Hanna looked in both directions again and there was still no one in sight. "I don't know," she replied, "but like I said, we are truly blessed."

THE END

A NOTE FROM AUTHOR MICHAEL LINDLEY

Thank you for reading **THE COULTER LEGACY**. I can't thank you enough for your time with my stories.

When we released Book #1 in the *"Hanna and Alex"* series, *LIES WE NEVER SEE,* in 2018, we had no idea the stories would come to be the #1 bestselling mystery series on Amazon on numerous occasions with over 10,000 five-star ratings on Amazon and Goodreads. There are now ten books in the series and I'm already off working on #11.

It has really become a labor of love as the characters of Hanna Walsh and Alex Frank have developed over the years and new stories come to life in the glorious Low Country of South Carolina.

For those who haven't discovered my earlier *"Troubled Waters"* collection of three novels, I would encourage you to check out THE EMMALEE AFFAIRS and THE SUMMER TOWN, and Book #3 in that series, BEND TO THE TEMPEST, featuring Hanna's distant relation, Mathew Coulter, whose family controlled the liquor trade in the South during Prohibition. We revisit Mathew's story beginning in 1939, in a dual narrative in this latest *"Hanna and Alex"* release.

You can find all the *"Troubled Waters"* novels in both eBook and paperback formats at my own online store, on Amazon and all major book retailers. Even your local bookstores can order them for you.

Michael

Online, visit store. michaellindleynovels.com/

IF YOU DON'T WANT TO MISS THE RELEASE OF MY NEXT BOOK...

We all know that Amazon lists literally millions of new novels each year. I'm so glad you found your way to reading mine!

If you would like to know when I release my next novel, rather than leave it to chance, if you haven't already subscribed to my Reader Group mailing list, drop a quick note to michael@michaellindleynovels.com to sign up for my *BEHIND THE SCENES* monthly newsletter. We will keep you up to date on new releases, special offers and a look inside the "*writing life*."

We will also send you a free digital eBook copy of the "*Hanna and Alex*" intro novella, *BEGIN AT THE END*.

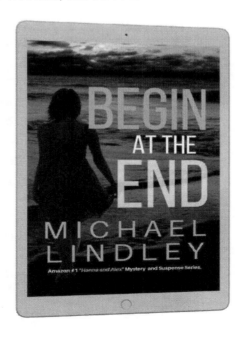

Other novels by Michael Lindley

The *"Troubled Waters"* Series

THE EMMALEE AFFAIRS

THE SUMMER TOWN

BEND TO THE TEMPEST

THE *"Hanna and Alex"* Low Country Mystery Series

LIES WE NEVER SEE

A FOLLOWING SEA

DEATH ON THE NEW MOON

THE SISTER TAKEN

THE HARBOR STORMS

THE FIRE TOWER

THE MARQUESAS DRIFT

LISTEN TO THE MARSH

THE FIRM OFFER

THE COULTER LEGACY

Your reviews on Amazon and Goodreads are always appreciated.

Michael